RESONANT SOLACE

USA TODAY BESTSELLING AUTHOR

TIYE

Copyright © 2025 by Honey Magnolia Media

Cover design by Qamber Designs
Print book interior design by Qamber Designs

Honey Blossom Press
www.honeyblossompress.com
@honeyblossompress

ISBNs: 9781967565061 (trade paperback), 9781967565078 (ebook)
Printed in the United States of America

HONEY BLOSSOM PRESS

Dedicated to my grandfather,
who lived and breathed Memphis.

ONE

Sophie

The echoes of a baby's loud cries awakened me. My eyes popped open, and the burn from the bright sun forced them closed again. Disoriented, I reflexively held on to my womb, locked in the place between sleep and awake. Such a nonsense habit to protect my stomach when nothing grew inside, no matter how much I longed for the opposite. I should've been married with two babies by now, and I was four years past my self-imposed deadline with no man or dating prospects. Then again, even the thought of giving my heart anytime soon made me cringe.

The piercing wail of my neighbor's new bundle of joy traveled through the thin, shared wall, pushing me fully into consciousness that I was in my bed in my apartment.

Where else would I be?

I'd been a hermit for months, only leaving my place to spend time with my family in Gatlinburg until being around my happily married sisters and their babies became too hard to bear. Burying deeper under my comforter, I flipped on my side, willing myself to return to sleep. Must have had a dream that I was somewhere else that I'd probably recall months later when I was least expecting it.

The thick fabric covering my ears was no match for the howling infant who continued expanding her lungs. Hunger cry? No, no…she needed to be changed. Over the past three weeks, after helping my sisters with their infants, I'd identified the baby's language and recognized and understood her sobs and cries. A warring mix of annoyance and an aching need to hold and comfort a baby I'd never met kept me from falling back to sleep. Curving my body more protectively, I squinted at the early light peeking through the blinds and sighed that another day had begun. A new beginning. A fresh start.

Mornings used to be my favorite time of day. Maybe because my father was such a spirited and energetic person at the crack of dawn, his infectious, sunny disposition passed down to me. He used to tell me whenever I walked into the kitchen to eat breakfast with a frown that I had no reason. Each morning was akin to the sun after a rainstorm. I'd heard that so much as a teenager that it became my mantra, and I seldom woke up upset or sad, no matter how I ended the previous night, until a love so consuming swept in like a tsunami and left the ravages of my heart for me to be whole again. And though the once-stabbing aches were more like an occasional prick now, scars remained. Lately, a new morning meant another day of nothingness.

Staring at the lens of my iPhone, barely registering my appearance, I snapped my daily picture and tossed the device to the side, ignoring the numerous missed texts from concerned family and friends. No music. No pressure. No expectations. No guilt. No regret. No matter whose text or call I answered, feelings I didn't want to experience would rush to the forefront of my mind. Responding to the outside world meant heartache and loss. Safe in my apartment, I could pretend I still had sunny mornings and lament freely about a love lost and never to be found again.

For most of my life, music had cured my soul. A rhythmic verse became my balm when life cut too deep. The twang of my guitar, the shrill of my tambourine, and the melody of my voice always healed my wounds. Because of him, I hadn't touched an instrument or sung a note in four months. Because of him, I no longer had a purpose. Because of love, my existence seemed meaningless, and I had no clue how to start again. No motivation or desire to perform, much to the chagrin of my best friend, Amara Johnson, a county star on the rise, who relied on my backup vocals and guitar during her first nationwide tour. I hated talking to her. Guilt that somehow we'd let each other down, though she hadn't done anything wrong, stilted our flow. I broke my contract and word to her and to Jake, my boss and manager, who'd become like my family over the past six years. How could I tell two people I loved dearly that their tangible, passionate love for each other tortured me? Trying to survive heartbreak had that green-eyed monster chasing me away from my friends and family. I promised myself I would be truly happy for my friends when I stood by Amara's side at the altar. I prayed that time wouldn't make me a liar.

Tension from a restless night and abruptly being awakened tightened my neck and shoulders. I pushed from the bed and eased down to the floor to stretch. I had never been a fan of jogging or any strenuous exercise, but yoga refreshed, stretched, and toned me. Moving onto all fours for the cat pose, I rounded my back toward the ceiling and dropped my head to the floor. *Inhale slowly, breathing in life, and exhale even slower. Inhale. Exhale. Inhale. Exhale.*

Being complacent for the last four months had made this more challenging than I remembered. Just because my mind was almost ready to return to the living didn't mean my body believed the same. I flopped on my back, the soft carpet pillowing my body. Sweating from five minutes of yoga? Staring at my recessed ceiling, I pondered, as I had these last few weeks, what now? What would the next phase of my life be like? All I knew was music, which reminded me too much of *him*. I'd saved enough that my hiatus from life hadn't impacted my ability to take care of myself. Yet. I had to make sense of my existence, regain purpose, and soon, or I would have no choice but to return home, and I didn't want to return to small-time life when I'd become a city girl.

The three heavy knocks on my door startled me. My heart fluttered with possibilities, no matter how I tried to temper the unrealistic, hopeful direction of my thoughts. I pushed up from the plush carpet and hurried through the joint living and kitchen area. Steve Urkel snorted from the TV mounted between my black-and-white photo collection of myself, my four sisters, and my parents. I grabbed the remote from the walnut coffee table in front of my sofa to turn off the TV I'd left on all night and then tossed the remote on the chaise longue next to my bay window, which beckoned me daily to rest and nap. Inhaling hope, I peeked through the keyhole. Disappointment dropped my forehead to the door briefly before I opened it.

"So, the cavalry decided to send you?" I stared warily at a smiling Nathan, the only friend who hadn't left a text or voicemail, probably because he'd been too busy traveling to notice my absence. "You can tell everyone I'm good."

He placed one tattooed hand on the jamb, rightfully expecting me to close the door on him. "I will once I believe that's the truth."

I folded my arms and jutted out my chin. "It's the truth. I just needed a break."

"Then you won't mind if I bring you back to civilization." His easy smile and affable nature pushed through my stubbornness to shut him and the rest of the world out again.

"Did Jake or Mari send you?" Nathan was Jake's old college roommate and best friend, who frequented the studio when he moved to Nashville. We'd hung out several times, usually with Jake and the band, and he'd seen me perform solo around the city.

"Does it matter who sent me?" Nathan glanced past my shoulders. "Is there some man waiting to jump me if I set one foot inside? Blink twice if you're being held captive."

"I'm not holed up with a man. Is that what everyone thinks?" I retorted, and at his raised brow, I apologized, "Didn't mean to snap at you."

"Can you let me inside? I'm freezing." He shivered, rubbing his bare arms that peeked from underneath his black-and-red Tupac t-shirt. "No one told me I should have worn pants instead of shorts today."

A reluctant giggle escaped my lips. "Why are you this way? You're standing in a hallway and it's at least eighty degrees at the end of the summer. You are not cold."

With one finger, Nathan pushed up his gold wire-rimmed glasses on his wide nose. "When the Sophie wind chill factor hits, it feels like fifty degrees."

"Ha. Ha." I stepped back to allow him inside. His toned forearm inadvertently brushed against my right breast, and my stomach clenched. I quickly hugged my chest protectively. I'd forgotten I wore a thin nightshirt that stopped at my upper thigh.

"Sorry. My bad," Nathan said, though I saw a spark of something in his eyes. "Probably need to put on actual clothes, since you didn't expect company."

"Yeah, yeah, take a seat… I'll be right back. Do you want something to drink or eat? I don't have much in the fridge. You can have whatever you see." I kept one arm across my body as I gestured to the attached kitchen. "Or you can turn on the TV. I also have a few magazines and books on the table. Um…I didn't expect company." Embarrassed by my cluttered area. I picked up a blanket off the floor and an empty pizza box off the table. "The remote is on the lounger."

Nathan jammed his hands in his cargo shorts and chuckled. "Stop being Ms. Southern Hospitality and get dressed so we can talk."

"I'm not going back on the road with Mari. If that's what you're here for, might as well turn back around." I planted my hands on my hips.

He pointed in the direction of my bedroom. "Don't know why I have to say more than one time to get dressed."

"'Cuz you're not my father," I retorted, tugging down my sleep shirt as I headed to my room, feeling the heat of his gaze on my bottom. "Stop staring."

"Then put some damn clothes on."

Surprisingly pleased that he didn't try to deny that I'd caught him checking me out, I slammed my door and leaned against it, breathless. Expectant energy buzzed around me. I hadn't seen Nathan since we were in Memphis five months ago, helping Jake throw a surprise party in which Jake proposed to Amara. Nathan and I had made a good team and had fun for the two days it took to arrange an impromptu gathering at the Peabody Hotel. We'd been amused at how nervous the usually unflappable Jake had been and how love had changed him.

Nathan, an award-winning freelance journalist, had left Memphis the following morning after the proposal to work on a story out of the country. And everything for me shifted a month after that. I'd been siloed from everyone else for so long that his teasing, familiar presence charged my social battery, and I wanted his unexpected company.

Catching my reflection as I passed my full-length mirror, I did a double take and snatched off the colorful satin bonnet I'd also forgotten about.

This is what I looked like when I opened the door?

Only my family and Amara were ever supposed to see me with this on my head. I released a calming breath. At least I'd washed and French-braided my hair last night. I wasn't a total mess.

Why did I even care? It was just Nathan, a man who was like my big brother. A man I'd known for the past two years, when the world traveler decided to chill in Nashville. Admittedly, he was attractive, with muscles that flexed without effort, a low-cut fade, and a groomed mustache and beard. Smooth skin that tanned chestnut in the summer. If I were into older men, which I wasn't, he might be kind of hot.

Still. Nathan was, well…Nathan.

Then why were my cheeks flushed and my eyes bright like I had a date waiting for me in the other room?

Comfort food and long days in bed for the past four months had thickened my belly, thighs, and ass. Even my breasts and cheeks were fuller and rounder. *Necessary added weight,* my mother, whose body lovingly carried the evidence of bearing five daughters, would argue. Nathan, a tall and rugged man who loved cigars and adventure, seemed the type to prefer Megan Thee Stallion over Tyla. Maybe that's why his glance and touch now affected me differently than in the past. Or maybe it was because I so longed for a man's touch that a man I'd only considered a friend seemed more at home in the confines of my living space.

I rushed to my disorganized closet, rummaging through some of the clothes that had fallen from the hangers the last time I searched for something to wear. Choosing something shouldn't be too hard, since I wasn't trying to impress or entice anyone—but my still-tingling body told another tale, so I grabbed one of my sister's baggy, black sweat suits. I needed to keep us in the friendly zone.

Nathan's eyebrows were drawn together while his hands were in sudsy sink water, washing dishes from the last four days. I scanned the room, and he'd made the magazines and books neat and tidy on the table. He'd already wiped the counters in the kitchen. Either he was a fast cleaner, or it'd taken me longer than I realized to get showered and dressed. Admittedly touched by this domestic side of him, I eased onto the island's barstool across from him.

"I do have a dishwasher right next to you."

"Machine never gets them as clean as my hands," he replied.

"You really don't have to clean up. I would've eventually gotten around to it."

Nathan rinsed off a wine glass. "You have a rack somewhere?"

"No. I usually put my glasses in the cabinet."

"I'll have to buy you a rack and install it right here." He gestured with his head to the light fixtures above. "Probably can figure out a space to place it. Then easy access."

"I don't need a rack," I said. Butterflies tickled my stomach at his offer, which seemed too much like a man trying to secure a spot in my life, unlike the nomadic Nathan I'd known.

"No one ever needs a rack, but this is the fifth wine glass I've washed. Threw two bottles away. You obviously love wine." He took a towel to dry off the glass and placed it on the island beside the sink next to the other glasses.

"Seriously, you're my guest. I know you didn't come over here to clean or make home improvements." Guiltily, I scanned the open area between my kitchen and living room to detect if there were any more wine bottles for him to discard. Wine, takeout, and solitude had become my norm.

He started putting the glasses away. "I think the words you're looking for are 'thank you' or 'appreciate you,'" he said, sounding like a parent.

I rolled my eyes and reluctantly said, "Thank you."

"You hungry?" His back was turned to me, giving me a second to admire his toned calves and that his cargo shorts fit his taut behind nicely. I quickly averted my gaze before he caught me ogling him.

"Is that your way of asking me to cook? I need to order groceries. I can probably scrape something together." I pulled my cell out of my sweatpants pocket.

"No, that stove hasn't been touched in years. Think I'm good on you cooking for me." Nathan's lips curved, though he had yet to look at me.

"I would be insulted and tell you I can bring *it* into the kitchen if you weren't right. I've been living here for over a year and may have used the stove a handful of times. Too busy to cook even if I enjoy it." The stainless-steel stove mocked me daily when I overlooked it to warm and prepare food in the microwave above it.

He placed another glass in the cabinet. "Too hungry to wait around anyway. Figured we can grab lunch while we catch up. Might have some work for you."

"What kind of work?" I hesitantly asked. Was I really ready to leave the cocoon of my home for more than a moment? Then again, I needed to do something, *anything* to get me out of this rut.

"Rather explain over lunch." He turned around and rested against the counter. "Humor me, okay? It has nothing to do with performing or the tour."

I looked down at my faded sweatshirt. "Oh…then I better change. I didn't realize we were going anywhere."

Nathan glanced at my attire and chuckled. "Doing your best to hide from me."

I hopped down from the stool. "I'm not hiding from you. I'm right here."

He tilted his head. "You know what I mean?"

"No, I don't." Although I did.

"Then why the too-big clothes when I've seen you wear a lot less? I'm here as a friend only. Don't change up on me because we haven't been around each other in a while. Wear something that makes you feel pretty."

"I am good, for the last time," I tossed back at him.

"Well, you almost look good for someone who vanished off the face of Earth.." He grinned. "I missed you, Twinkle."

"Ugh…not that damn nickname." Gripping the edge of the island, I said, "You're like the pot calling the kettle black. You disappear all the time. Did you really miss me? I don't recall a text or a call. Not even a funny meme or video in my DMs for me to heart or laugh."

"My bad." He dropped his gaze for a second. "I met up with Jake and Mari in Sacramento last week to catch her show, and I asked about you. Jake told me you dropped out of the tour a few months ago and that neither he nor Mari had heard from you except for a dry text. They were worried, and I told them I would check on you when I returned to Nashville." He crossed his ankles. "What's up? Not like you to ghost people."

"I didn't ghost anyone. I told Mari and Jake I needed a break from touring. Mari might have just started touring with Jake, but this is year five for me backing up his other artists."

"It's not just the tour. You haven't been performing anywhere in the city, and you're not even responding to Tavion's texts." Nathan twisted the worn leather band around his wrist. "And you two are tight."

Tavion was my best friend and bandmate. I didn't feel like hearing his straight-from-the-hip honesty that I should've known better than to fall for another musician. At first, he'd called and texted nonstop that I was making a mistake to potentially ruin my career over a man. Tavion didn't and never would understand that I didn't care about my future in the music world or any particular job. Lately, he hadn't called, and his texts were few and far between. Although I missed him and his friendship terribly, I wasn't ready to rehash everything that had happened between Omar—my ex—and me, a necessity if I wanted to get back in Tavion's good graces.

I shrugged. "They all want me to be on the road with them. Not feeling music right now. To be honest, not sure I even want to perform anymore."

"Twinkle, who do I need to fight, because I can't imagine you never singing or playing again. Before I left, you kept a guitar in your hand." Lines crossed his broad forehead. "Did a hideous, jealous troll say something about your singing, or did your man demand you give it up for him?" He narrowed his gaze. "No…he broke your heart, and in a big way."

My eyes widened, and I could barely hear myself ask over my thundering heartbeat, "How did you know about him? Did Tavion or Mari say anything?"

"No. It's always a man when a woman does a disappearing act, whether it's to relish being together or to nurse the wounds of a breakup." He glanced around my space. "This seems to be about the end of a relationship. No judgment. Promise. I'll treat you to some barbecue, and we can talk about him or whatever you want to talk about. I feel like brisket and sweet tea. If I remember correctly, you love brisket too." He pulled out the stopper in the sink.

"I do." I nodded, willing my body to relax. I had to stop reacting like that about a man who probably wasn't thinking about me anymore. "And I don't want to talk about him. It's been months and he's ancient history."

"I did say we could talk about anything. You changing or nah?" Nathan asked.

"I happen to like what I have on," I quipped, though I wouldn't be seen in public in these sweats.

He walked past me, wiping his hand on my sleeve. "This thick and fluffy material is perfect for warmth and drying. I'll need it to wipe that barbecue off my fingers."

"Stop it, Nate. You play too much." I slapped his hand away from me. "You know I'm not leaving my house looking like this. I just don't like men telling me what to wear."

"Say less." He chuckled. "Next time, I won't say anything about your raggedy nightshirt or the puffy bag you had on your head."

"You better not tell anyone you saw me like that. I'm serious." I punched his shoulder, and he rubbed it, laughing.

"I won't," he promised as I rushed back to my room to find an outfit that made me feel beautiful and ready to face the world. His uninvited yet comforting presence had lifted my mood, and suddenly, I couldn't wait to see what job he had in mind.

TWO

Sophie

Over the noise of the early dinner crowd and the young woman at the counter yelling customer orders to the cook, I gripped my fork, straining to hear Nathan, who was sitting across from me in a booth. "It's loud in here. This may not have been the best place to talk."

He scanned the usually laid-back barbecue joint full of people sitting at picnic tables or booths. "Didn't think it would be this busy in the middle of the week, and it's not even dinnertime." Nathan dipped his fork in his green beans before adding mac and cheese and gulping the mix down. "Do I need to repeat myself?"

I leaned closer to him. "Let me get this straight. You want me to go with you to Memphis and take pictures with my iPhone for a documentary on the blues? Sort of like the same lie I told Mari when she asked why I was in Memphis when we planned her proposal party?"

He finished chewing on a bite of brisket and wiped his mouth. "Yes, or I can buy you a camera if you prefer."

"My phone. It might take me too long to figure out how to use a camera if all I'm doing is taking pics for social media or a Pinterest board."

Nathan placed his hands on the table near where mine rested next to my food. "I want you to do more than take pics for social media. The images you capture will continue to inspire me as I write and direct what we want in the documentary. With all this attention on Stoney and his stolen legacy, Mari believes that anything I write will garner attention for the proposed documentary on the lost souls of blues."

Stoney Johnson, Amara's estranged grandfather, was a blues singer and musician who wrote songs for other artists. The recognition and money he deserved for creating award-winning hits had only happened after his death, when Amara found his old guitar, a worn journal, and love letters. Nathan had been instrumental in assisting Amara and Jake in finding out the truth about Stoney and writing a feature story about him that spread through the world like wildfire.

"*Lost Souls of the Blues*. Nice title." I slurped the rest of my Dr. Pepper.

Nathan tilted his head slightly. "The documentary isn't named yet. Still working that out with Mari. The lost souls of the blues is how I envision the project. We want to shed light on eclipsed voices in the industry. Jake is funding our research with the hope that a studio will take an interest. Even if we can't get a buyer, we all believe in this documentary and are prepared to do it ourselves. I'm going to Memphis to do some preliminary work, gather background information, scope out the locals and the musicians, and explore the history of Memphis. Stoney mentioned a couple of songs in his journal, attached to musicians. I plan to start with them."

"The project is perfect, and it will definitely sell. But I'm not a photographer. I dabble. My iPhone is my camera. How can any pictures I take do justice to what y'all trying to do?" I placed another forkful of the baked beans in my mouth to quell the growing excitement. Interesting and important work that didn't involve me performing. Still.

"Well, I'm not a filmmaker, either. I write. You have an eye, Sophie. Your pictures are what helped Mari's social media blow up. Jake's management company wouldn't be as sought after if you didn't document the details. You didn't just take pictures of Amara or Jake on stage and off. You captured them as people everyone wants to know them." He picked up his cell and scrolled on his screen for a few seconds. "See this pic you took of Mari while she sang karaoke in that bar? This had ten million likes. Why? Your lens caught pure joy on her face. Happiness is universal. An emotion that, for most people, is fleeting. When we see it, we try to hold on to it. I need you to find the humanity in the people and places in Memphis. I want people to see our pain and our triumph as theirs."

I stared at the beautiful picture of my friend as Amara finally shed the last of her nerves to showcase her God-given gifts. "I took this photo without thought. You're asking me to be intentional. I don't want to mess this up for you or them. My gut leads my choices. I don't know if I can trust it anymore." I passed his phone back to him. "I know this was Mari's idea to get me out of a slump, trying to help me. I'm flattered she thought of me, but I'm not the person for the job."

"It was my idea, and they agreed." He pushed his empty plate to the side. "Sure, I can find a professional photographer easily. Already have a few in mind for the music magazine I want to publish in the future. But you're Tennessee through and through. Born in Knoxville, raised in Gatlinburg, and now a resident of Nashville. This is your home state, and your gut will dictate what images are important for this project."

"Memphis is a different beast from anywhere I've lived."

"Stop making excuses. Memphis is still Tennessee." Clasping his hands together before him, he firmly added, "And I can't let you continue to wallow over a man who's not worth it."

"You can't *let* me?" Nathan didn't flinch at my rising voice. "You said no judgments, remember? I've said nothing about him or our relationship. I needed a break. Period."

The ends of his brows dipped behind his glasses. "Two weeks is a break. Hell, I'll give you a month. It's been four months, Sophie. We've been here for more than an hour, and from what I can tell from your conversation, you haven't done much except hang with your family and then binge-watch mindless TV for the last few months. Maybe read a book of substance or two. You're way too young and talented to give up on everything because of a broken heart. What if he's not the last man to hurt you? Huh? Is this how you'll react every time a relationship ends? You can't keep shutting everyone out."

A passing couple holding trays of food looked at us on their way to a nearby table. The noise in the restaurant had quieted while our voices remained raised.

"You think I *like* how I am right now? That I can't seem to let go of what could've been? This was different. He was different. I thought he was the one," I spat. "But I bet you wouldn't know what that feels like. How you ache from the moment you wake up until you fall asleep at night, knowing that you can't ever touch that person again, and the life you envisioned no longer exists. Hell, I doubt you've ever stayed in the same place long enough to fall in love."

He stared at me for a long second before lowering his voice. "I struck a nerve because you know I'm right. You're ready to get back out here and live, so you're sitting across from me. You just don't know how to do it. I'm offering you a rope. Take it or leave it. I won't ask again."

"Then don't." His demanding tone tugged at my pride and stubbornness.

Our chests heaved in unison while time seemed to stand still. His eyes finally yielded.

I pushed my basket of uneaten food to the side and softened my tone. "I appreciate the opportunity, I really do, but I'll figure it out on my own, as I've always done since I left home at eighteen."

Nathan's cheekbones never seemed more pronounced than while he gathered the remnants of our meal. "You finished?"

"Yeah. You can throw it away. Lost my appetite."

With our baskets in his hand, he pleaded, "Sophie, maybe I came across a little too strong because I care. This opportunity isn't just about getting you out of a rut. I really could use your help. This project has the potential to be bigger than Stoney's."

I stared silently at him, pushing down the anticipation of doing something new and different stirring in my body.

"If you change your mind, you have my number." His ramrod shoulders drooped in defeat as he headed toward the trash receptacle in the corner of the restaurant.

In his absence, I drew in calming breaths. He *had* struck a nerve. This recent, purposeless life had drained me of my natural zest and motivation. Nathan's words and ultimatum rattled around in my head before settling in my heart. What he asked of me, I could do without thought. Taking photos had become second nature, like my guitar playing, and all the solitude had become exhausting. The idea of spending endless days hiding from the world no longer appealed.

When a somber Nathan stood over me, ready to go, I sank back in the booth, lifted my chin, and asked, "What's next?"

The stern set of his mouth contradicted the gleam in his eyes. "We go to Memphis tomorrow in time for the weekend. Maybe stay a week. Maybe longer. Hotel and food on Jake's dime. He said to check your bank account for payment tonight. If you don't like the pay, he'll adjust to what you believe is fair."

"Leave tomorrow?" Lowering my eyes to slits, I asked, "When did Jake decide this?"

"When I texted him and said you're on board while you were changing into that pretty dress." Nathan's expression relaxed into a wide grin.

"How did you know I would agree, *and* agree to leave so soon?"

Nathan lifted one thick brow. "What else do you have planned for the next week? You can ride down with me, or I'll pick you up from the airport if you'd rather fly."

"Why aren't you flying?"

"I love driving. My creativity flows when I'm behind the wheel. Flying might get us to our destinations quicker, but there's way too much involved to catch a flight. Security checks, long lines, and annoying people. Most of my assignments require airplane travel, so when I get a chance to drive, I seize it."

Allowing the tension of the last few moments to dissipate in the space between us, I returned his smile. "Feel the same. What time are you trying to get on the road?"

"Crack of dawn. Want to hit the city running." He retrieved a leather wallet from his back pocket to toss a twenty-dollar bill on the table, though no one had served us. "You riding with me or flying?"

Contentment flowed through me at finally finding ground after floating these past few months. "Think I need to stay close to earth." I scooted out of the booth and faced him.

"I'll pick you up around six thirty. Something tells me you need to leave a little later than dawn. Bring your guitar."

I scowled. "Haven't played since I left the tour."

"Not even at home?" Nathan's eyes widened.

"No. Not bringing it."

He jammed one hand in his pocket. "This whole project is about music. You don't think there's anything or anyone who will inspire you to play? From one creative to another, I can't travel without my laptop or a notepad and pen because I have no idea when something will strike me, and I have to write it right then and there. Whether you ever play the guitar or sing again, you're a musician as much as I'm a writer, even if I never write another word."

"I don't want to feel pressured to play." The whine in my voice annoyed me. I sounded like a spoiled child instead of a woman certain about why I didn't want to bring my guitar.

"I'm never going to pressure you or expect you to play. I'm looking out for you. What if we're jamming at some bar or with a musician? You'll wish you had a guitar on you, or at least back in your hotel room. Trust me on this."

Since I couldn't think of a valid reason against bringing my guitar, I pointed at his chest. "It has to be my playlist. I don't want to hear Motown's greatest hits all the way." I laughed at the deep frown on his face.

"You have serious jokes. The driver chooses the music, and it's hip-hop all the way." He moved toward the door and waited for me to join him.

"That's not fair. I don't want to hear old-school rap. That's got to be the fourth Tupac shirt I've seen you wear." I glanced at him. "I bet you're the type that refuses to let a woman touch the wheel."

"I don't know any woman who wants to drive on a road trip when there's a man around." Nathan pushed the door open. "Am I wrong?"

"No," I reluctantly admitted. "But if you want me to stay awake and keep you company, it has to be my playlist. Sexyy Red all the way."

He groaned loudly. The bright sun glinted off his glasses, and I could see my reflection there. I'd unbraided and finger-combed my sandy-colored hair into wild, wavy tresses that flowed over my naturally sun-kissed face to shoulders left bare by my pink halter dress. Was this how I appeared to him at this very moment? Sexy. Confident. Happy.

Squinting to look up at him, I said, "You look handsome in those. I didn't realize you wore glasses."

His lips twitched. "Need a prescription for my contacts, and there's a lot you don't know about me."

"That's a true statement. You're like this mysterious figure who dips in and out and saves the day." I headed to his gray 4Runner parked next to the curb. "Do you purposely keep people except Jake at a distance?"

Nathan quickened his steps to reach the passenger side first. "Habit of a military brat. We used to move so much, and I didn't try to make friends, because what was the point?"

"Is it a habit you want to change?"

Nathan opened the door and rested his hands on top of it. "I'm here when I could already be in Memphis working. What you think?"

"Guess we're about to find out about each other." I gripped the top of the door, our knuckles almost touching. The faint scent of his cologne, or maybe his soap, wafted in the breeze. "Like, why do you call me Twinkle? Is it because you think I should be a star like Mari?"

He tilted his head. "Maybe one day I'll tell you. Does it bother you?"

I made a small space between my index finger and thumb and replied, "Bothers me *that* much."

Nathan cracked a smile. "That much, huh?"

"I kind of like that you have a nickname for me. You and Jake are the big brothers I always wanted."

Nathan bit the corner of his lip. "I'd rather you see me as a friend."

I tapped the hand that rested beside mine. "I already do. Thank you for thinking of me for this project."

"Most welcome." He winked and strolled to the driver's side.

I eased down in the passenger seat and buckled up with new hope that this trip would be just what I needed to move on from the sadness and grief and remember the mornings.

Long after Nathan dropped me off, I reclined on my chaise longue, staring out my bay window. I watched the orange-pinkish sky transition into midnight blue. I'd been offered a lifeline from the least expected person. The disappointment that squeezed my heart that it wasn't Omar had lasted until Nathan smiled at me. I wasn't foolish enough to believe that my spirit's lifting at his presence meant anything.

I looked around the room that he'd tidied up for me, the cluttered space that mirrored my thoughts. I'd been touched by the caring gesture that subconsciously opened my mind to him—his quiet insistence that I change clothes and that I had to let go of my despair. His belief in my ability to assist him in such an important project moved me. I would be a part of history as we told the story of brilliant, unheralded musicians.

The longer I stared out the window, the more energy shifted in my body like the last notes of a song I wished had only just begun. Then the sweet, sweet giddiness once I remembered that any song could be enjoyed over and over again—how life was meant to be lived. Nathan had reminded me of that in a few short hours after I'd been trying to remember for the last four months. I'd meant it when I said he was this mysterious man who dipped in and out and saved the day. With Nathan's impeccable investigative and writing skills, he'd unveiled the hidden legacy of Stoney Johnson to the world. And now he wanted to shed light on others like Stoney.

Others like me.

My heart thumped against my chest, and I swung my feet over the chair to stand. Had I become like all the other faceless musicians who gave up on their talent? Was this the real reason Nathan had thought of me? Was it because he wanted me to see myself in the people we would meet? Or was it simply a coincidence? My mind settled on that thought. He didn't know I'd completely given up on music or that a successful career was never my end goal.

Nathan would learn soon enough not to equate me with unsung musicians, since we would spend hours together with no one interrupting us for the next several days. I couldn't let the yearning feelings he aroused become anything meaningful, because then I would become that desperate woman who jumped from man to man, hoping one of them would love her. No matter how much I longed for happily ever after with a husband and family, I wanted it to be with the right man. Nathan loved adventure too much to be content with the life I dreamed of. Whatever chemistry and attraction flowing between us would eventually die down the more we learned about each other, and I could forevermore keep Nathan in the friend zone.

Resolved in my decision, I picked up my cell as I headed to my bedroom to pack for the start of a new journey.

"Squirrel, you better be calling me to tell me you're on the way here," Mama demanded as soon as she answered. "If it's not why you're calling, then it better be to say you worked it out with Omar or you're back on tour with Mari."

"You only met Omar once to wish we were still together, and I'm not going back on the tour." I cradled the phone to my shoulder to sort through my clothes in my closet, her overt reminder that I needed a man sticking like a thorn in my side. "But hey, I can stop calling you until I meet said conditions."

She clicked her tongue. "You better call your mama anytime. Just worried about you, like I always do. You're my only baby I can't touch if I want to." Of her five daughters, I was her eldest and the only one to leave Gatlinburg when I saved enough money from working at nearby Dollywood as a waitress. "You left out of here like a bat out of hell the last time you were here. I assumed you were running toward someone."

"No…just got to be too much of a reminder of what I don't have." I tossed a formfitting yellow maxi dress and a black, short one on my bed from the closet, perfect whenever we hit the nightlife of Memphis. Never knew who we might see or meet. A little flirting here and there with Nathan and other men wouldn't hurt a fly.

"Aw, baby, you will have what they have if you want it," Mama promised me, as she often had once my younger sister married her high school sweetheart six years ago, and my even younger sister married two years later.

"For the last time, I do want a husband and a family. It just hasn't happened." I balled my hands into fists. "Before we start another debate about my singledom, I only called to tell you I'll be in Memphis working on a documentary. I leave tomorrow."

"Memphis? I wish you'd moved to Memphis instead of Nashville. Might have found you a husband there easier," she said knowingly.

She won't stop. I pulled the phone from my ear and gritted out, "Do you want to know more about what I'll be doing or not?"

"Stop getting mad. I was just about to ask you. Is this a project with Jake?"

Cooling my irritation, I replied evenly, "It is. Mari too. There will be a documentary about the blues inspired by Stoney Johnson. I'll be there to take pics of the sights and sounds of the music of Memphis."

"Taking pictures and not performing? Who are you going with? For how long? When did you decide this? And are you sure it's okay with Jake? I'm only asking because I thought Amara was still on tour." She was sputtering as if she sensed my patience was wearing thin.

"She is. I'm working with a friend of Jake's. He's the one who wrote the article about Stoney. He's won awards for his writing and everything."

"Is he single?" She practically sang her question.

I rolled my eyes. "Not the point, Mama."

"Or it's the exact point, since he must be single. Don't let the old love stop you from a new one."

"What if I told you he was knocking on sixty? Is he still a catch?"

"For your auntie, he would be. A writer who's still single. Ooh, wait until I tell her," she exclaimed. "What's his name again? Maybe you can invite him here for the holidays. I can make my famous ham and get your aunt to make her sweet potato pie. Nothing like good food to get a man's attention." Mama was a notorious matchmaker, proud that she'd connected several couples in our town—which really wasn't that difficult when the population was less than five thousand.

"Mama…stop. Stop. Stop. He's Jake's age."

"Ooh, then he's perfect for you."

"You know I like men to be my age."

"If he's Jake's age, then that man can't be more than five years older," Mama scoffed. "See, this is why you're still alone. Coming up with stupid reasons not to date an eligible bachelor. Most women would jump on this. If he's a friend of Jake and looks remotely like that beautiful Black man, he definitely has potential. Don't block your blessings, Sophie."

"Bye, Mama. I love you. Will see you soon. Tell Papa I'll buy him a new Grizzlies cap. I gotta run." I clicked off the cell before I rudely reminded her that I'd left home as soon as I could because of her meddlesome ways. I didn't need to feel worse than I already did, that my mother and sisters could hold on to love, and I couldn't.

My phone buzzed.

Proud of you, no matter what you do or who you decide to be with, my talented firstborn. Sorry.

Mama's text watered my eyes. No matter how much she frustrated me and went overboard in her matchmaking schemes, she meant well. She only wanted whatever I wanted for myself. And right now, I wanted to be in Memphis, creating history with one Nathan Price.

I returned to my closet and stepped over discarded shoes and clothes to get to the back wall. My pink guitar case stared forlornly at me, half hidden by my wool coat. I dragged the case out of my closet and plopped down on the carpet. I opened the case carefully as if what was inside would frighten and not comfort me. Only emptiness and numbness stared back.

I shut the case and huddled in a ball, hoping morning would come soon.

THREE

Nathan

An explosion rattled my body. I popped up in bed, grabbing my ears from the expected pain of the sound waves from the blast, sweat dripping down my face and chest. I pressed my ears flat to my head as I scanned the room, waves of dizziness making it hard to remain upright, frantically searching for anything that would firmly plant me in my safe environment, not the dangerous ones I had the misfortune to inhabit. My desperate eyes grabbed the cover of *The Nickel Boys* by Colson Whitehead on my wall. I fixed all my attention on the red-and-white cover with the two Black boys in the corner until my mind and body rejoined me in my conscious present.

Taking a deep, relieved, and settling breath, I remained still until the dizziness subsided. I shook off the remnants of my troubled sleep by dropping to the floor to do my daily routine of push-ups and sit-ups. Years of repetition had negated the need for a gym or free weights to maintain the physique I'd earned from maturation and years of running to and from danger, both in the harsh, violent urban areas of the States and the warring countries abroad. All in the name of finding the cold, hard truth. I'd learned that aggression knew no color or gender and was an innate part of us, easily triggered into violence given the right circumstances. If some random person cut us off on the road, we flipped into a murderous rage after being at peace a few seconds prior. The young man who'd just killed another under the auspices of serving his country in the military was an innocent senior in high school a few months ago. An unremorseful woman stabbed another woman for taking her man, as if we somehow have ownership over another human being in the first place. Child soldiers took the lives of others without having the cognitive development to understand the permanency of their actions.

I'd grown weary of living on the edge and seen enough of the worst of human nature that I now longed for the best. The stolen legacy of Stoney Johnson had brought different attention to my work, and human-interest stories regarding music had become my spark. Music, like the concepts of God, love, and family, was universal, no matter the genre.

I collapsed flat on my back after my two hundredth sit-up, panting. The daily exercises served me mentally and physically. The burst of energy also lifted the heaviness of my violent past, which often descended while I slept. Without checking a clock or a watch, I knew it was four thirty and not my usual five a.m. wake-up time. My body recognized that I needed the extra time to relax into my day, since I'd told Sophie to be ready by six thirty.

The familiar thrill of the chase coursed through my blood, sparked by my charged interaction with Sophie. I'd been up late drafting ideas and writing. I wasn't sure if the zestful interest in this was about spending time with Sophie or the actual project. I'd noticed her as any man enthralled with a woman's beauty might the first time I watched one of Jake's artists rehearse at Evelyn's studio.

Of course I'd noticed Sophie strumming her guitar in the booth, head bowed, focused. Beautiful. Talented. Sexy.

Her natural, sensual femininity allured. Sophie lit up any room with her warm, wide smile and affectionate nature. She bounced with every step, like she remained open and ready for whatever was next. It didn't hurt that she had curves she loved to show off and pretty brown eyes that fluttered flirtatiously when she wanted something. The blonde and bright-colored wigs she preferred complemented the warm honey tone of her skin, though I longed to wrap the real, silky strands she'd allowed me to see yesterday around my finger.

I longed to do so much more when she'd opened the door wearing hardly anything, and I had to control my impulse to kiss her. I'd always kept it light and friendly because she was the type of woman a man made a wife, not just for sex. Cleaning up her space was more for me than for her. I needed to do something productive with my lustful energy and not scare her away. When she'd changed into that drab and unflattering outfit, I thought I had, and that saddened me.

In Sophie, I always saw hope. She had this vibrancy and this genuine expectancy that only good things happened, a belief and faith that even when hard times occurred, there was a better tomorrow. Her light tickled my darkness, reminding me there was still good in this terrible world. For the last two-odd years, whenever I encountered Sophie, she brightened my day. She probably still believed I called her "Twinkle" because I saw her as a star. Not the pop singer kind, though she had enough talent in her pinkie to be that kind of performer. No, her easy, sunny disposition made a grouch like me smile.

When she'd opened the door to her apartment, Sophie seemed a hollow shell of herself. No longer alight with the glow of possibilities, she'd lost a part of herself. I'd become more determined than ever to help her regain her natural light. I would as a friend. And though I'd been attracted to her from the moment she hugged me instead of shaking my hand when I first met Sophie, I had no intention of ever pursuing her. She was a forever woman, and I was only a temporary man.

After an extended hot shower to relax my muscles, I pulled on shorts and walked across from my bedroom to the office, then sat down in my cushioned chair and clicked the laptop on. The names, places, and concepts scrambled around in my brain. Claudette Saint. Stoney Johnson. Withers Collection. Stax Records. Elvis. Beale Street. Peabody Hotel. B.B. King. Soul. Rhythm. The Pyramid. Lorraine Hotel. Mississippi River. Memphis Blues. W.C. Handy, the father of the blues. What was my angle? What was the point of this story? Who cared about these people? Who cared about this city of mostly Black folks named after the ancient capital city of Egypt, which most associated with Graceland and not Beale Street? No one listened to the blues anymore. No one cared about history anymore, especially *our* history.

I pushed back from my desk. I needed to care. I needed to feel the rhythm of the city in a snapshot. I needed to believe that the people in that storied city mattered. If I didn't believe it, it would show in my words. Three years ago, I'd lost my edge, my passion for the truth. Writing Stoney's story had challenged me and reinvigorated my quest for knowledge, my desire to write informative stories that could help people make sense of the crumbling world around us. Country music and the Nashville scene started it all. Maybe the soul and blues of Memphis would finish it. This project might be the key to unleashing the last creative blockage hindering me from the ultimate prize, the Pulitzer. With an eye for capturing emotions, Sophie might be the key to making all this happen.

My cell rang, and I answered without noting the caller. I assumed it was Sophie wondering what time I was headed her way. I often got lost in my work, and time would slip away, which was another reason I hated flying. I was confined to a schedule.

"What did she say?" Jake asked anxiously.

His gruff voice startled me, and I rechecked my cell. "I told you, she already agreed yesterday."

"And I know how you do. She probably didn't agree until after you sent me the text."

I chuckled. "We know each other too well, and we're getting on the road in a few. Why are you even up at five in the morning?"

"We haven't been to sleep yet. Mari had a show, and then there was an after-party. It's three in San Diego."

"How did she do?" I smiled, already knowing the answer. Amara Johnson was an undeniable star.

"Man, she gets better and better." I could picture Jake's dimpled smile. "She's getting a lot of love throughout the country, which has helped settle her nerves that people will accept her."

"I'm glad. I never wanted her career to be impacted by what I wrote. Congrats on another stellar show." I pulled my chair back up to the desk, feeling once again grateful that my exposé of a country legend hadn't impacted Amara Johnson's career in a world that traditionally didn't accept people who looked like her.

"Thanks." He paused before announcing, "It's Nate on the phone. Sophie is going with him to Memphis. They're getting on the road this morning."

Amara shouted her approval, and a few seconds later, her raspy songstress voice caressed my ear. "Nate?"

I smiled. "Heard you were amazing."

"Thank you. Thank you. But I don't want to talk about me. How did Sophie look? I haven't seen her face in months. Is she mad with us, or did Jake do something that pissed her off? You know how he can be." Her rushed words told of her concern, worry, and love.

"Hey, I didn't do anything to Sophie," Jake complained in the background.

"Trust, I do know how much of an asshole he can be." I chuckled again. "It's not about you or Jake at all. She's not into music right now. Healing from a broken heart. Her ex must have done a number on her. I don't think she was happy to see me at first. Had to talk her into Memphis." I closed my laptop. "Please make sure Jake puts money in her account in case she needs it. She hasn't performed anywhere and doesn't even play her guitar."

"I knew she and Omar had broken up, I just didn't realize she was that hurt," Amara said. "Why couldn't she tell me she needed time? I would've understood."

Hearing the name of Sophie's ex caused a twinge of jealousy, though I didn't know him. "My guess is you're engaged and happy, and she didn't want to bring you down. She also might be a little bit jealous. It can't be easy for her to be around you and Jake."

"I hadn't thought about how our engagement might bother her when she wants to be married more than anything." Amara sighed. "I hate that I couldn't be there for her like she's been there for me. You think she'll take my calls once you get to Memphis?"

"Give me a couple more days. By the time I dropped her off back at her place, she seemed more like our Sophie. This project is a good move for her." My phone beeped, and I checked the screen.

Bags are packed and I'm at the door. ETA?

I returned my attention to Amara. "Listen, I need you to send me information about Claudette Saint. I want to start with her. Stoney mentioned her name in his song journal, though I can't find anything about her on the Internet."

"I'll send you her daughter's information. She's excited about talking to us. From my understanding, Claudette doesn't want to relive her past but is willing to sit down with us, since she considered my grandfather a friend. She'll still need convincing."

"I love a challenge. I want to make her the focal point. Similar to what I did with Stoney. I don't want secondhand information from her daughter or what I might find in Memphis when Ms. Saint is still alive." My wheels started turning. "Then again, maybe Memphis is the point."

"Not following you."

"Not following myself either right now," I admitted. "I need to mull a little bit longer before I share what I'm thinking. And I need to get off the phone because Sophie is waiting for me."

"Wait, Nate. Jake wants to speak to you again."

Now I was running behind. I strode back to my room, placed my phone on speaker, and tossed it on the bed as I pulled on a short-sleeved red polo shirt, followed by my jeans.

"Hey." Jake's voice was lower.

"I'm here. What's up?"

"Listen, Sophie is vulnerable right now."

"Why are you telling me this?" Perched on the edge of my bed, I donned my red Jordans. "I'm not trying to push up on her. That would be you before Amara."

"She's like my little sister, and I don't want to see her hurt any more than what this dude did to her."

"It's been months since they broke up, and she's not much younger than Mari," I reminded him.

"Your point?" he practically snarled.

"She's a grown woman." I grabbed my duffel and rolling bag out of my closet. "You don't need to warn me. I care about her too, and I won't hurt her."

"I'm serious, Nate."

I picked up my phone and turned off the speaker. "I am, too. Why all this concern?"

"Because I know you. I hear the eagerness in your voice, and it's not all about this project. You're both single, and it's just you two in Memphis. Eventually, she'll want more than you can give her."

Instead of arguing, I said, "I'll text you when we make it to Memphis and update you in two days. Later."

Jake tersely responded, "Later."

Pushing our tense conversation to the back of my mind, I slipped the phone in my back pocket and hurried out of my house with my bags. I had no intention of trying anything with Sophie, and I couldn't wait to prove Jake wrong. I threw my bags in the trunk and drove the fifteen minutes to Sophie's place, determined to ignore any attraction I sensed between us.

Sophie was patiently waiting in the parking lot in front of her apartment. The fitted white tee twisted in a knot at her waist, and her jeggings emphasized that her hips and thighs had gloriously thickened since the last time I saw her. Her natural hair had been shaped into springy curls that framed her oval face, enhanced only with gloss and eyeliner—simple yet beautiful. And that was before she held up her guitar case and smiled at me.

Sophie once again brightened my day.

FOUR

Sophie

"**K**endrick Lamar is it for me," I said as we neared Memphis. "Come on, how can you not see his greatness? He won a Pulitzer Prize for his words. What did Tupac win?"

"I never said Kendrick wasn't great. He achieved an unheard-of feat when he won the prize at thirty-one. Tupac was stepping into his shine as an actor and an activist when he was gunned down at twenty-five. We will never know how far he could have gone." Nathan hit his steering wheel for emphasis. "Kendrick wouldn't be who he is without the influence of Tupac, who spat real-life shit in ways that enthralled the world. Kendrick is one of the best to ever do it, no doubt. He's just not the GOAT."

"I hate that terminology because the definition of greatness changes with time."

"No. 'Greatest of all time' encompasses all times. Period and end of story. Mic drop. The crowd roars. Tupac is the GOAT." He gave me a sidelong glance. "Bet you think that LeBron is better than Michael Jordan?"

I shifted in my seat and taunted him, "Because he is."

He gestured to the floor. "Yet you're wearing Jordans on your feet right now."

"And? I also have LeBrons, Kobes, and Kevin Durant's shoes at home. My Serena Williams Nikes are in my bag," I said, ticking off my fingers.

"Wait." He took his eyes off the road to incredulously ask, "Are you a sneakerhead?"

"Proud, card-carrying member," I boasted. "Fifty-six pairs in my closet."

"Seventy-eight. Do you have any Air Jordan 3s?" He arched a brow.

I jerked my head back. "What do *you* think?"

"Twinkle," he exclaimed, raising his hand for me to slap. "I'll have to show you my original Air Force Ones when we get back to Nashville."

"1985?" Nathan nodded vigorously, and I squealed, "Impressive. Can't wait to see them in person." I rubbed my hands together. "If you travel so much, where do you house your collection?"

"I might travel all the time, but I choose a home base every so often. Right now, it's Nashville. It might be London or San Francisco next year. I wanted to take a break from being overseas a couple of years back, and Jake suggested I stay in Nashville, since I love the music and energy. When the mood strikes, I'll pick a random bar, grab a beer, and listen to live music."

"Okay...okay, Nate." I wiggled my shoulders. "Might be more to you than this serious vibe you give off."

"What? Is it the glasses? I'm always joking or teasing you." He sat back in his seat, wearing a slight frown.

"Like the big brother you claim you don't want to be," I reminded him. "But other than that, you're quiet. Reserved, almost. Used to wonder how you and Jake got to be best friends. He's so...so..." I searched my brain to find the right words.

"Larger than life," he finished without any hint of envy or jealousy that one might expect when his best friend seemed to have it all. The way I sometimes felt about Amara, no matter how I fought it.

"Exactly. Besides the properties everywhere, the flashy cars, and the expensive clothes, everyone notices when he walks into any room like he's Morris Chestnut or Michael B. I bet that was before he became an agent or his mother married his rich stepfather."

"All true. I doubt we would've become best friends if he weren't my roommate. I'd already befriended a guy who was more my speed and met him during a special early admittance during the summer. I've never been one who needed a group. One or two good friends are all I need." He chuckled softly. "I thought Jake was white at first."

"Really?" Grinning, I turned slightly to rest my back against the door.

"His stuff was already in the room when I moved in. He had expensive suitcases, and his name was labeled or stitched everywhere. His stepfather stopped in the room because Jake had a meeting for business majors and had forgotten his ID. Mr. Barnes, a friendly white man, shook my hand and wished me good luck in college after retrieving his son's ID. Later that evening, when Jake returned to the room alone, I thought he was *looking* for Jake. It took me a minute to realize that he *was* Jake Barnes and my new roommate. He had all this energy and was excited to be on his own, while I missed my brother and father terribly—they lived in San Antonio, where my father was last stationed."

A soft smile graced his handsome profile as he reminisced.

"Jake immediately took me under his wing, though I'd been acclimated to campus a whole month before him. He had the gift of gab and understood how to navigate between white and Black worlds, which was necessary as a student of color at a primarily white university—especially a private one like Tulane—to be successful. I'd lived in and been exposed to other cultures, but I didn't have his ease with people. He loved that I cared about the news and was a communications and African studies major. I challenged him intellectually, and he challenged me socially. Dating was never an issue, hanging out with Jake. We've been tight ever since."

"It's so cool to hear about Jake from way back when. Didn't realize that colleges existed that long ago." I pushed his shoulder playfully.

"Yes, along with the invention of the telephone and airplanes. Imagine that," Nathan wryly commented, and glanced out of his window.

I giggled as I picked up my Dr. Pepper bottle from the console. Our three-hour drive had been relaxing and fun. I'd forgotten how I enjoyed Nathan's company. Our flow had been natural and unforced, like we'd known each other in another lifetime. I would've missed out on spending this sunny day and this potentially life-changing opportunity if he hadn't insisted that I join him.

"Have you ever been with Jake?" Nathan focused on the road and quickly added, "If you want to say 'none of my business,' I receive that."

"No, it's a fair question, since he has messed around with women he's worked with in the past." I twisted off the top of my soda and sipped from it. Wiping my mouth with my hand, I continued, "Never been anything between us. Even if he were ever attracted to me, I prefer a low-key family man. A more traditional man who wants to protect and provide for me and our children. I'm old school like that. I actually love the idea of a man keeping me barefoot and pregnant."

"Get the fuck out of here." Nathan looked at me. "With your mad photo skills, your incredible voice, and that you can play the hell out of a guitar, being a housewife is your end game?"

"Taking care of home is one of the best jobs a woman can have." I tapped the console for emphasis.

He scoffed. "Not for a woman like you."

"Explain." I crossed my arms. "I'm listening."

"Let me preface my next statement with the fact that I loved that my mother stayed at home raising me and my younger brother."

"So did I. Mama loved being there for me, my sisters, and my dad."

Nathan's grip tightened on the wheel. "Mine didn't. Because my parents married young and my father was in the military, she had no choice but to focus on her family. I didn't realize she felt anything but happiness until I was seventeen. She said she tried to stay until my younger brother, who'd just started high school, finished. My father was blindsided, and he demanded that if she left, she couldn't take us. He could be a hardass and had the money to make it difficult. She didn't want to fight him, so she left us and became an epidemiologist. She's up in the D.C. area working for the CDC. She seems to be happy now."

"That had to be tough." I could picture a young Nathan hurt that his mother, who'd been there every day of his life, had suddenly stopped being there.

He admitted quietly, "It was. Still dealing with it in some ways, though I have a relationship with both my parents."

I squeezed his knee. "Your mother felt forced into it. I *want* to be a full-time wife and a mother."

He shrugged. "That isn't enough for you. You have way too much talent and would get bored."

"Trust me, it is," I said firmly. "Moving on to another conversation."

Nathan pretended to zip his lips. "Won't mention it again, because you would make a good wife and mother to the right man."

"Thank you." I chuckled. "Though how I feel right about now, I'm not ready for anything serious. Need to protect my heart for a while. Give it a chance to fully heal."

Nathan tapped the steering wheel. "So, swearing off men?"

"No. I love men way too much to deny myself. Just going to have some fun and not get caught up. You were right—I can't stop living because everything doesn't go according to plan. I don't want to go through what I just did again with my ex. I have to be careful, pay attention to the signs the next time I'm interested in a relationship."

"Did you ignore the signs that your ex didn't want what you wanted? Or did he change up on you?"

"A question I've asked myself over and over again." Surprisingly, talking about Omar with Nathan didn't hurt. I pulled one leg underneath me. "When I think about our relationship, his actions didn't match what he told me. I cursed myself for ignoring the red flags."

"Believe what a man shows you," Nathan said. "Believe what people show you, period. We've all been guilty of ignoring what we want to ignore because we want what we want."

"Hmm…we've been talking about me this whole time. What do you want, Mr. Price?" My discerning gut prevented me from asking what he had ignored to get what he wanted and who had hurt him in the past.

"I want my writing to matter." He met my curious gaze. "No more. No less."

Nudging his right hand that rested on the console, I said, "All work and no play makes Nathan a dull man."

"Oh, I play, Sophie. I play."

His eyes traveled over my body enough for me to look away from him and try to ignore the unexpected heat between us. A heat I could act on if I chose to, without any guilt. I was beholden to no one. Too focused on the hurt and disappointment of what I thought was a promising future with a man, I'd forgotten that there were some perks to being alone. The sunrays trickling through the car mirrored the light that now spread through my chest. For once, I liked that I wasn't obligated to a man or a child. That I was completely and totally single, and I could decide on a whim to be in Memphis for a week or two. I could choose to be gray or what had always felt more natural to me.

Pressing the button to roll my window down, I stuck my head out and closed my eyes. The wind hit my face and blew through my hair. I yelled, "I'm free."

Nathan chuckled beside me. "Yeah, you are. Free to do whatever you want."

With the air whipping on and around my face, whatever lingering sadness of the past few months coursed out of me and blended with the wind. "Feeling inspired. Let's hit Beale Street tonight. Catch the vibe. Begin our journey with a bang."

He enthusiastically nodded. "Figured we would hit it up anyway. Can't write a story about the soul of Memphis and not include Beale, right?"

Excitement filled me as I propped my arms on the open window and watched the fast-approaching skyline. "This is going to be your best writing yet, Nathan. I can feel it."

"With you by my side, capturing the moments I might forget about, there's no way we'll fail."

I returned my attention to the window, wondering how long before either of us addressed the elephant of our growing attraction in the room.

FIVE

Nathan

Memphis. Such a far cry from the glitz and showiness of Nashville. A working man's city. A city of lost and fulfilled dreams nestled on the banks of the mighty Mississippi. A city where Black people comprised almost sixty-five percent of the population, compared to only a quarter of the population in Nashville. A musical city without the allure and sensual vibe of New Orleans, the history-making soul sounds of Detroit, or the grimy glamour of the five boroughs of New York. Yet this seemingly unassuming city had birthed legends and the beginnings of blues, rock and roll, and soul.

Sophie appeared to be in a contemplative mood as she rested her head on the open window, the warm air blowing through the car, cooler because of the speed at which we traveled. I remained on I-40 through Memphis and didn't stop until I neared the Hernando de Soto bridge that connected the city with Arkansas. I pulled off the highway to an area where tourists and residents could park and see the river up close.

She sat up and pulled out her cell to take a snap out of her window. "Why are we stopping here first?"

I stared at the murky brown and blue water of perhaps the most well-known river in the world besides the Nile. "It's the beginning of our journey."

"And not Beale or the Rock 'n' Soul Museum?" Sophie held her phone out of the window and took another pic before exiting the car. "Do I need to roll up the window?"

"No. We won't be here long." I shook my head and held her hand to assist her walk over the grassy path.

She asked no further questions and followed me down from a high bluff overlooking the river to the banks.

I released her hand, and her shoulder touched my upper bicep as we admired nature. She teased, "Oh, deep one, why are we here, besides getting sweaty and the delightful pleasure of getting bitten by mosquitoes?"

"What do you know about Memphis?" I picked up a rock and threw it at an angle to make it skip twice across the water before sinking.

Sophie shrugged. "I guess what everybody knows. Where the blues started, where Martin Luther King, Jr. was killed, and the land of Elvis and Graceland. Home of Three 6 Mafia and the movie *Hustle & Flow*. Love. Love that movie. Oh, and that weird pyramid in the middle of the city, because Memphis was also the name of ancient Egypt's capital. I've visited Memphis several times because of Jake and the band, but never did the touristy thing outside of bar-hopping on Beale."

Incredulously, I asked, "You've never visited anything here besides Beale Street and the Peabody Hotel?"

"Already told you that I don't know Memphis. I'm from a small town and have lived in Nashville for years."

"Is country music the only genre you sing? I already know you like other genres of music. My ears still hurt from your playlist."

She jabbed my shoulder. "Whatever, dude. You knew the lyrics better than I did for most of my ratchet playlist. Your skills are not too bad either. I ought to tell Jake on you. I can sing other genres but chose country because it's what I listened to the most growing up and what many of the bars in Nashville prefer."

"I know you can sing the hell out of any genre. I'm asking if you do." I loved the quiet strength and sultriness of her voice. Whenever I heard her sing, my eyes would inevitably close, and whatever troubles I had floated away. "I used to visit the studio just to hear you sing, even in the background."

Sophie smiled softly before turning back to the river. "At home, in the car, in the shower, for fun. Never performed anything in public except country music."

"Maybe you'll sing some blues or some soul for me while we're here." I snuck a glance at her to gauge her reaction. She frowned slightly and hugged herself.

"I'm not performing."

I stepped slightly in front of her, partially blocking her view. "Asked you to sing for *me*. Not for an audience."

She faced me, and lines appeared over the bridge of her nose. "Is that why we're here by the water? Some sort of ancient ritual, and you expect me to sing?"

I grinned. "Yep. I'm Prince, and you're Apollonia. And this is our Lake Minnetonka. You have to purify yourself before we go any further." When she continued to frown, I gently pushed her folded arms open. "I'm kidding. I'm too tall and will never wear my ass out to ever be Prince, and you can sing circles around Apollonia. I didn't stop here so you could sing. Only wishful thinking on my part that I'll get to hear your voice at some point while we're here."

She grudgingly smiled at me, and I turned away from her tempting allure to admire the water. "Our enslaved ancestors probably set foot right here off some boat in chains. Memphis was a major port in the slave trade, like other Southern cities near a large body of water. Years later, we're staring down the Mississippi River wanting to tell their story through their descendants who have also lost so damn much. Music has always been a way to communicate our needs. Our joy. Our sorrow.

"From the negro spirituals used to pass secrets between the enslaved or to uplift us when we wanted to give up. The feel-good music of Motown in an era of turmoil. The self-love of the seventies through James Brown, Earth, Wind & Fire, and Isaac Hayes. Or the storytelling of Pac and NWA letting the world know of the injustice and horror of growing up poor in the inner cities. Music is a malleable form of culture that flows from one generation to the next—just like this river." I scanned the horizon. The sun drifted closer to the middle of the sky. "Our ancestors understood the magic and power of water."

I squinted out at the vastness of the river. "It's always funny when I hear that Black folks don't like water or that we don't know how to swim.

And maybe some of us unconsciously don't because of our forced trip to this country from our homelands across the ocean. Or we consciously know we weren't allowed or didn't have access to public pools to learn how to swim for years. But our ancestors loved and embraced water. They understood the power. Just like they understood the basic rhythm of any song starts with a heartbeat." I squatted and held my hand in the tepid water, beckoning a reflective Sophie to join me.

She lowered herself beside me and placed her hand in the water. "Are we about to do a libation or something?"

"Yes. Before I start any journey, I give thanks to the people who have traveled the road before me. Instead of pouring from some other source into the earth, I wanted to use this river that holds so many memories of those long gone." I cupped my hands, and she followed suit. "In honor of the souls of our ancestors, we thank you for your strength and infinite wisdom. May you watch over us on this uncharted path." I looked at Sophie. "Anything you want to add?"

Sophie studied her entwined hands that slowly leaked water. "If we forget our purpose, may the ancestors remind and guide us that this water transcends time and space. Your sacrifices won't be in vain. You will always live on through us."

We both scooped the water and allowed the river to flow from our hands into the ground. We were silent as we both raised our heads to the heavens, giving praise and ready to receive whatever our ancestors offered. A peace blanketed me, reassuring me of my choices thus far that led to this very moment. I lowered my head first. The tears that trickled down her cheeks from her closed eyes touched me more than any words.

As we returned to the car, Sophie took my offered hand and asked quietly, "Why did you choose African studies?"

"Wanted to learn more about our history. I've lived on three continents with my parents and been exposed to different traditions, languages, and rituals. Yet, in some form or another, it seems to all link back to Egypt or Kemet, the original name of the natives before the Greeks renamed it as Egypt. This project, which on the surface appears to be about forgotten blues musicians like Stoney, is so much more. Last night, and when I first woke up, all of these thoughts crashed around in my head about the *why* of this story."

"So did mine. Had trouble sleeping because I do feel like we're on the verge of something great. I woke up early, though I didn't fall asleep until late. Eager to get to work."

I squeezed her hand. "I love that you're including yourself on this project, because it's not just about what I see, what I believe or know. You have a unique perspective as a musician, a singer, a Tennessee native, and as a Black woman. I wouldn't be a fair journalist if I didn't try to include your thoughts while you're here with me. Thank you for trusting me. Your voice is an integral part of this work."

We made it to the car, and still holding her hand, I opened her door. The heat from the midday sun that blazed our skin cooled in comparison to the energy coiling between us. Her questioning gaze rose to mine, though I didn't know the answer or what she silently asked. Or maybe I did and wasn't ready to answer. I might never be ready.

I cleared my throat. "We'd better go. Check in the hotel, eat lunch, and plan from there."

She dropped my hand and eased into the car. "Where are we staying? The Peabody?"

"Nope. The Peabody is Jake and Amara's story. We're staying at this hotel within walking distance of Beale. Might as well immerse ourselves and live and breathe the heart of Memphis. We can drink and be merry without worrying about driving. Thought it would be a kick to stay there while we're here."

Sophie's lips curved into the widest smile. "So, you really do play? Game on."

I closed her door firmly and took a deep breath, hearing Jake's concern and warning to leave Sophie alone. I guess he knew me more than I knew myself.

After a day of driving through the city, noticing spots or places to visit that weren't already on the list, like the Withers Collection, I waited in the modern, chic lobby of the River Bend Hotel for Sophie to have dinner and hang out on Beale Street. She and I had always spent time as a small group and never just the two of us. The only time we had ever done anything together without Jake, Amara, or the band was the planning of Amara's surprise proposal party. Even then, we were so focused on ensuring everything went off without a hitch that we didn't focus on the fact that we gelled well.

In the last thirty hours since I knocked on her apartment door, we'd seemed to connect on more than a surface level. We had more in common than differences. Our banter and conversations were easy; even when confusion or disagreement interrupted, we could continue without an argument. Like we just *got* each other. Understood boundaries. After all was said and done, I imagined our friendship would deepen. I didn't have many friends, and Jake was my best friend forever. And if I could ignore the maddening attraction, Sophie could become one of my best friends, too.

The question about Sophie's closeness to Jake had always been in the recesses of my mind, but I'd had no intention of ever asking it. We'd both had our share of women through the years, but Jake hadn't always been thoughtful about his choices—some because of his arrogance, some because of his too-often inebriated state, and others simply because he could. I'd assumed that he and Sophie had been sexual with one another at some point, though I'd never asked him, and he never spoke of Sophie in any way except as a highly valued member of his team.

The question had slipped from my lips partially because of Sophie's obvious affection for Jake and his warning that lingered. His concern came from a place of love and didn't feel territorial.

Still.

I'd had to know if he'd ever been with her. If he had, I had another barrier to keep her and me in the friend zone. Jake and I didn't swim in the same water. Period. I had been prepared for Sophie to either refuse to answer or admit they'd had a short fling. I bit down on the relief and hope that threatened to show through my smile when she'd denied any interest or involvement with Jake. The genuineness with which she answered halted any further thought. I believed her.

I should've known that he and Sophie had never been intimate. If they had been, I doubt she would've become best friends with Amara or been a part of her band. Jake would've never allowed that to happen, which would have placed Amara or Sophie in a potentially awkward situation. He might have been out there bad for years, but he was a traditional man at heart who believed in being loyal and taking care of his wife and family.

I'd sensed a difference in him the day I asked about a viral video of him and an unsigned Amara giving an impromptu performance at a bar in the Peabody Hotel. He couldn't stop staring at her while she sang. The old Jake would've seized the opportunity and stopped at nothing to get Amara on contract and in his bed. His hesitancy and uncertainty in reaching out to her had surprised me. Even more surprising, once Amara agreed to travel to Nashville, he was like this giddy teenager who was fascinated yet intimidated by this talented, beautiful, and humble woman from Atlanta. And now she would be his wife, and I couldn't be happier for him.

Thinking of my friend, I pulled out my phone and texted him.

We are settling here in the city. Drove around, mapping out our stops while we're here. Now we're about to hit Beale Street. Sophie is cool people, but I also know I'm not what she needs or wants. You can chill on that. I'll call tomorrow and update you after I meet with Sweetie Jay at the museum.

My cell beeped almost before I finished sending it.

I'll chill. Tell Sweetie that Mari and me still owe her drinks.

I smiled. We were good again.

"Who has you smiling? Better not be a woman ready to fight me over you because we're here together in Memphis. If you're seeing someone, hope she knows that this trip is only business," Sophie's soft voice teased.

With a snappy retort ready to fire back, I looked up, and the words caught in my throat. Sophie had gone to her room as a pretty woman and returned as a tempting vixen. The little black dress understood the assignment. The red heels strapped around her ankles, matching her red, pouty lips, iced the look. She'd even thrown on a honey-brown wig that flowed down her back. Damn it, I shouldn't have sent that text to Jake reassuring him that I wouldn't try her, when Sophie had sealed the deal in this outfit.

She cleared her throat, and I dragged my gaze from her body to her face.

Sophie smugly said, "Cat got your tongue?"

"You might want to use another phrase right about now," I replied, forcing myself to focus on her face and not drift back down to her cleavage.

"I must look damn good for you to say that to me." She walked over and grabbed my hands, pulling me up as I openly appreciated her beauty and flowery perfume.

"No comment."

She batted her long lashes. "Try to keep your eyes in your head tonight."

I slowly shook my head. "Then you better walk beside me and definitely not in front of me."

She wrapped her arm around mine. "You clean up nicely, too. Decided not to wear glasses?"

"Since I'm not driving, figured I could swing it. I only need glasses for long distances. Like driving, or if I have to read off a board." I'd changed into dark slacks, a black polka dot Tom Ford shirt, and black Timberland boat shoes. "I haven't had time to get a new script for my contacts."

"I love this hotel. The suites are so spacious, and I can't wait to wake up and walk out onto the balcony, taking in the morning sun. I feel like I'm at home. It was a struggle not to dive into bed and sleep." We walked toward the sliding doors.

"We could've stayed in tonight, since we'll be here for a few days. It's not too late to eat at one of the restaurants here," I offered to be polite, though I had too much energy to be caged in my room or the hotel.

"Looking like this?" Sophie gestured at herself and me. "We have to hit up Beale Street."

Internally, I breathed a sigh of relief. "Same page. We have plenty of time to sleep. Although the walk isn't far, you probably need to catch a shuttle, looking at those oh-so-sexy heels."

"I always knew you were a smart man." She batted her lashes again, holding on tighter to my arm as the balmy night air swaddled us.

"The shuttle is over there." I led us toward a small silver van waiting to transport guests to and from Beale Street.

"So pretty," Sophie squealed when she looked up. She pulled out her cell from her sparkly wristlet and took a pic of the Memphis Pyramid in the near distance, gleaming in the late summer night, before we stepped into the shuttle.

"Trying to catch a woman tonight?" Sophie scooted to the window, and I sat beside her, nodding to the couple sitting at the back of the van.

I replied in a low voice, "Didn't you just accuse me of already having someone?"

She arched a brow. "Doesn't mean that you don't want to meet someone else, since you're not the marrying kind."

"I may not be the marrying kind, but if I'm in a relationship, I'm committed," I replied.

"When's the last time?"

"I don't want to hear your mouth, but my last relationship was my college girlfriend."

"I wasn't going to laugh." She tapped my thigh, which pressed against hers. "What happened?"

"We tried to make it work for about three years after graduation. I thought we might even get married. But I realized that with all the traveling my career required, it wasn't fair to her or any woman. I saw what happened to my parents. Most women want their men home, just as much as men want their women home."

Sophie added, "Except you. Would you care if your woman's job required her to travel?"

I shifted to see her face. "I might seem like a hypocrite, but I don't see how a relationship would work long term if we were both traveling, unless we were doing it together most of the time. Maybe one day I'll be ready to stay put."

Her forehead wrinkled. "So, you would want your wife to follow you everywhere?"

"No. I don't want a woman to follow me. She's her own person and shouldn't have to give up who she is or what she wants because she loves me." My face grew warm, and not from the summer air. "Why all the questions about my dating life?"

"We're getting to know each other, right?"

"Yeah."

"I'm only trying to figure you out. You're a contradiction. Most men who don't want marriage love women too much to settle down with one. But that's not you. You really just want to be free to move without any obligations or guilt, and ain't nothing wrong with that." She kissed my cheek in acceptance, and the tension in my body released.

"Stop trying to block me from other women. Got lipstick all over my cheek," I grumbled.

She pecked my cheek in two other places before she laughingly rubbed her temporary marks with her thumb. Her flirtatious playfulness blew another hole in my quickly crumbling resolve to remain only her friend.

Sophie leaned on my shoulder and wrapped her arm around mine. "Thank you. I needed this more than you know."

The need to always take care of Sophie overwhelmed me as I allowed myself to rest my head on top of hers for the brief ride to Beale Street.

SIX

Sophie

eale Street. The home of the blues. A historic street that ebbed and flowed with tourists and natives. The brightly lit, colorful signs of the bars and lounges were similar to those of Broadway in Nashville. The streets differed by the genre of music—soulful voices that echoed through the streets, backed by horns and the piano, and not the twangs of a guitar or a banjo, greeted us. The electric energy of the sights and sounds pulsed through me as nightlife always did.

"Strange how Memphis and Nashville are the mirror images of each other," I commented while we strolled down the street after a simple dinner of burgers and fries at Dyer's. "Both are in Tennessee, anchored by music. One focuses on country, and the other on blues, lamenting love and life's ups and downs. Nashville is majority white, and Memphis has us. Broadway and Beale. Two streets that are the heart of the city, bustling with this spirit and determination to survive no matter what. Whether they're thriving is another matter. Country is no longer the subgenre it used to be. In some circles, it's as pop as Sabrina Carpenter. Between Miley Cyrus and Taylor Swift, who crossed over, and Teddy Swims and Chris Stapleton, whose soulful voices made us listen." I glanced around at the bars. "While blues has all but died out. Everyone remembers B.B. King, but who really knows the musicality of Fantastic Negrito or that the most popular blues performers nowadays are white, like Marcus King, and that the music is often infused with rock and country?

"Hell, all of the genres nowadays are so entwined. The distinction can be so minute, and I don't understand why people get up in arms when artists explore areas other than the music they're known for. Or maybe I should say when Black artists explore areas other than R&B or blues. *Cowboy Carter* was pure genius, but Beyoncé's decision to create such an album was questioned, though she was born and raised in Texas. Artists like Reyna Roberts or Tanner Adell would probably rival Queen Bey herself if they chose any genre outside of country. Hoping they still can with all the attention on artists like them now. And new singers like Amara, who didn't even grow up with country music," I proudly finished. "She's proving once again that we belong in any genre."

Nathan walked quietly beside me. "Why do you perform?"

I thought about his question a beat before I answered, "At first, it was a way to be close to my father. He loves the guitar and thought he would have a son to teach him how to play one day. After the fifth girl, he realized he was fated to be a girl dad. I was twelve when my youngest sister was born, and he started teaching me. Despite my love of the guitar, I had no interest in a music career. I earned decent grades and spent most of my childhood helping Mama with my sisters. The guitar became my escape from all the responsibility, eventually leading to a way to pay the bills."

"Are you saying that you play for the money?"

The chatter of passing pedestrians and musical notes of Beale Street faded the more we walked and talked, becoming an island of two.

"I play because it's an honor. We were never allowed to touch my father's guitar until we were older because he wanted us to respect instruments and the gift of music. My mother was the disciplinarian in our household, but we knew not to test him about Queenie."

"He named his guitar?"

I beamed. "Yep. Named mine Princess, since I was the only one he taught."

Nathan smiled. "Fitting for that pink velvet case and pearly-white guitar."

"Princess is pretty, isn't she?" Guilt pricked my heart. For so long, my guitar was such a part of me, and now Princess seemed a distant memory.

"My father didn't aspire to play professionally. He loved that with the magic of his fingers striking a certain string, he could relay the deepest of sorrows, the highest of joys, and the emotions in between. Imagine my excitement the day he handed Queenie to me and asked me to play instinctively."

"A child prodigy?" His brows lifted.

I laughed loudly. "Hell no. I was horrible, terrible, and no good like Alexander's very bad day. Eventually after hours of practice, frustration, and sheer will, I got it."

Nathan curved his arm around my waist and pulled me to his side. "Your father was a good teacher. Love to hear you play, especially when you and Mari are together. Simply beautiful."

At the mention of Amara and how we complemented each other, guilt and regret battled for first place. "Thank you." I tapped his broad chest, and he released me.

"Speaking of great artists who name their guitar…" He smiled and opened the door to B.B. King's Blues Club.

We squeezed into the crowded bar, managing to find two leather stools beside each other. We drank and flirted with the people around us. We sang at the top of our lungs to the band playing covers of popular blues, country, and soul music. At one point, Nathan dragged me off the stool to dance to "Love" by Keyshia Cole. He kept dipping and spinning me, making me laugh, which drew attention from an attractive woman with thin braids twisted on top of her head. While he excused himself for the bathroom, she was bold enough to ask if we were together, and I told her to go for it. Once Nathan returned, I winked at him and moved to another part of the bar while the woman conversed with him.

I danced with a college student from Phoenix, chatted it up with two older women from Chicago, and laughed with the cutie bartender about where to find men and fun things to do while in Memphis. The entire time I snapped pics of the restaurant and the live band—I even took one of Nathan smiling at his new friend. I quashed the twinge of jealousy that he and the woman seemed to be caught up in one another, and took a selfie kissing the cheek of the bartender and one laughing with the eclectic group of people at the bar. *This* was me. Not the mopey woman who'd been hiding out for months nursing emotional wounds and blaming myself when what I'd lost wasn't fully in my control.

When I stumbled trying to dance with an older man whose wife clapped along to the music, I knew it was time for me to go—I'd had one cocktail too many and needed fresh air. I eased up behind Nathan and wrapped my arm around his taut waist while he engaged in conversation. *Mm.* He smelled and felt so good.

I whispered in his ear, "Had too much to drink. I'm going to catch some air, and an Uber is on the way. You stay. I'll see you in the morning."

Nathan twisted his neck to whisper, "I'll go with you. Give me a few minutes."

He turned away before I could protest that he should stay. I walked toward the exit to give him privacy. Did he realize how close our lips were when he turned his head to respond? One inch to the left, and we would've kissed.

I balled my fists and hugged myself. *Nope. I will ignore the tingling I've felt since yesterday and how his pleased gaze heated my body in the lobby.*

When Nathan joined me at the door, I gestured to the bar and the woman who still watched him. "I'm fine, Nate. Go have fun."

"It's late, and you wobble when you walk. Someone could take advantage of you." He guided me out of the bar with a possessive hand on the small of my back. A hand I welcomed.

"I'm wobbling because these heels were only meant to walk from the valet to the table. I'll be fine." We exited into the cool night. I grimaced with each step on the hard concrete. "That woman wanted you. She's not your type?"

He shrugged. "She was cool."

His pace was too fast for my throbbing feet, and I stopped moving.

Nathan frowned. "What?"

Gripping his shoulder for balance, I lifted my right foot. "Need to take these off. Used to wearing my boots."

"You're going to walk around barefoot on this street?"

"Yep." I struggled to unbuckle my strap. "I grew up a tomboy playing in the woods, the mountain my backyard. This concrete will feel a lot better than these shoes. We only have to walk a few blocks to the car I ordered."

"Put your foot down, Twinkle."

"Give me a sec." I tried to lift my leg higher.

Nathan sighed then moved my hand from my shoe and knelt before me. I admired the waves in his hair as he placed my foot on his thigh and unbuckled my right heel and then did the same with my other one.

"Ooh…I feel like Cinderella, except in reverse. Thank you."

His hand lightly touched my left calf as he rose to tower over me. "I've been up since four thirty, and I drove from Nashville. I'm tired, too." He glanced around and pointed to an empty table and chairs outside a bar. "Let's sit here, and text the driver and see if we can persuade them with a few extra dollars to come here. This street is too hazardous for you to walk barefoot."

The waiter approached as we sat down, and Nathan pulled a twenty-dollar bill out of his pocket. "We only need to be here for a few minutes. Her feet hurt."

The man nodded, took the tip, and left to assist customers.

I looped my arm around Nathan's and rested my head briefly on his shoulder. "Beale is not much different than Broadway. I walk that street all the time by myself at night, sometimes barefoot. I would've been fine. You didn't have to go through all this trouble."

"Well, we're not in Nashville. Besides, I'd rather be with you." He pointed to my purse. "Text the driver."

"Okay…okay." After I texted the driver, I snuck a glance at his profile as he people-watched. His lips were curved, and the diamond stud in his ear glinted. Nathan looked good tonight. "You might be able to get some from her if you go back right now."

"And not from you, right?" His eyes were hooded, maybe from alcohol or exhaustion. *Desire*, a tiny voice added.

"You are way too old and grumpy."

He touched his chest, wearing a wounded expression, the edges of his lips turned down comically. "I'm old at thirty-four?"

"When I'm newly twenty-nine, yes, you are too old for me. I've never been interested in older men. The average woman lives almost six years longer than her man. So, my future husband has to be my age or even younger if we're going to grow old together."

He patted the arm he held. "Spoken like a twenty-something."

I arched a brow. "What's that supposed to mean?"

"You believe you have forever. No one is promised tomorrow. Wives have died before their husbands, even when that man was a lot older. If you're going to dismiss a man because he's older, at least let it be a valid reason. Like he's too controlling or doesn't know how to have fun."

"Okay, when do you think you'll want to get married?"

"Huh…what? We're not…talking…what…marriage? I thought we talked about that earlier." Nathan stumbled over his words like he'd stepped in a hole on the sidewalk.

I chuckled. "I might be twenty-something, but I know not to waste my time with a man who doesn't see marriage and family anytime soon. Even if your age didn't bother me, your aversion to marriage and family does."

He moved his arm from mine and entwined our hands. "It's not an aversion…just not for me. You also said you weren't looking for anything serious."

"What does that have to do with you and me?"

"After tonight, you have to admit that we click…that we're chill with each other." Nathan grinned and winked. "Thought it might be cool to dive into this city, kick back, listen to some good music, and have a little sex and a lot of fun while we work."

"I love how you slid in the 'sex' part." I giggled. "I at least need to be attracted to you, Nate."

He slanted an amused gaze at me. "So, you're not attracted to me at all?"

I squeezed his hard bicep. "I think you're cool. I even understand how other women find you attractive, with these muscles and a bright smile. But I only see you as my friend."

"Really? Not *remotely* attracted to me?" he asked as a black Tesla slowed down in front of us on the street. Nathan held my heels and purse as he helped me to my feet.

"Yep," I said, although I liked how my palm fit neatly within his and the ease and comfort with which he held it. I felt protected and safe in his presence.

"If you say so." He opened my door before strutting to the other side.

On the short ride back, we were quiet. I strapped on my heels again, and he looked out his window. Was I attracted enough to have sex with him? The chemistry was most definitely evident, and it had been months since Omar. Until yesterday, I hadn't thought of Nathan in that way before. Maybe because now we'd been in such close proximity that my curiosity about him sexually had been piqued.

Or maybe I was horny and he was a ready and virile man.

My stomach clenched when we arrived at the entrance of the hotel. Would he make a move, or would he accept my answer? I honestly didn't know which option I preferred. Right or wrong, I enjoyed the flirty banter between us. His admiring gaze and attention boosted my waning ego. I'd chosen my dress with Nathan in mind for the reaction I expected and received. We were acutely aware of each other at the bar tonight, even when we were talking with others. I had been pleased that he chose to leave the bar with me.

Nathan didn't speak or touch me, though he held my purse while we headed to the open elevator. Once the doors closed and we were the only inhabitants, his free hand curved to my waist. "Kiss me."

"I don't kiss my friends." I wrinkled my nose, though I couldn't drag my eyes away from his mouth.

"Humor me, since you're already thinking about it." Nathan grinned.

I crossed my arms and finally met his teasing glance. "I'm not kissing you, Nate, to prove a point. Take what I say at face value."

"Yet you haven't pushed me away." His brown eyes danced before he removed his hand and stepped back. "All right, all right, Soph. We're working on this project together. Strictly professional from this point on. Forget I said anything."

"Now it's going to be awkward between us," I complained, missing the heat of his hand on me. "I still want us to have fun."

"Nothing has to change. I tried. You're not feeling it. All good. We'll still have fun." He leaned against the back wall, his expression pleasant and relaxed.

I frowned. "Why are you so cool about me turning you down? Were you just messing with me?"

Nathan crossed his ankles. "Not at all. What's the point in being mad or disappointed or feeling rejected? Too many beautiful women for me to get my feelings hurt if one doesn't want me."

"Are you going to call that woman we just left?" I accused lightly, hating the jealousy that flamed. "Are you about to go to her?"

His eyes sparkled. "Why do you care what I do with another woman?"

"Because…" My words faltered. I couldn't have it both ways, reject him and expect him to yearn for me. Nathan could do whatever and whomever he wanted. "I don't care. It's not my business."

The ping sounded, and the elevator opened. He held my purse out to me. "Your floor. I'll call you for breakfast around eight, and then we can head to the museum."

After being with Nathan all day, I wasn't quite ready to leave his presence and damn sure didn't want him to go back out. I stared at him, not sure what to say or do.

He quickly blocked the closing doors with his arm. "Sophie?"

At his questioning gaze, I patted his chest as I exited the elevator. "You're not going to walk me to my room?"

Crinkles appeared in the corners of his eyes. "The room that I can see from here?"

"I mean…what if someone is lurking, ready to get me while I fumble looking for my key card?" I reasoned, trying to prolong the night with the flimsiest of excuses. "I won't feel safe until you check around my suite."

He followed me to my door. "Is that all you want me to do?"

"Maybe I'm not ready for you to go. I haven't had fun like tonight in a long time." I reached into my small purse and pulled out my card to unlock the door. He placed his hands on either side of me, compressing the air between us.

"Look at me," he commanded softly.

Okay. I wanted him. My knees almost buckled at the timbre of his voice. This side of Nathan tempted and scared me. Too afraid I would succumb if I complied, I opened the door. "Why?" *Damn it. Why did my voice have to squeak like that?*

"I want to be clear about something before I set one foot inside your room."

Not quite trusting myself not to kiss him if I turned around, I looked over my shoulder. "What?"

His gaze zeroed in on my lips. "That whatever happens, it won't change how I see you or our friendship. No awkwardness, disappointment, or anger. Just Sophie and Nate enjoying each other. I need to know that I'm not taking advantage of you in any way."

"Are we speaking in third person now?" I smirked.

He didn't respond. The fiery gleam in his eyes relayed that the time for teasing and joking had passed.

Our gazes locked, and the nervousness faded. After the pain of the last few months, maybe all I needed was a temporary pleasure with a man I instinctively trusted. I boldly faced him. "You mean, don't get any ideas about us ever being serious?"

He nodded. "The last thing I would do is add to your hurt. Be honest with me. If all you want to do is talk in your room, we can go back downstairs and hang out at the bar to avoid temptation. I want you too much to pretend that I can be in your hotel room and nothing will happen. Whether it's a conversation between two friends or I'm in your bed, I'm not ready for the night to end either."

Grabbing his bearded chin, I stared into his eyes. "No worries, I'm a big girl. You can't hurt me, Nate, because I can separate the two. We wouldn't work long term anyway. I want my man home with me most nights, and staying put in one place is so not you. And I really don't want Jake or Mari all in our business, trying to make something happen between us that never will. It's just a little fun while we're in Memphis. One night."

Nathan lowered his head to kiss me. "We're here for days."

"One night is all you get."

His lips descended on mine, capturing my last word in his mouth.

The vibration of his deep chuckle traveled through me, inflaming the sexual urge that had started on the walk outside of B.B. King's place. I suddenly desperately wanted him, and only the present mattered.

"Mm," I purred at the intoxicating blend of his warm, soft, yet insistent kiss. "No one told me that you could kiss like this. I've been missing out."

"Glad you finally recognize." Nathan used his whiskey-flavored tongue to open my mouth, drawing me closer and closer into his realm.

His palm drifted to my neck, and his thumb caressed my shoulder while his other hand opened my door without breaking the sensual kiss. He backed me into the suite enough for the door to close with finality behind us. His hand traveled over the curve of my ass to press me into his erection before Nathan lifted his head, his gaze drunk with alluring need searing right through me.

Touched that he would seek my consent again and incredibly turned on by his lustful desire, I backed up a few inches from him and pulled up my dress enough to hint at my green lace panties. "Fuck me."

Nathan's chest heaved up and down before he crashed his mouth into mine, kissing me fervently and deeply like I were his oasis in a desert. I slipped my hands under his shirt, exploring the contours and ridges of his muscular chest. The contrasting smoothness and dips of his skin fascinated me. I broke the kiss to lick his belly button, which tasted sweet when I expected salty, before meeting his lips again. He moaned, ripping the strap on my dress in his impatience to push down the top to indulge in my breasts.

I giggled as Nathan mumbled apologetically, his lips now wrapped around my rigid nipple, pleasure pulsating through me, coaxing me to submit to him, to lose my inhibitions with every teasing suck. I reached down between us to grasp his bulge through his slacks, practically salivating in anticipation of his thickness and length.

Touching his erection seemed to be his undoing. Nathan tugged my panties over my feet and pushed me down on the bed with my dress hiked up, baring the most intimate part of me. His heated gaze devoured my writhing body as he removed my heels and tugged off his shirt, revealing a chest sexier than I'd imagined, tatted and muscled—an unexpected edge, reminding me of the rugged man who loved adventure and cigars, and not the thoughtful, glasses-wearing man he'd been with me. He had my undivided attention as his slacks and boxer briefs dropped next and he sheathed his throbbing manhood. He seemed more than up to the challenge to please me thoroughly.

Clasping my hands together above my head, I permitted him to do whatever he wanted to do to me. Nathan dragged his tongue down my neck and between my breasts before he opened my legs with his knee, his hands pressed on either side of me. When he thrust inside and started pumping hard, fucking me instead of making love, as I'd requested, I adjusted to his girth. My center filled with a spiraling, sensual tension that forced me to shut my eyes and moan loudly, begging for the sweet torture to end.

I needed this. I needed the satisfying release that only sex provided. I needed to remember that I was still a vibrant, desirable woman who enjoyed life. With every stroke, I relished the feel of his throbbing manhood inside of me—the naughty freedom of being intimately wild with no expectations except a fun time.

He thrust harder and harder, twisting my body impossibly tighter and tighter. I clutched his strong biceps as Nathan pressed my thighs open and sped up his rhythm. His eyes were closed, and the determined lines etched into his face relayed that he wouldn't be a selfish lover. I shut my eyes and allowed the rapturous sensations to unleash and crash over and through me as his incessant pumping pushed me over the climactic threshold.

Within seconds of my shuddering release, Nathan stiffened as he finished with a loud grunt and slumped on top of me, spent. I hugged him and kissed his neck, appreciating the soothing comfort of his body pressed to mine.

SEVEN

Sophje

hat would my boss say if he knew that I slept with his best friend?

The next morning, I cracked open one eye, hoping that what had occurred between Nathan and me was the wet dream of a crazed libido after all the drinking, flirting, and touching we did last night.

The rumpled sheets and my deliciously sated body told another tale. Hot sex was definitely what I'd needed to truly remember that I was still a desirable and alluring woman.

I popped up, covering my naked chest, and searched around the bedroom. The bathroom door was open. Where was he? Did he sneak away in the middle of the night and return to his room?

"Wait…is this my room or his? Note to self: stop after one cocktail."

"You do know I can hear you?" He chuckled from the balcony. The sliding door was partially open.

Wrapping the sheet around myself, I ventured to the balcony and chose a chair across from him. Thankfully, he'd pulled on his boxer briefs before walking out here. His bronzed, naked chest and the intricately designed tats that covered his left shoulder and right pec reignited my fire in the light of day, and we'd already agreed that last night wouldn't happen again.

Well, at least *I* had.

"Any regrets?" he asked quietly.

"It's funny you ask… My first thought when I woke up was that I'd slept with my boss's best friend and what he would say." I tightened the sheet around my body.

Nathan whistled, propping his arms behind his head. "He would probably be pissed, because he told me to stay away from you. I told him I would, but your body in that dress made a liar out of me less than twenty-four hours later."

"Why would he say anything? He needs to mind his own business," I testily said. Jake's arrogance grated on my nerves at times. He really was like an annoying big brother.

Nathan glanced at me before refocusing on the scenic view of the Memphis skyline and Hernando de Soto Bridge. "He's afraid I'll hurt you because he can tell that I like you and can't give you what you really want."

I scoffed. "That's because Jake has me in a box like you men like to do. He probably can't imagine that I have had no-strings-attached sex before. And as much as I want more from a man one day, like I already told you, I don't want anything deep anytime soon. Last night was last night."

He continued to stare out at the horizon without any further comment.

After a few seconds of more silence, I asked, "Do *you* have any regrets?"

Nathan gave me a sideways glance. "Not about being with you. I was supposed to prove Jake wrong. Can't lie—it bothers me that I don't have as much self-control as I would like to think I have." He chuckled. "I thought that woman at the bar would be a good distraction, and then you had to whisper in my ear."

"What else was I supposed to do? You couldn't hear me over the band." I innocently shrugged.

"Oh, I definitely heard you say I smelled and felt good."

I gasped. "I said that aloud?"

"Yeah. You did, and I immediately got hard. I don't even remember if I told the woman goodbye, trying to pay the bill to get to you."

"Oops, sorry." I covered my mouth, giggling. "Wasn't trying to turn you on."

"Stop lying, Twinkle, denying you were attracted to me when you kept touching me every time you had a chance last night. You knew what you were doing just by wearing that dress, braless, that I happily snatched off you. By the way, how much do I owe you?"

"Ooh, at least five thousand dollars. It was an expensive Givenchy that didn't have to be ripped." I winked.

"Worth every penny," he quipped, knowing damn well I didn't spend that much on that dress. We'd had conversations in the past about my frugality.

I allowed the sheet to slip lower, hinting at the swell of my breasts. "The dress was short. Next time, just push it above my stomach."

Nathan quirked a thick brow. "Glad you recognize that last night won't be the only night."

We shared wide, cheesy grins. The morning was off to a brilliant start.

I yawned and stretched my arms. The sheet almost dropped to my nipples. "What time is it?"

"Almost eight." The heat of his gaze on my bare skin aroused me again.

"How long have you been awake?" My voice sounded breathy.

The corner of his lip curved. "Five. A habit after being a military brat and then a journalist, traveling the world with all the different time zones. I'm used to getting by on less sleep than most people."

"We didn't go to sleep until after two," I reminded him.

Nathan stretched his legs out in front of him. "Doesn't matter what time I close my eyes. They open at five."

"I'm a morning person, too."

"It figures."

"What does that mean?"

"You have this positive energy, infusing drops of joy in anyone you meet. You have a calming effect on people." He steepled his hands on his chest. "Even seen it with Jake, and we both know when he's in asshole mode, it's hard for him to come out of it. You have a way with people that draws them in."

"I might be able to draw them in, but apparently I can't keep them. I wouldn't still be single and childless." I looked away from his softening gaze and studied my bare nails. "I don't know how I could have been so wrong about Omar. I thought we were on the same page."

"Maybe you were, and things changed for him. Or maybe you wanted to believe in him, no matter what he showed you. Men are simple when it comes to love. When we want to be married, you know."

"I guess I keep getting it wrong because I'm almost thirty and no man has ever wanted to make me his wife. This is Mari's second proposal, and two of my younger sisters are already married." I blew out a ragged breath. "Sorry… sorry. I know comparing myself to anyone steals my joy, but sometimes it's so damn hard."

"Come here," Nathan quietly demanded.

I wiped my eyes with my pinky fingers. "I'm fine where I am. You don't need to feel sorry for me."

He grabbed the arm of my chair and pulled me and the chair to him. "Ain't no one feeling sorry for you. For the last four months, you've been in your head with all these negative thoughts, with no one to remind you how great you are. I've seen some bad shit in my life, so I know an amazing person when I see one. You haven't met that man who's right for you yet. Take something from every man you dated and learn from it. But don't stay stuck over this dude or any other man who isn't deserving of you."

Nodding, I replied, "I'm trying."

"No, not try…*do*," Nathan said before holding me and the sheet over his shoulder. "Guess I didn't do my job last night. I was supposed to make you forget him."

I squealed in surprise and laughter. "Yeah, think you might need a little more training on how to make a woman forget her name, too."

He popped my ass. "Oh…I need more training?"

"Yep, at least a couple of more sessions," I said as he dumped me on the bed and hovered over me. I rubbed his forearms and looked up at him.

Two lines creased his forehead. "What?"

"You better not catch feelings for me either. You and I are only temporary, remember?"

Instead of responding, he blanketed me with his body and sucked on my right nipple.

EIGHT

Nathan

The last time I'd visited the Memphis Rock 'n' Soul Museum to research Stoney, his exhibit was a small corner of a section of local musicians. Since then, his life and works had been expanded to feature prominently on half of a wall. I admired the display of his "lost" songs that told of the awards won and how the hits he'd written had catapulted a relatively unknown Evelyn Hart into superstardom. The wall also now held pictures of his family.

Sophie began snapping shots of Stoney's exhibit, including a photo of his renovated home in West Memphis. Other pictures included Stoney teaching a young Amara how to play the guitar and an adult Amara singing at the famed Ryman in Nashville. Platinum and gold records also graced the wall to commemorate the hit songs he'd written for Evelyn Hart.

"Nate, you did this. This is all you."

I shook my head. "Not all of me. I wouldn't have had a story if it weren't for Jake asking me to help and Amara's willingness to share her grandfather's life."

"Exactly. All Amara wanted was to know more about her grandfather. It was your words, your storytelling, that snatched our hearts. You made us stop, pay attention, and empathize with a lonely old Black man. Yes, Jake and Amara brought Stoney to you, but you brought him to the world." She squeezed my bicep. "Take your props like a man."

"I will when you admit you're far too talented to never perform again." I pushed my glasses higher on my nose. "You could have a wall here one day."

She lowered her iPhone from her face. "Don't use me to deflect. Be more original."

"I don't know how much more original I can be than to state a fact."

Sophie's cute nose wrinkled. "I thought you weren't pressuring me to play?"

I glanced around the room. "How am I pressuring you when you don't even have an instrument and we're in a museum? If you want me to take credit for something that wasn't completely all my doing, you take credit for something that's all you."

"I swear you get on my nerves," she complained before she abruptly snapped a shot of me with what I could only assume was a smug expression on my face.

"Nathan?" a woman's voice called from behind me.

I turned around and smiled when Sweetie Jay, Jake's friend and the museum curator, approached me with an outstretched hand. I grasped it warmly, covering hers with mine. Sweetie Jay effused Southern hospitality with her wide smile, deep twang, and firm insistence that whoever she encountered was family. "The young woman at the entrance said you were on break," I said. "Sorry we just dropped in on you."

She waved a hand. "Please, you're welcome anytime. There's no need to call ahead. I'm here every day, like this is my house."

I gestured toward Sophie. "This is Sophie, and she's helping me on a new project. I don't know if Jake had a chance to talk to you."

Sweetie Jay grinned wider as she shook Sophie's hand. "Good to meet you." She squinted. "Wait…aren't you in Mari Johnson's band? I've been following her ever since she started performing."

Sophie smiled. "I was. Now I'm taking a break and helping Nathan out here while he's doing research for his next story."

She lowered her eyes briefly before returning her attention to me. "Jake didn't give me details. Just told me you would be visiting soon. Tell me how I can assist."

"Right now, we're just touring the museum," I said. "If we need anything, we'll let you know. Writing Stoney's story opened the door to so much more."

"Who are you telling?" Sweetie Jay looked past my shoulders. "How do you like Stoney's wall?"

"I was just telling Nate that without his story, this wall wouldn't exist, and he refuses to accept praise," Sophie said as if she were telling on me.

Sweetie Jay's eyes widened. "She's right. The demand to know more about Stoney has risen in the last year. Without your article, I wouldn't have been able to secure more space. I've always been a fan of his. Just glad that everyone else is aware of his immense talent."

"That's right—you knew him." I made a mental note to review the information relayed by Jake and Amara about this museum and Sweetie Jay.

"I met him a few years ago when we first added his exhibit. I only knew the bus driver and not the songwriter and musician he once was. He didn't show up for the exhibit reveal, but he would pop in from time to time and visit. He was reserved and quiet, though always polite." She clasped her hands together and shook her head slowly. "I knew he was great. I didn't know the depths of his talent. He deserved to be celebrated, and now he is. So, yes, Nathan, be proud of what you did for Stoney and his family."

Sophie's lips curved into a triumphant smile as I graciously accepted praise for my work. "I am. Thank you."

A dark-haired woman whose hair was pulled into a sleek ponytail stepped closer to us. "Did I hear correctly that you were the journalist who exposed Evelyn Hart?"

"I rather think of it as telling Stoney Johnson's truth," I quipped as we caught the attention of a couple of other patrons.

"At the cost of her career." Her red-stained lips pursed.

"So, you are the journalist?" Another woman walked up with a curious expression, seemingly more friend than foe. Time would tell if my assessment was correct.

"Yes, we are honored to have Mr. Nathan Price, an award-winning journalist, here at the museum for a visit," Sweetie Jay confirmed.

An amused Sophie took pictures the entire time the small, growing crowd gathered around me, knowing that, like her, I was used to the background. Most writers were introverted, and though I considered myself more of an ambivert, the questions thrown at me as if I held a press conference were rather daunting. All I yearned to do was slink in the corner and move about unobtrusively.

"Were you ever worried that you could potentially damage your career once you released your article? After all, Evelyn Hart was America's sweetheart," a man with long locs commented.

"I've never shied away from the truth because of any fallout. My only concern was for possible repercussions for Amara Johnson, her career, and her family. If she told me not to write it, I wouldn't have. Once I had her blessing and trust, I took special care to ensure her grandfather's memory and legacy would be held in high regard. So far, I believe it has been." I gestured to the wall behind me.

"If you were worried about his reputation, why include that he cheated on his wife with Evelyn?" asked the original stern-faced woman—probably an Evelyn fan, or simply someone uncomfortable with the insidious truth that race played a factor in Stoney's and countless other musicians' ability to obtain commercial and financial success.

My jaw tightened before I released it. "Again, it was the truth. I wasn't trying to paint anyone as a bad or good guy. I simply relayed what happened and why it happened. Without the love affair, maybe his just dues and credit would've been given to him back then. Maybe not. He wasn't the first, and unfortunately, he probably won't be the last to be taken advantage of by the music industry because of his skin."

"I love everything you write, and I'm a fan. I read your article on the combat zones in the inner city a couple of years ago and found your style riveting," the other woman gushed.

Okay. This curious woman might be a friend. Sophie snapped a picture of her. We didn't need to receive permission for these shots, since we wouldn't use any of them to sell the story. This was simply background fodder to help me remember and inspire me at the end of every day.

Her green eyes gleamed. "Are you here researching another story? I already know it's going to be good."

"As an investigative journalist, I'm always doing research. Even talking to all of you is a part of my process," I smoothly answered, not yet wanting our documentary to be public knowledge. "I hadn't seen the updated exhibit of Mr. Johnson until today. Thought I would stop in, since I'm in the city."

The dark-haired woman scowled. "Have you spoken to Evelyn Hart since everything happened?"

The woman had become an annoying thorn in my side, and I prayed my expression didn't reflect my irritation.

"No, I haven't," I responded evenly.

She crossed her arms. "Isn't your friend Jake Barnes, who used to be her manager? She had to feel so betrayed by her inner circle."

"I can't and won't speak for Ms. Hart or Mr. Barnes." My gaze found Sophie, who stood behind the group, and she shook her head subtly. "Thank you for your questions and comments, but we really do have to keep moving. You can reach me via my social media. I'm @NathanPrice everywhere." Internally sighing with relief, I smiled and waved.

"Ladies and gentlemen, we need to allow Mr. Price and his companion to continue their visit," Sweetie Jay said firmly. "They are tourists just as you are and have limited time. Please allow them privacy."

The small group of people clapped for me, and I nodded at them as I followed Sophie, who'd already moved toward another hall. I caught up to her, and she whispered, "You okay?"

"Yeah. I don't know why I'm always caught off guard when someone recognizes me and has legit questions. Stoney Johnson has placed a spotlight on me, whether I want it or not." I glanced around us to make sure no one could hear us. "And I plan to use it to get this documentary made. Imagine the attention this film will receive if I got so much from a freelance cover story."

"Nathan?" Sweetie Jay hurried to us. "I apologize for the disturbance. It was my fault for announcing who you are. I know you need to be able to gather information in peace. Do you want to return sometime early next week, after hours like I did with Jake and Amara when they visited? Then you can do whatever you need to do without watchful and lurking eyes."

Sophie touched my forearm. "I think she's right, because people will try to figure out what we're doing here, especially with me taking pics. It might be just my phone, but it's obvious that I'm capturing something."

"I didn't think about reserving a time for the museum. Never had to before." I whistled in frustration, ready to dive into my work.

"We can hit up the Stax Museum instead and come back here later, since no one knows or is expecting us." Sophie turned slightly toward the older woman. "When is a good day to return?"

"Are you going to be here on Monday? Now that the summer is winding down, we don't have any summer camps or groups coming. That might be the best day for me to open early or stay later for you. Tomorrow or Sunday might be too hectic."

I answered, "Monday works. We can arrive early or stay late—whatever is easiest on your schedule."

"Then let's do it late. Maybe stop here around three and stay. I have work to catch up on. It should be practically empty around that time."

"Appreciate your flexibility. We can pay you for your time or donate to the museum," I reassured her.

She waved her hand. "Jake donates regularly, and your work has brought new attention to the museum. I'm sure whatever you're working on next will only shed more light on the influence of this city on music."

"That's the plan."

I smiled as Sophie took another pic of me and Sweetie Jay, who grinned. "I feel like a celebrity around you two."

"Because you are. Your job every single day is to make sure musicians are remembered." Sophie started snapping pics and moving around her playfully while Sweetie Jay complied. "Strike a pose. Supermodel. Vogue for us. You just had a hot-girl summer."

The patrons who wandered into our section and I clapped at Sophie and Sweetie Jay's antics.

Yep, my intuition had been right about my asking Sophie to accompany me to Memphis. She had the charm and persona to switch a room's energy from dull to lively. Sophie was a light who didn't quite know or accept her power over people.

Sophie walked backward to face me as we toured the Stax Museum of American Soul Music. "I can't believe I never knew about this record label. I would've so wanted to be here instead of Nashville if I were born two generations earlier, like you."

I snickered despite my best attempt not to humor her ageism daggers.

She gestured with her arms at all the colorful displays of albums and singles produced by Stax Records in Memphis lining the walls. "I could so easily imagine myself playing my guitar with Isaac Hayes in the studio. People slept on his talent. Listen to the complexity of music in *Shaft*'s theme song. In-cred-i-ble." Sophie hugged herself. "Otis…O-T-I-S, are you freaking kidding me? A limo driver working for Johnny Jenkins and the Pinetoppers somehow gets into the studio and becomes Stax's biggest artist before perishing in a crash too soon. Imagine what hits he left on the table. Or that Booker T. & the M.G.'s were like me and The Crew, a house band for the label who recorded their own songs. And I had no idea the Staples sisters were a band with their father. Their story reminded me of me and my father playing together." She suddenly twirled around. "I feel so alive here. I've never been this moved in a museum."

"Because you are a musician, Sophie." I pointed at the album covers. "These people are your people. Your kindred spirits. I wish you could see how animated your expression is right now. You're like a big kid in a toy store with an unlimited budget. Don't give up on yourself."

She stopped walking and grabbed my forearms. "Whether I ever play music again isn't me giving up on myself."

"Then what would you call it?" I stared down at her pretty face, which was made impish by the cleft in her chin.

"A space of transition. You fail to see that there's more to me than a woman who sings and plays her guitar." She released me and walked beside me. "Music doesn't define me. It never did."

"If you say so." I shrugged. I'd learned in these two days with Sophie that she was as stubborn as they came. "I just know my face has never looked like yours walking through a museum about an old record label in Memphis. I do know that."

"History and learning about music excite me. You're reading too much into my reaction," she retorted, moving away.

I pointed to Isaac Hayes's custom Cadillac Eldorado. "The fact that both Isaac and Booker T. and the MG's were studio musicians for the label and later had their own careers doesn't inspire you in the least bit?"

"No. Women can't have it all like men can."

"What about Amara?" I placed my hands behind my back, watching her slowly walk around the Cadillac.

Wrinkles crossed her forehead. "What about her?"

"She's on a successful tour, is a millionaire, and is engaged to a rich man. To most, she has it all. Isn't that your dream?"

"I'm happy for my friend. But that's not *my* dream." Sophie stopped moving and planted her hands on her hips. "And what happens once she has a child? Huh? Jake's career won't miss a beat. I guarantee hers will. Mari knows this and isn't trying to be a mother anytime soon. As much as I like to believe otherwise, it's still very much a man's world. We have to make sacrifices men don't. I've met men who think it's cute, like you do, that I sing and am in a band. But what happens when he wants me at home and I have to be on tour, then what? Men can be selfish creatures. And what if I have a banging-ass career as a singer? Is that supposed to take away my loneliness or my yearning to be a mother? I've been a paid musician for years, and it hasn't gotten me closer to a husband or a baby." She hugged herself and turned away from me, but not before I saw the sadness in her eyes.

"Hey… Is that really what happened with you and Omar? He ended things because he thought your career was more important to you?"

Sophie walked in the opposite direction.

Cursing myself for my need to prove a point, I started after her. Then stopped. She needed space. I wanted to take back my words. Who was I to tell her that her desire to have a husband and a family over a career was wrong? Sophie deserved love and would make some man deliriously happy.

My chest tightened. The thought of her being with any other man besides me struck a jealous chord, and I abruptly headed the other direction, placing my AirPods in my ears, immersing myself in the sounds of my Stax Records playlist. Coincidentally, Sam and Dave's "When Something Is Wrong with

My Baby" played. I quickly pressed skip and attempted to clear my thoughts to Rufus Thomas's dance song, "Walking the Dog."

Bothered by my irrational jealousy, I wandered through the museum to refocus on my purpose in being in Memphis—which was *not* to fall in love. I pulled out my phone and used my stylus to jot down notes. Work erased the lingering pangs of hurting Sophie's feelings and the inevitability of her being with another man.

"What are you writing?" Sophie said by my ear as I sat in a chair near the gift shop an hour later.

I ignored the thrill that coursed through me at her now-familiar floral scent and replied without looking up from my screen. "Piecing together bits and parts. According to her daughter, Claudette Saint used to be part of the studio band, performing background vocals during the Isaac Hayes era. I had hoped to find some evidence of her work here at Stax. Figured I would see a plaque or a statement or see her name somewhere around."

"Why?" Sophie shifted from one foot to the other.

"Stoney used to be a songwriter, too, and he didn't work with Stax Records. So, I wonder if he wrote any songs for her, and if he did, where are they?" I slid the stylus slid back into my cell and stretched my arms when I stood up.

"Another lost song." Sophie's lips slowly spread into a smile. "A song potentially worth money."

I nodded. "Probably why the daughter wants us to visit their home against her mother's wishes. Stoney's legacy is worth a couple of million now. Imagine what an unreleased song from back in the day might be worth, especially if it's sample ready."

Sophie clasped her hands together. "Mari would be so thrilled to find yet another of her grandfather's songs. I bet it was fire. Shit, I still sing the songs Stoney wrote for Ms. Evelyn, and country wasn't even his favorite genre. You might have another mystery on your hands."

"Maybe or maybe not. I just want to know if my gut is right and Claudette Saint is the story."

We wandered back toward the only entrance. The gnawing disappointment of the lost opportunity to investigate and write at the Rock 'n' Soul Museum had subsided once we'd arrived at Stax, where no one knew us. We were able to move freely about and take our time exploring.

Impulsively, I pressed my lips on her temple and said, "Sorry for earlier. I didn't mean to upset you. Sometimes I can press too hard, a hazard of being an investigative journalist."

Her soft gaze slid to mine. "I can be way too sensitive."

"You and Erykah Badu are sensitive about your shit. I get it." Sophie laughed and pressed her hand against my chest as I looped my arm around her neck. "Thank you for helping me pivot to another choice. I was beginning to think that today had been a waste until you suggested Stax. I'm so glad you're here with me."

She blushed and couldn't quite look me in the eyes. "You're welcome."

"Seriously, we make a good team."

Sophie nodded and walked ahead of me, pushing through the glass door. "We do. It's getting late. We've been here for hours."

"You hungry?" The heat of the humid night hitting my face and the sounds of cars driving past reoriented us to the present after spending hours in the past.

"Yes, but I'd rather eat in the hotel. Need to get some rest. Somebody kept me up late." She sang the last words.

"Who, me?" I grinned and lifted my bag higher on my shoulders. "I was willing to go to bed by myself until you persuaded me otherwise."

"That's not true. You came on to me first," she accused playfully, and snapped a pic of me.

The crawling sun making way for the moon cast a honeyed tint to our skins while we strolled to our hotel a few blocks away, heightening the growing sexual tension, and I understood why she'd grabbed that photo.

My smile widened. "No, Twinkle, you knew what you were doing wearing that dress and whispering in my ear from jump. You were so worried about me going to that woman, you couldn't think straight."

Our eyes remained locked while pedestrians moved between and around us on an early Friday evening. After all the emotions we'd experienced today, we needed this light, teasing energy.

"That's not true." She jabbed my side.

"I wouldn't have tried you if you didn't give me the green light."

Sophie gasped and covered her mouth briefly. "You would've tried me eventually. Don't act like you needed the green light from me to make a move."

"We agree to disagree." I gripped the straps of my backpack. "I've already learned I won't win an argument with you."

Sophie impishly smiled. "Glad you recognize."

We approached the revolving doors of our hotel, and I suggested, "Maybe tonight we have room service and chill. Got a lot to think about. Need to figure out the best way to approach Ms. Saint by Sunday."

"Sounds like a plan. I really am exhausted." She slid in one of the openings and yawned as if on cue.

Her sleepiness didn't deter my desire. I wanted her again, and her soft touches and flirty banter as we walked back to the hotel had told me she felt the same. Like last night, I would drop back and let her decide whether we had sex. Sophie was the kind of woman who would retreat if I pushed too hard, even if she wanted what I wanted.

My already aroused body stiffened when Sophie's pretty eyelashes fluttered as the elevator landed on her floor. She pouted. "Tonight is the last time. I'm serious."

Feeling like I'd won a prize after a hard-fought contest, I nipped her lips, tasting the last of her peach-flavored gloss. "Okay. Okay. After tonight, we're back to friends without fucking benefits."

She grabbed my hands and tugged me off the elevator. "You only said 'fucking' because you know that word turns me on."

"Does it? I hadn't *fucking* noticed." I wrapped my arms around her waist as she searched for her key in her shoulder bag. She emitted a low moan at the feel of my hardness pressed into her ass.

"You're such a liar." Sophie pushed open the door and waited for me to pass her. This time, the brush of my arm on her breast was intentional. And unlike the last time, she didn't hide that my touch thrilled her as she began pulling my shirt off my body before we even closed the door.

NINE

Sophie

The warm water cascaded over my head and shoulders while I hummed "Let's Do It Again" by the Staple Singers. The visit to the Stax Museum, the subsequent interview of some of the studio band members who still lived in Memphis, researching old blues legends like Eddie Floyd and Memphis Minnie, a guitarist and singer—it had all stirred my musicality. We'd even made a stop at Royal Studios, home of Hi Records, arguably Stax's biggest competition, and label of Al Green. The history of those soulful singers with such rich voices and the sheer talent that graced Beale Street inspired me to rethink how I'd viewed my career.

I wanted to sing again in some capacity, though I wasn't quite ready to tell Nathan he'd been right. The pieces were slowly coming together. If only I could figure out how to fit marriage and family into this new puzzle. I'd meant what I told Nathan—I didn't believe I could have this amazing musical career and be the type of homemaker I envisioned. But I could no longer ignore that I wanted to perform again, and maybe on a different stage.

The air cooled around me, and I waved my finger at a naked Nathan. "This is why I wanted to take a shower in my room. We have to get going."

We'd slept together again last night, though we didn't do much sleeping, amped up on the success of the day. He had amazing stamina and probably could've gone another round or two after giving me back-to-back orgasms.

This time, we'd slept in his room at my request. Nathan attempted to honor what he believed I wanted and had bidden me goodnight in the elevator on Saturday evening. But the idea of spending a night alone after so many nights together didn't appeal, and I'd pressed the button to close the doors without exiting.

"I'm trying to save time. You take long showers and forever to get ready. I'll let you remain in front and use most of the water." Nathan slid in behind me. "Pay no attention to me. Did you find my soap in my bag?"

"Yeah." I grabbed it from the holder before me and passed it to him.

"I like your hair like this." He ran his hand over my braids.

"These cornrows help my wigs fit better. I don't wear these outside." I flicked my tongue at him.

"I know. But I like that I see all of your beautiful face." He kissed my cheek.

"And though you're adorable with your glasses, I like when I can look directly in your eyes." Turning my head back around, I welcomed the water soothing my body.

"I'll have to get more contacts as soon as I return."

"You do that. But I'm still wearing my wigs." I rested my head on his chest, letting the water strike my face. His presence comforted me, and I closed my eyes, enjoying the weightlessness of no burdens or worries.

He chuckled. "Please keep humming. You sound so good. I could easily get back in bed and sleep to your voice."

"Can you guess the song?" Surprisingly, I wanted to sing for him. Maybe because he didn't make a big deal about hearing me hum, or perhaps because it felt right.

"No. Just loved how happy you sound." He wrapped his arms around me and kissed my nape.

"I'll sing it to you, and you guess." I smiled as we rocked together. "Except all I know is the chorus. Didn't exactly grow up listening to this music. Shared a kinship with the Staple Singers, though this song wasn't recorded with Stax. Did a deep dive on their music and now I'm positively hooked."

"Make up the lyrics as you go." He tightened his arms around me, and his thick erection pressed against my back. "I could listen to your voice all day."

With his encouragement, I sang the words I knew and improvised the ones I didn't know about enjoying good sex. A perfect complement to what we'd been doing for the past few days. While we grooved to my voice, Nathan lathered his cloth and washed my body. I returned the favor, and we danced, sang, and hummed together in the shower until the heat between us ignited. He lowered himself to his knees and lifted my leg on his shoulder. His mouth assuaged my aching center after the strenuous fucking of last night. I caressed the soft waves on his head, luxuriating in the sensual feel of his tongue on the most intimate part of me. *Hmm.* This man could devour me anytime.

We didn't have expectations, and for once, I could see the freedom in being this way with a man. I didn't second-guess every thought and search for signs he wanted commitment. I knew where Nathan stood, and honestly, he was just what I needed: a man with whom I felt safe and cared for, satisfying my physical needs. I wanted to focus on the present and not think beyond today, and the man between my legs slowly mended the jagged edges of my broken heart.

After I lustily returned the favor, we exited the shower. I wrapped a towel around myself and headed to the side table. "I forgot to take my daily selfie."

Nathan finished toweling himself. "You take a picture of yourself every day?"

"Every morning for the last two years. Started because I saw something in a magazine that said that often our internal thoughts don't match our external appearance. We're walking around all incongruent and wonder why communication always breaks down. I wanted to let the truth show in the pictures before the mask dropped. It became a habit, and I do it without much thought." I picked up my cell and smiled at my reflection. My face glowed with sexual satiation.

"Why wear a mask at all?" He dug in his bag for boxer briefs.

"Sometimes you have to. Who really wants to know that you're hurt or sad?" I asked.

"I do." Nathan pulled up his underwear. "You never have to wear a mask around me."

I bit back my words, ready for a snappy retort that he shouldn't talk like that if he wanted us to remain casual. Real friends believed in creating safe spaces for the people they cared about, and wasn't that who we were? Unsure how else to respond, I deflected and picked up my jean shorts from last night. "Ugh. Don't want to put this back on."

"I'll grab you something to wear from your room." He donned a red, green, and black Bob Marley t-shirt and jeans while I fished around in my shorts and held out my key card.

When he grabbed the card, I held up the phone to capture him, too. Nathan pressed his cheek to mine, and I snapped a photo. Once he left the room, I admired how good we looked together. His eyes twinkled while I smiled at the lens. Despite my best intentions, the flutter of possibilities tickled my belly.

This was morning.

We pulled up to a small, old—though well-maintained—ranch-style house in Imogene Heights, a neighborhood with sparse trees and unevenly kept lawns in North Memphis. As Nathan and I gathered our belongings from his SUV, a woman around the same age and build as my curvy mother stepped outside of her front door. Her lips curved to reveal a gap between her front teeth, adding warmth and beauty to her round, brown face. "I can't believe you're really here. I'm Annie Wesley. Please call me Annie."

I smiled and walked across the broken concrete walkway to her as Nathan shut the back passenger door. "We're happy to be here. Thanks for meeting with us. I'm Sophie—"

She cut me off with a dismissive wave. "I know who you are. Sophie Turner. I follow you and Mari Johnson on IG. You sing and you're a part of her band."

Annie beckoned us to her door. Nathan joined me and placed his hand on the small of my back. A rather possessive move he'd been doing for the last four days, seemingly without thought. And I secretly loved it every time he did it.

He greeted her, "She is, and I'm Nathan Price. We appreciate you taking the time to meet with us to answer a few questions."

We followed and stepped inside her modest home, which smelled of potpourri and food seasonings. The wall unit in the window blasted cold air above the worn yet clean sofa. "My mother is here, though I'll warn you she doesn't like to talk about that time. She said she would meet with you as a favor. Offer you a Sunday supper. She can be a little ornery. I'm hoping she'll be more open once you talk to her about what you're doing."

"Nice home." Nathan admired the small, neat living area with a brown leather recliner facing a large TV on top of a dark console filled with pictures and vases. Framed portraits of Annie, Claudette, and other family members covered all the walls. "Thank you for allowing us into your space." He'd offered to arrange a private room in the hotel to meet with Claudette and her daughter, but Annie had insisted we meet at their home.

She smiled kindly. "I had no choice, honestly. It's the only way I could get Mama to agree to see you. She doesn't really like to leave the house except for doctor's appointments or family events."

"Where is she now?" Nathan asked.

We remained standing rather awkwardly. Or at least that was how I felt. Nathan seemed comfortable with his easy smile, reminding me he'd been in much more dangerous environments to interview people. This aging home in the middle of a Memphis neighborhood was probably a cakewalk to him.

Annie gestured toward the back of the house. "In the kitchen about to cook Sunday dinner. I told her we could get takeout or delivery, but she wasn't trying to hear me."

"Is that her favorite place to be?" Nathan pushed his glasses on the bridge of his nose. "If it's okay with you, I think we should pick a place where she feels most comfortable to talk."

"That would be the kitchen," Annie replied.

"Kitchen it is." Nathan smiled again and waved his hand for Annie to lead the way.

"Is it okay for me to record?" I asked. At Annie's nod, I hit record on my phone, visually documenting our path through her home.

"Mama is always experimenting with food." She led us through an archway to the kitchen. I'd forgotten that once upon a time, kitchens were separate from living areas. Even the house I grew up in had an open floor plan, which worked with our busy, loving, large family. We could cook, wash dishes, do homework, and watch TV in the same large room. What type of house did Nathan grow up in? Probably the opposite of mine, given what he'd told me about his parents and his stance on marriage and family.

A humming Claudette Saint stirred a boiling pot. Probably a gospel song, based on her cadence. The short, round-faced woman, wearing a honey-brown bob and a black velour jogging suit, moved briskly between the yellow counter where she prepped and the gas oven where she cooked. After Annie introduced us, she half turned to greet us without shaking our hands. "I'm cooking, you understand. Call me Ms. Claudette. Saint is too formal in my house, and my ex-husband's name."

Standing just in the kitchen doorway, we both nodded like children asking for permission to enter.

I held up my cell. "We'd like to snap candid photos and video you while we're here. It helps us recall the people that we meet and what was said so that Nathan can be more accurate when he's writing. You signed an agreement that it was okay to take photos and record you. Is it still okay?"

"What do you plan to do with the photos?" Ms. Claudette placed one hand on her ample hip, her frown crinkling her otherwise surprisingly smooth face. Only the lines in her neck revealed her advanced age.

"We just wanted to take a few pics…maybe a little video using my phone while we talk and you cook. Something to remember this moment. I do occasionally post pics on social media. We won't post anything if you don't want us to," I reassured her.

"And I won't publish anything you say or do without your final approval." Nathan took a step into the kitchen. "We're transparent about everything. No secrets or ulterior motives here." At her doubtful expression, Nathan smiled as he rubbed his stomach. "Mm-mm. You haven't even started cooking, and it smells good. Please say you're about to fry up some chicken. Got my stomach growling."

She beamed, temporarily forgetting about her question. "I just started. Best fried chicken in Memphis, besides Gus's."

Nathan moved to the square wooden table and placed his leather bag on the floor next to a chair. "We haven't tried Gus's yet. Do you think we should?"

"You have to try it, and then you can see I'm right about my food."

I interjected, "We can't impose. I'm sure you didn't plan to cook a meal for us. We have a few questions, and then we can be out of your hair."

Nathan's brow furrowed and then relaxed, his only sign that I'd overstepped. He'd been more than open to my participation in everyone we interviewed, but he'd cautioned me to allow him to take the lead with Ms. Claudette or anyone else who seemed hesitant to speak with us. I had to quell my nerves and not feel compelled to speak for our musicians or fill silences with nonsense chatter, a habit I'd only noticed in the last few days.

Ms. Claudette picked up a bowl of batter. "No bother at all. No one's here but me and my daughter. I don't mind feeding you, so ask your questions and"—she glanced at me—"you take your pictures."

"Is it okay if we sit down?" Nathan asked.

"Unless you want to stand up looking crazy this whole time when I have a perfectly good table right there. And why are you trying to sit in that chair, when men sit at the head?" She sucked her teeth as she started battering her chicken. Water in a pot boiled loudly, and a dull grater stood on the counter.

"Yes, ma'am. I didn't want to presume." Nathan shifted to sit at the end of the table and pulled out a notepad, since he preferred writing to recording and playing back conversations. He believed his method helped his subjects relax, knowing he could share what he'd written at any time.

"Please, tell me you're making mac and cheese?" From behind my phone, I squealed. "My favorite in the whole wide world. I haven't had any homemade since last Thanksgiving. What else do you have on that stove?"

Nathan gave a subtle nod.

"Just some of my cabbage with some turkey necks thrown in, and corn bread. I have an apple pie I baked this morning." Ms. Claudette practically glowed. "Go ahead and ask away. I like people who love to eat."

Nathan and I exchanged smiles. "Then he and I are in the right place."

Her daughter joined Nathan at the table. "I would help her cook, but Mama hates it."

"I really do. She gets in the way. She learned nothing from me. Can't cook to save her life." Ms. Claudette turned up the burner under the black cast-iron pot. "The oil is ready. Might as well talk, because once we eat, we don't talk business."

"Understood. Reminding you again that although you signed papers to talk to us and for Sophie to take pics and videos, we won't include anything you don't want to be said or seen. The documentary is about the unsung talent here in Memphis." Nathan tapped the yellow paper with his mechanical pencil.

"There are plenty of people like me who didn't make it. We come a dime a dozen around these parts. Why do you want to know *my* story?" She dipped the chicken in batter before placing it in the sizzling grease.

Nathan scooted his chair closer to the table. "Your daughter reached out to Amara Johnson, and a large part of why we're even doing this documentary is to expand upon Stoney's legacy, here in Memphis. He kept a journal of songs. Some had the singer's name attached, and some didn't. We interviewed Mac Wilson, one of the interns at Stax when you were there, who spoke about knowing you as a background and studio singer at Stax. He believed you'd worked with Stoney before you stopped singing."

"That scrawny kid with the too-big glasses held together by tape?" She smiled. "He was a sweetheart who kept hoping for his lucky break in talent management. What is he up to these days?"

"A car salesman at a Ford dealership," Nathan responded evenly.

Ms. Claudette twisted her lips and scoffed. "Told you there's plenty of us out here."

"I mean no disrespect to Mr. Wilson or any other person who might not have ended up with the life he or she wanted, but you are different," Nathan insisted. "You worked directly with Stoney. We assumed that he wrote a song or two for you. Given his track record with creating hits, we wanted to know what happened with your songs, if there are any?"

Her back faced us as she stood at the stove. "My story isn't going to be like Stoney's. I sang at a few clubs, tried to get signed on as an artist at Stax, and settled for being a part of the house band. It paid the bills most days. I got married and had my Annie here. End of story. I don't have any deep, dark secrets to tell. No lost songs or a family member who sings like me. No stash of money to leave my family set for life. My husband and I divorced years ago. It's just me and my daughter here now. My grandson is finishing up pharmacist training at some Black school in New Orleans."

"Xavier, Mama. I keep telling you he's at Xavier." Annie sighed.

"As long as you know the name." Ms. Claudette shrugged, still facing the stove. The weight of retelling her unfulfilled dreams drooped her shoulders.

Annie rolled her eyes. "Mama, you told me years ago that you had music you wished other people heard. What happened to that song you used to sing around the house?"

"Some lyrics I wrote. Never recorded them. Just played around in the studio." Ms. Claudette stirred the boiling pot and lowered the blue flame underneath. "Sorry, I can't really help you."

"Mama, those were Stoney Johnson's lyrics, and I know you remember the words. Nathan can match the lyrics to one of the songs in the journal." Annie looked at us for guidance. "That should be enough to prove that he wrote music for my mother."

"We wrote them together," Ms. Claudette corrected her sharply while pouring yellow cornmeal into a waiting cast-iron skillet.

I glanced at Nathan, who held his pencil over the pad, quietly waiting for Ms. Claudette to continue speaking.

She shoved the skillet into the oven. "Stoney didn't believe in making any song without the singer's blueprint. Each song he wrote uniquely told the story of that artist."

"Did you know him well?" I asked before I could stop myself, refusing to acknowledge Nathan's disapproving frown. Instead, I snapped a pic of her turning over the chicken in the pan.

She glanced at me with lines crossing her smooth forehead before returning to the stove. "Everyone knew Stoney. He tried to help any hungry artist he could. After his wife and son left him, he wrote songs for free. Probably tons of unrecorded songs out there. He didn't even care about making money once he lost his family. Even the two he wrote for me. I begged him to take something for the time he spent, but he said he no longer cared about creating music for the money. It was his gift and passion, and it made him happy to write for others." She used gray oven mitts to pick up the pot to drain the noodles through a strainer in the sink.

Her lips curved into a proud smile, and she looked at Nathan. "Man, he could sing. He had such range. Pitch perfect. The first time I heard his granddaughter sing on the radio, I cried happy tears. That was Stoney's styling, and his rhythm brought back to life through his bloodline."

Nathan jotted down notes. "Do you still have the music you and he created together? It doesn't matter if it was never recorded."

She waved her hand. "I don't know where it is. It's been decades, and I'm sure it got lost during one of our moves from house to house. My daughter thinks the songs are worth money."

He nodded. "His songs are valuable, even if it's only to the Johnson family. Can you remember any of the lyrics? We can match them to the journal or dive deeper into finding the music again."

She poured the noodles into a large baking pan. "No."

"But Mama…" Annie protested.

Ms. Claudette glared so deeply that her grown daughter bowed her head. "I said no."

Nathan continued, "We still want to include you in the documentary, whether you have proof he wrote songs for you or not. We would love to know about your journey. If you prefer to talk about your relationship with Stoney and not the music, you can."

She placed the back of her hand on her hip and chuckled. "Let's be clear. Never had a relationship with him. We were strictly friends. He was handsome as the devil, but he wasn't paying any women any mind. Only his wife mattered to him. I've often wondered what he did to make her leave him like she did, because we all thought he loved her and that boy of theirs dearly. Everyone loved Stoney, and we thought she was the luckiest woman. Figured it might be a side woman, but back then, women didn't leave their husbands because of cheating, especially when he was as fine and talented as Stoney. You stuck it out. We imagined all kinds of reasons when she and that boy of theirs just disappeared."

Ms. Claudette started humming the tune from earlier as she grated cheese. The three of us watched as she layered the cheese and macaroni.

She didn't speak again until she added the pan next to the skillet in the oven. "Once I found out what actually happened, I understood why she left town. He could've been killed if anyone knew he was seeing a white woman during that time. After everything we suffered and endured here in Memphis, including Dr. King's assassination, how could he even think of leaving his wife for her? I would've hightailed it out of there, too. No way would I have ever stayed with a man who forgot that Black men were lynched in this very city for looking at a white woman, even if it weren't true." Her brow furrowed. "Will any of the pictures you're taking today be included in the documentary?"

I moved beside her to show her. "Recorded you for a little while. You can see it. Whatever picture or video you want me to include, let me know."

She shook her head. "I trust you. I heard you sing, too, and I know you play with Stoney's granddaughter."

Nathan proudly smiled at me. "She's one of the best, too. You should see her perform."

"Oh…a man who brags about his woman. You'd better keep him. It's not easy finding a man who supports your career. Men want their women at home waiting on them hand and foot." She slanted a flirty gaze at Nathan. "And he's all strong, handsome, and smart. A good man."

"We're not…" I swear my face reddened as I gripped my phone to stop the nervous tremble at her assumption.

"If I were ten years older, Ms. Claudette, you would give Sophie a run for my attention." Nathan smoothly interrupted my stammer by teasing the woman who was easily in her seventies.

"You couldn't keep up." She winked and laughed loudly.

"He can barely keep up with me," I slipped in slyly, and he twisted his mouth at me. I would play along, since he hadn't corrected her about our relationship status, for now.

"Where can I buy your music?" Annie took down four white plates from the cabinet.

My stomach flipped. "Um. I don't have any songs. I just do background for Mari Johnson."

"You do more than that. You also perform on your own in Nashville." Annie placed the dinnerware on the table and looked at me for confirmation. "I'm a fan…Told you I follow you on Instagram. I love to watch your shows. You haven't posted in a long time. I thought maybe something happened to you. I was so glad when Mr. Price told me you would be with him."

Nathan's gaze lingered on me, though I didn't return it. I had a small following of thirty-six thousand on Insta, and somehow, knowing that strangers missed me hit different. It meant I mattered to more than just my family and friends.

I lowered the cell and touched Annie's forearm. "Thank you for being a fan. Just needed a break."

"I hope you don't take too much longer."

Nodding, I raised my phone back up like it was my shield, warding off the emotions stabbing me from different angles.

"Oh…leave her alone. She'll be back when she's back." Ms. Claudette held a platter of steaming chicken, and Nathan quickly retrieved it from her to place it in the center of the table. She wiped her hands on her apron. "The mac and cheese won't take as long as it normally does. I'm baking it at a higher temperature. The cabbage and corn bread will be ready in a few minutes."

Shaking off my tumbling thoughts, I swallowed a deep breath. "You made a whole meal from scratch in forty minutes? And I'm always saying I don't have time to cook."

"Would've been less than thirty if I were alone in here," she bragged. "I'm the original thirty-minute-meal cook."

"My mother used to make dinner fast like you until she started working. Being in here while you cook reminds me of my childhood," Nathan observed as he settled back in his chair.

"I bet it felt good to have home-cooked meals." Ms. Claudette used a fork and placed a large piece of chicken on the plate in front of Nathan. "You look like a breast man."

"It did feel good, and I am. Love when they're plump and juicy." He chuckled and took a bite while sneaking a peek at me. Last night, he'd praised the fullness of my body through the heat of his sexy gaze and his treacherous mouth.

I shook my head at his naughtiness and took a shot of him eating the crispy meat with relish.

"Sophie, can I ask you something?" Ms. Claudette held the serving fork up.

"Anything." I snapped another pic of her before sitting in the chair beside Nathan.

"You just told my daughter you were taking a break from music. Is it because you don't have a record deal?"

My stomach lurched. "Why do you ask?"

"I remember when I took a break and never returned." Her eyes softened. "All I wanted was a chance. That's it. All my life, I heard this voice calling on the angels in heaven. I moved here from across the river when I was seventeen to sing with the greatest, against my parents' wishes. I played in local clubs for a couple of years and finally landed an audition for Isaac Hayes to be a background singer when he was a part of the studio band for Stax. I worked for and with them for years. Those were good days."

"And you got to sing once with B.B. King, Mama." Annie rose to her mother and slipped an arm around her. "Met Elvis when he stopped at the bar where she sang, and he praised her voice."

A soft smile graced her lips.

"I met a lot of good people, most of us living on hope and a prayer in a time when this country didn't believe we had the right to dream." Ms. Claudette pointed the fork at me. "You're lucky you were born in a better world than your parents and grandparents. Don't give up. My daughter showed me some of your videos. You play and sing so beautifully that some record company is going to snatch you up soon. Traveling with Mari Johnson can't hurt either."

I lifted my chin. "I hope I don't seem disrespectful, but I've never wanted a record deal."

Her head jerked back. "I don't know any singer, especially one who lives in Nashville, who doesn't dream of a record deal. Is that what you tell yourself so you never have to be disappointed? I've been there, tricking yourself into believing it doesn't matter if you never make it because you sing for the passion of it. Then it hits you when everyone around you shines and you're in the background. That it matters."

Her eyes focused past my shoulders. She was no longer talking about me. "Day after day, you try to figure out how you can be different, how you can be noticed, and wonder why it hasn't happened for you yet when you've grinded harder than those who made it. Or at least it feels that way. Going to bed crying and waking up, pushing through the negativity, only to receive another rejection. Do you know what it does to your soul when hope gets trampled on?" Her chest heaved, and she gritted through her teeth, "And when you finally get an opportunity, those bastards snatch it away."

Tears sprang from her eyes, running like rivers down her cheeks, and she jabbed the fork at her daughter. "Why didn't you just listen to me? I told you that I didn't want to talk about this. Why would I want to revisit a dream that never came true?"

Annie grabbed the fork from her mother's hands and stood up. "Because it wasn't your fault, Mama. You marched with King on behalf of those sanitation workers. You heard him speak the day before he was assassinated, and he inspired you and your music with Stoney, remember?" She spoke rapidly as she glanced at Nathan. "Mama, now is the time to tell your story— whether we ever make any money, I want your sacrifices to be known. That you had this amazing life here in Memphis and a chance at a record deal, but found out you were pregnant. Don't change the truth because you're afraid of the pain. You taught me that."

"Enough," Ms. Claudette said.

Annie blinked rapidly. "Tell them your story, please."

Nathan rose and picked up Ms. Claudette's hand with both of his. "That's exactly the point, Ms. Claudette. It's about righting the wrongs of the past. Too many of our ancestors sacrificed so that we, their descendants, could have better. We want to make dreams finally come true, even years later. Stoney died before he could see the fruits of his labor, and we don't want that to keep happening to our people. You're here and alive. Let me hear your voice…your words. Let me hear *you*, Claudette Saint."

Ms. Claudette suddenly seemed her age as her eyes glistened with regret and sadness. "I need to take the corn bread out of the oven before it burns and ruins our supper. No one eats cabbage without corn bread." She wiped her tears and squeezed Nathan's arm when she passed him. "My voice stopped mattering years ago. But I'll share my experiences with Stoney because he was a friend, and I'm happy that he finally got the justice and the accolades he deserved."

Nathan dragged a hand over his head and down his face. He eased back into his seat at the table and threw her a lopsided grin. "Ms. Claudette, I believe I just had the best fried chicken of my life. You'd better hurry with the rest of the meal before I eat all this on this platter. Sophie, you have to try it." His bright and cheery tone didn't match the dullness in his eyes. I felt and understood his disappointment. And also became keenly aware of how my decision not to perform might affect others, known and unknown, who care about me.

Ms. Claudette sniffed before pulling out the pan of mac and cheese from the oven. "Wait until you try this. Come on, Sophie. Time to put that phone away and eat. You can ask me anything except about myself after supper."

"Yes, ma'am. I can't wait." I sank back in my chair, deflated.

Nathan patted my thigh underneath the table. His empathetic gaze warmed my heart as he used his thumb to wipe the tears I had unconsciously shed.

Anne dried her wet cheeks with a paper towel, straightened her shoulders, and finished setting the table.

Later that night, alone in my room, I restlessly paced. My jumbled thoughts were unyielding. I couldn't relax and focus on anything coherent. My music. Princess. Omar. My parents. My family. This project. Ms. Claudette's palpable remorse of a dream deferred. Her daughter's frustration at her stubbornness. What I'd lost. What I may never have again. Rising fear that my mind would revert to the numbness and loneliness I'd experienced before Nathan convinced me to come to Memphis spurred me to go to him.

I knocked on his door, and he opened it shirtless. His eyes were red and worn. I scooped my arms under his, and he backed up, holding me, and allowed the door to slam behind us.

"I can't function right now. My mind is spinning and I don't know what to do. Is that why you look like I feel?" I asked, hoping he would say something to comfort me. To acknowledge all that had happened today so that we could process it together.

He inhaled and exhaled deeply. I lifted my head to look into his now-hooded eyes.

"What's wrong?"

His arms tightened, though he wouldn't look at or acknowledge me.

"Nate?" I tried again, wanting him to say or do something that would make me feel better. Make us feel better.

A strong hand rubbed my back while he continued to avoid eye contact. "I'm okay."

"No, you're not. You said nothing on the ride back or in the elevator."

"Thought I would give you the space you've been asking for," he said weakly.

"You wanted space tonight. Not me." I stepped from his embrace, and he dropped his gaze to his bare feet. "Why won't you look at me? Talk to me? I know you were disappointed by Ms. Claudette. We can figure it out." Nathan shifted away from me, and my heart dropped. "If you want me to leave, I will. Just wanted to talk."

He didn't say anything.

"Got it." I backed away, and he grabbed my wrist. I twisted out of his grip. "I'm good. See you in the morning. Sorry to bother you."

I walked back out the door and to the elevator. Nathan didn't come after me. I hated that I cared and was embarrassed by my need for him. We were just friends with benefits. I didn't have the right to be upset or hurt. It wasn't like he'd asked me to join him in his room to reject me. He hadn't done anything wrong. I needed to share my day. My confused emotions. He didn't. Simple and plain. I had to brush off the feelings of rejection because we differed in how we coped.

Today had been a tough one for both of us. Claudette Saint's story wasn't just about a woman who never broke into the music business. It was so much more, and we might never know how much more. In her age-old wisdom, she'd posed a question that had the potential to shift my own paradigm. My reason for existing.

Had I been lying to myself about a music career?

Jake had jumped on the opportunity to sign Amara, and he'd never offered to sign me in the five years I worked for him. Was I lying to myself when I said my end game was marriage and family? Was I content with being adjacent to superstardom? Had Nathan accurately judged me when he didn't believe marriage and family would be enough for me?

He had been dealt a blow today, too. I'd seen how his shoulders dropped when it became apparent that Ms. Claudette wouldn't talk to us about much. He'd wanted to center the story around her because of her past in the civil rights movement, her connection to Stoney, and her career as a blues singer. She had been our first roadblock when everyone else we'd spoken to welcomed us. Nathan had anticipated her hesitancy but been certain he could convince her to share. Still, his reticence in his room seemed deeper than a potential subject's unwillingness to cooperate. Nathan didn't want me to see him like that. Perhaps he didn't want me to truly see him, period. Maybe this was his way to remind me that we had different paths, and this was simply a moment of convergence.

Needing fresh air, I grabbed my guitar case, walked out to the balcony, and tucked my legs under me. The summer breeze cooled my skin, and with trembling hands, I opened my pink case and stared at the smoothness and shine of the wood used to make the instrument. Since I was twelve, I had played the guitar every single day. First it was Queenie, and then my own Princess.

After.

I couldn't even bear to pick up my instrument that I carried everywhere. Music no longer appealed. I'd broken my playing streak and didn't care. Had I unconsciously given up my music because I didn't want another disappointment? Was my unwavering desire for my own family an excuse I could use if I never made it in the industry?

I placed my hand on my empty womb and the possibilities of pregnancy. No. I *did* want my own babies and a husband one day. That wasn't a lie. Yet I couldn't reconcile that with why I didn't expect more from my music when it'd been so much a part of me.

A soft knock interrupted my musings. I walked back into the artificially cold air, placed my case next to the bed, and ignored the warmth that spread across my heart that he had come for me. I cracked open the door.

Dressed in a black hoodie and red basketball shorts, a somber Nathan stared back at me with his leather satchel in his hand.

"Can I work in here with you?" He looked past my shoulders like he expected someone else in my room.

"I don't know," I replied honestly.

His gaze darted back to mine. "I'm sorry."

"I don't need an apology." I gripped the knob and searched his face. "Did we make a mistake sleeping together? It's been four nights when we said one time, and now we're at odds."

"Are we really going to have this conversation while I'm standing in the hall?"

Nathan caught the door I widened for him, and I perched on the edge of the bed. He placed his bag on the desk in the sitting area before flopping flat on his back beside me. He pulled me to recline with him, and we faced each other.

His finger twirled the string on my pajama bottoms. Intense heat rose between us. "Why do you think we made a mistake? I tried to stop you from leaving."

"Nate, you didn't mean it. You wanted to be alone, and there's nothing wrong with that. I didn't have the right to be upset." I captured his finger, too close to my tingling sex, and pushed his hand back to his side. The flame lowered to an ember. "Thinking my feelings were only hurt because we'd been intimate."

"Yes, you did have the right because of how I handled it. You are my friend, first and foremost. You would've been hurt even if we'd never slept together. It hurt worse because we have. I shut you out after being so open with you these past few days." His sigh squeezed out of his lips, almost sounding like a whistle. "Years of solitude make it a challenge to explain myself to someone else when I'm troubled."

"You don't have to explain," I reassured him, though I wanted him to talk to me. His friendship was starting to mean the world, and I wanted to be there for him when he needed.

"The fact that you're second-guessing me tells me I do." Nathan caressed my cheek with his hand. "Maybe I'm being selfish to want you when I know I could hurt you."

I pushed his glasses higher on his nose. "I told you, I can handle it. I needed a moment. You and I would've been good even if I didn't see you until the morning. Thought maybe you regretted being with me and didn't know how to say it."

"Never. I don't care if you end up hating me and want to kick the shit out of me. I will never regret the gift of having Sophie Turner in my bed." His gaze drifted from mine to the space between us. "You might have disappeared for months because of love, but I disappeared because of my career. I love what I do, and I keep hoping that my work matters not only to the people I've interviewed but to the world. Yes, I've won awards and been acknowledged by some pretty important people, but..."

"You want more," I surmised softly, tucking my arm underneath my head.

His eyes met mine. "I want to win a Pulitzer Prize. You might call me selfish or think that my work is a means to an end."

"No, I don't think that. You've risked your life because you care. Wanting to win a Grammy doesn't negate a musician's desire to make music."

Nathan slowly nodded. "When my vision doesn't go quite as planned, it takes me a moment to adjust. I'd been lost and wondering what was next for me when Jake invited me to Nashville. When he asked me to look into Stoney, I did it as a favor, but the more I studied his letters and the journal, the more curious I became. I found my footing with Stoney and Evelyn Hart, but I could find myself again with this project. Today was tough because everything in me knows that Claudette Saint *is* the story. Without her, I'm not sure we have a heart."

Before I could respond, he draped his forearm across my waist. "What she said got to you too. I see your guitar. Did you play it?"

"No. Still can't play it."

"Why?" Nathan shifted, and his face relaxed. As he had done earlier with Ms. Claudette when he mentioned how good her food smelled, he was steering the conversation in a different direction, and doing it so disarmingly that I didn't want to push him to talk more about himself. Instead, I wanted to share.

I propped my head on my arm. "Jake has never offered me a contract. That has to mean something, right?"

"Only if you want to make it mean something."

"I don't know what to think." Doubt curled like spoiled milk in my stomach, and I flipped to my back.

"Then how would he know if you're unsure what you want?" Nathan grabbed a pillow and tucked it under his head.

"Amara wasn't even trying to be a star, and he went after her when I've been right there in the studio with him," I reminded Nathan.

"That's not completely true. He said he saw her as another good singer for the studio and gave her his card. He also wanted to know Stoney's granddaughter better. It wasn't until she approached him at the Peabody asking for his help, and she sang in the bar, that he saw something different. You don't think Jake would've helped you, if you asked?"

Memories of my work with Jake flashed. He spent countless hours in the studio and on the road with one of his stars, always relying on me to match their rhythm, not mine. He reserved praise and criticism for them, rarely for me or the band, because he didn't expect anything from me except to do what I was told. He'd known before Amara that I wrote songs and performed solo throughout bars in Nashville and never ventured to see me until she and Nathan invited him out.

Slamming the pillow over my face, I mumbled, "Maybe I was too afraid to ask when he could see my talent."

Nathan removed the pillow, his face full of concern. "I couldn't hear you."

"I didn't want you to hear," I glumly replied.

"I can respect that." He opened my clenched fist and traced the lines in my hand. "You have a bright future, Sophie Turner."

"Geez, please don't tell me that another one of your talents is reading palms." I giggled.

"You didn't know? I can read minds, too." He narrowed his eyes and pressed his index finger against his temple. "You're afraid to know how big you can be."

The accuracy pierced the expanding balloon of jumbled emotions and thoughts, and I hit the space between us with my palm, words gushing out of me like water from a burst pipe. "Day in and day out, he hears me sing and play that guitar and has told me nothing. He knows I write songs and has never asked to hear them, though he appreciates it if I help Mari finish a song when she's stuck. For five years, I worked with that man, and he's never been excited for me like he has for his clients." I pushed out a breath. "The funny thing is I can't even tell you if I'm more afraid he would reject me or develop me into the star that Amara's becoming."

Through my tirade, Nathan continued to trace lines on my palm. "Being too big means you don't get to have the marriage and family, right?"

"Mari lost Phillip because she decided to pursue stardom, but gained Jake in the process. Everyone can't be that lucky to have a man by your side as you rise to the top." I averted my gaze from his discerning, unnerving one to the recessed ceiling. "Four months of racking my brain about who I am and what I want moving forward, and I'm still stuck."

He gently tugged my chin back to him. "Bet you're closer than before you came to Memphis."

"Maybe," I answered grudgingly.

Nathan popped up and pointed at my face. "I found the chink in that pretty armor. You hate to admit when you're wrong."

I grabbed a pillow and hit him in the head, knocking his glasses off his face. "Oops, sorry."

"Huge mistake. I always beat my mother and brother in pillow fighting." He growled, and I jumped out of bed, trying to find my escape from the pillow he now wielded like a tomahawk.

Prepared to evade him, I hunched down and opened my arms wide. "Nate, I was playing. You don't want to hit me with that pillow. I'm your Twinkle."

"Did you know I used to play football?" He knelt on the bed, trying to get his aim right as I rushed around the room laughing.

"Must have been pee wee football," I teased.

"Hey, I still played football." His thick brows dipped into a V, and when he aimed, I blindly ducked and dodged and squealed at the unexpected feel of his arms around me as he brushed my lips with his. "Are we good?"

"Yep." I kissed his chin. "The specks of gray in your beard make you look distinguished, like a professor at some Ivy League."

"I don't know if that's an insult or not coming from you." He studied my face.

"Trust, it's not." When he continued to stare at me, I asked, "What?"

Nathan shook his head. "Nothing." He released me. "I wanted to look at some of the pictures and footage you've taken to inspire me. Ms. Claudette knocked the wind out of me today."

The playful mood had transitioned in the blink of an eye. When Nathan worked, he became singularly focused. I bent to pick up my phone, which had fallen from the bed from our antics. I swiped through the pics and videos to the beginning of our trip and found the one I took as we stood next to the Mississippi River. The sun bounced off the water, highlighting the blue over the murky brown. I presented the photo to him. "This city that sits along the Mighty Mississippi is the story. Why don't you just make Memphis the focal point? Forget any musician or person who lived or rocked out here as the heart. The city itself has a story, from then to now."

He slowly nodded. "I've been playing around with that thought in my head, and it won't quite gel."

"You wanted Ms. Claudette to be the center because of her sociopolitical history in this city, because she represents Memphis. Then why can't we present Memphis and her complexities? The good, the bad, and the downright ugly."

Nathan picked up the pillow he'd thrown and tossed it on the bed. "Then we need to move our trip to the Lorraine Motel instead of the Rock 'n' Soul Museum tomorrow. I need to feel the injustice like I sensed in Ms. Claudette today." We'd planned to tour that museum on our last day, and allow the music, not the legacy of segregation, and the hard-won fight for our civil rights to lead the documentary.

I plopped down on the green sofa in the open suite. "Why do you keep calling it that instead of the National Civil Rights Museum?"

"Because what happened at the Lorraine Motel forever changed history. Made the world wake up to the hypocrisy of the country known to be the land of the free. A man who advocated and demonstrated peace in the face of hatred was killed violently while fighting for our right to be damn humans. I sometimes wonder if he hadn't been assassinated, would we still be openly practicing segregation?" His glossy eyes somehow still appeared dull.

Nathan averted his gaze past my shoulders and continued quietly, "When you've traveled the world like I have, you find two groups of people, those who hate America and those who envy me because I'm an American. Neither has a realistic view of this country. Hell, I was born here and have lived here longer than any other country, and can't explain the United States.

But that day, an assassin's hateful bullet cut down Dr. Martin Luther King, spotlighting this country's revulsion for people who were forced here in chains centuries before. Those same people who helped make this country, in particular the South, wealthy and powerful from their sweat and tears. I don't need to see the rest of the museum to know the impact of the tragic event at the Lorraine Motel on the civil rights movement." He grabbed his bag from the desk and pulled out his laptop, then turned his screen toward me. "Read and tell me what you think so far."

"I have a better idea." With all the reverence I'd ever given to my guitar, I retrieved it and carefully opened the case. I then positioned myself cross-legged on the sofa with Princess in my lap. "I'll play while you read to me and hope we're not disturbing anyone."

A smile brightened Nathan's face, and he began to read while I closed my eyes. I listened to his soothing voice relay the beginning of his next powerful piece of art and strummed mindlessly to his words.

TEN

Nathan

Boom.

People screamed and ran. I tried to run with legs too heavy to move, like my feet were stuck in wet cement. I couldn't move while chaos rained down around me. I covered my head with my arms, hoping that shrapnel or shards of glass from the blown-out windows of the nearby office building would miss me. I closed my eyes to block the destruction. Blood. So much blood everywhere.

Pop. Pop. Pop.

Gunshots whizzed near me.

Checking to see if an unknown enemy's bullet had struck me, I glanced down and my chest slowly spread red. Shit, I've been hit. *I kept touching myself, wondering why I didn't experience physical pain from the bullet that had pierced my skin.*

Because it's just a dream, right?

I glanced around at the people surrounding me. The faceless people that were being attacked now became somewhat familiar, cowering in the corner of the building.

Another boom shook everything around me, and a frightened Sophie appeared out of nowhere, running toward me for protection while a soldier pointed a gun at her.

Terror gripped me as I raced toward her, waving my arms, trying to distract the shooter. "Kill me. Kill me," I shouted.

Another voice quietly commanded, "Wake up."

I jolted awake. The sheets fell from my chest, the air conditioner freezing my heated, sweaty skin. Goosebumps crawled up my arms. My panting was so loud and fast, I was afraid I would hyperventilate. In the darkness, I looked around the room, trying to find my Colson Whitehead picture. Only a framed picture of a city's skyline came into view.

"Where am I?" I whispered, grasping for any orienting object. I had to find something tangible to ground me in reality, or I feared drifting back into certain death for me or Sophie.

"You're safe with me."

A cool hand touched my arm, and I jerked back.

"Nate, Nate. It's me. Shh…" A woman rubbed my back. "You had a nightmare. It's okay."

My ears finally focused on her familiar voice. Then her concerned face appeared. "Twinkle?"

"Yes, it's me." Sophie kissed my cheek and hurried out of bed, nude, to the bathroom. She returned with a warm cloth, wiping my face, chest, and back. "You were moving and mumbling in your sleep. Then you popped up like an alarm went off. It's okay. I'm right here. Shh…just relax. You need more rest. It's not yet three."

Though surprisingly more comforted than embarrassed that she'd witnessed the aftermath of my nightmares, I didn't want to admit I was afraid to go back to sleep. I'd almost forgotten about my nightmares sleeping beside Sophie for the last few days.

I mumbled, "I might as well get up and write. I'll go back to my room so I don't disturb your sleep anymore."

"No, you won't. We have a big day, and you need rest, Nathan. Two hours of sleep isn't enough, not even for you," she said firmly, and placed the cloth on the bedside table.

"I don't think I'll be able to fall back to sleep. Once I'm up, I'm up. I'll get rest later. I'm fine." I tossed off the covers. I was also worried she would want to know about my nightmares, and I didn't want to shut her out again. I didn't want anyone to know how the violence I'd witnessed haunted my dreams. That now she did too, and I had to protect her at all costs.

Sophie reached down on the floor, picked up my discarded shorts, and pulled out a condom from the pocket. "Figured you came prepared. I can fuck you back to sleep."

My breath hitched at the determination in the sexy glint of her eyes, and I slowly relaxed back on the bed, waiting for her to take care of me.

This woman. This woman. She was unlike any I'd ever met. She seemed to know when to push and pull back instinctively.

The rawness in my need for her and the firm hand that tugged my manhood brought my body quickly to life. She slipped the condom on me and slid down my erection. The tips of her nails dug into my chest, adding to the eroticism of her riding me relentlessly, demanding my release, taking complete control of my body. I was unashamedly hers for the taking. I closed my eyes and relished the feel of her special sleep aid until we both yelled in ecstatic pleasure.

The next thing I remembered was her shaking me, fully dressed, her beautiful face framed by the daylight. "Morning."

I grunted, not yet ready for the new day.

"Time to get up, Mr. Grumpy." Sophie's wide, bright grin rivaled the sun, invoking my reluctant smile.

"What time is it?" I tore my gaze away from her face to glance at the clock on the table.

"It's after eight. You officially slept past five."

"Damn, Twinkle. You know how to wear a brother out." I wiped my eyes of sleep and pushed up against the headboard while she did a happy dance around the room.

"I made Nathan sleep. I made Nathan sleep," she sang. "I got the goods. I got the goods."

Grabbing my glasses off the bedside table, I smiled and protested, "No, you don't."

The heaviness that usually followed a nightmare wasn't present. In fact, I felt rested and free, ready to face the world.

She continued to sashay around the room bragging about her good-good. I swear she'd become my morning.

"I still can't believe you thought of this." I ate another bite of flaky sausage-and-egg biscuit and touched her knee with mine on the Ida B. Wells Plaza bench. The soft breeze made it a comfortable summer morning to eat breakfast outside.

She swallowed her orange juice. "Figured you might need a little inspo from one investigative journalist to another determined to expose the truth one page at a time."

I smiled widely. "When I look at what she accomplished, I really have nothing to complain or feel sad about. That woman was ahead of her time. Born a slave in Mississippi, advocated for our rights and used her words to educate and amplify the injustice and cruelty of racism. She didn't allow threats to deter her, even after being threatened, the publishing company she co-owned being destroyed, and being forced out of Memphis. Still Ida kept pushing, eventually becoming the first Black woman to be a paid correspondent for a white newspaper." I stared at the statue in the middle of the small park area. "What happened yesterday with Ms. Claudette pales in comparison. Ida risked her life to write the truth." I nudged Sophie's shoulder. "I'm humbled at this reminder."

"You've risked your life, too." She shifted on the bench and passed me a napkin. "You have cheese on your lips."

"Thanks." I wiped my mouth and placed my balled napkin in the paper bag. "The difference is that I placed myself in harm's way to gather the truth. Every day she walked out of her door was a risk." I smirked. "And she married and had four babies while she traveled the world advocating for equality through her journalism."

Sophie pursed her lips. "Your point?"

"Maybe you can have it all, too," I gently replied.

Her jaw tightened. "How do we know she didn't struggle trying to have it all?"

"I don't know any marriage or family that hasn't struggled at one point." I squeezed her knee as I rose. "Stop being stubborn. You do want a family *and* this amazing career. It doesn't have to be one or the other. Iola knew what she was doing."

"You really know how to beat a dead horse. And who's Iola?" She passed me her empty Styrofoam container to throw away.

"Ida's pen name. Most of her writings are under Iola and not Ida—for her protection, I'm guessing." I tossed the trash in the nearby can and walked up to a replica of an old press of Ida's that made newspapers. "She made a difference."

"And you have too," Sophie reminded me.

"Maybe," I conceded.

She snapped a pic and showed it to me. "Is this how I looked at Stax Records?"

On her small screen, even the lens of my glasses couldn't hide the light and hope in my brown eyes. The slight, contented smile added emphasis.

"Yes."

She slipped her phone back in her pocket and made no further comment.

Sophie kept pace a few feet behind me, recording and snapping photos as I slowly walked through the National Civil Rights Museum with my AirPods firmly in my ears. We'd been able to block off four hours to be alone, and I'd chosen Motown hits to play, the songs of that era, while perusing the exhibits. This motel had been destined to go down in history books even if Dr. Martin Luther King, Jr. wasn't assassinated here. Local and visiting Black musicians and songwriters from Stax Records and Beale Street stayed at the Lorraine. Other famous singers like Nat King Cole and Aretha Franklin stayed here. King and other civil rights activists stopped at this motel when they visited Memphis. During segregation, they didn't have much choice.

I kept my hands behind my back and fought against the need to protect my ego and conscience. Anytime my gaze drifted from the exhibits and displays when the threat of hurt or anger assailed me, I forced my focus to remain, even if it triggered old trauma. My emotions and instincts needed to guide me. My intellect and rational side would resume when I gathered my thoughts later.

The first powerful chords of The Four Tops' "Reach Out I'll Be There" played as I walked through the slavery displays. My forefathers had been chained in ships under the most inhumane conditions because they were not seen as fully developed men, no different than cattle herded together before our culture and heritage were slaughtered. The soul-breaking statue representing the mother holding her baby on the auction block brought tears. She and her infant could be sold as a package deal. More often than not, they would be viciously separated. The husband and father were long gone from this woman, leaving her forever unprotected.

What did that inability do to a man whose existence was to defend and protect, and wasn't allowed to do what he was built to do? What did that helplessness do to a man's psyche and to his descendants' psyches? Did it make it hard for him to fight for his woman…his children? Intergenerational trauma continued to tug at the strings of the very fabric of our origins as a communal, open people, in which the family headed by men was the core of the village, slowly unraveling with each new generation of shattered dreams, unresolved pain, and hurt until we had nothing left of our ancestors.

The inside of my cheek hurt from biting it. My need to protect Sophie even in my dreams was instinctive, and she wasn't my wife nor the mother of my children. I would die trying to defend her.

As I slowly progressed through each phase of the museum, which began with the Middle Passage and ended with the assassination of Dr. King, a knot formed in my throat and only wound tighter the closer I drew to the last bed that he'd ever slept in. I pushed off the headphones to listen to Mahalia Jackson's incomparable rendition of "Precious Lord, Take My Hand," the song she'd performed at his funeral.

306.

Peeking into the glass of the last room Dr. King would ever inhabit, away from his wife and four children, seemed surreal. On April 4, 1968, he walked out onto the very balcony that I could see through the glass now and leaned over to talk to friends in the parking lot. An assassin's bullet struck him in the side of the neck, near his face, as he turned to go back to his room. He wasn't much older than I was right now.

The weight of a desperate and hurt people in search of hope burdened his shoulders. Dr. King was just a Black man with his own fears, guilt, and flaws. I pressed my hands against the glass and looked down at the parking lot, and then in the direction from which the bullet originated. His life was gone in a snap. I moved away from the glass, overcome with emotion, knowing firsthand the destruction of a bullet striking flesh.

Unable to hold me up a moment longer, my knees buckled and dropped right there. As I wept, Sophie's arms circled me, and she gripped me tightly. We rocked slowly together on the floor in front of the display of 306.

"It's been over fifty years, and the injustice he died for still exists. The haunted eyes of those street lords in Chicago or the child soldiers in the Congo or Somalia are no different than those of the young Black men of our past. I don't understand why the darkness of hate persists when the brightness of love soothes and heals. To be angry, to be sad, takes so much more energy than to express joy. All these years of being out there in the trenches, risking everything to make sense of this world and the same fucked-up shit that existed during Ida's time, through King's time, is still here. As much as mankind takes two steps forward, humanity takes a step back. Why do I even bother? Huh?"

Sophie pressed my hand against her heart. "Because if we stop hoping or trying, darkness will swallow the light that does exist. One of the reasons I want to be married is so I can share my joy and pain. Our ancestors weren't allowed the basic right to love another soul deeply. The slave masters didn't want us to have and hold each other because no one is more powerful than the Black family, sure of who they are and where they're from. Yes, what we just experienced is hard because we know this country has much more work to do, but we can't give up. If we do, then Dr. King and all of our heroes died in vain. And the oppressors win yet again."

My chest heaved as I stared into her beautiful, proud eyes. Her words broke through the despair that clouded my mind. I quietly replied, "Then you can't give up your voice. The blues originated from our pain. We needed something to hold on to make it to the next day, a way to express all the unfairness and injustice boiling inside of us. Music is and was our cathartic release. The way you sing and play the guitar is your gift, just as much as my writing. Now, I'm not saying you have to be this big star if that's not what you want, but you can't let your God-given talent wither away, either."

She shook her head and sank against the outside wall of the Lorraine Motel. "Man, you won't give up." She sniffed and wiped her eyes.

"Like you said, we can't let the darkness win."

Sophie sighed deeply and rested her head on my shoulder. Gratitude welled inside me—despite the trauma and tragedy of our past, we were still here, strong, brilliant, determined, beautiful, and proud.

And *I* could honor and protect this woman by my side.

ELEVEN

Sophie

His heavy body rested across mine. My breasts were his pillow while he slept.

The statue of the mother and her baby had wounded me. Seeing the tears fall when he zoned in on the same mother and baby touched a part of my heart I thought I'd hidden from him.

I'd quietly observed Nathan spiritually break down the longer he moved around the museum. His visible pain kept mine in check. I recognized before he acknowledged that the tears weren't solely for America's long history of insidious racism. He'd seen horrible, unspeakable acts of violence that probably caused him nightmares, though he had yet to tell me what caused him to yell in his sleep and wake up afraid. I rubbed his coiled hair softly and hummed "God Bless the Child" by Billie Holiday, a song my mother would hum whenever her babies were sick. His vulnerability, his honesty, and his courage drew me even closer than our admittedly amazing physical connection could ever do.

What did that mean?

The other side of me taunted that our closeness was an isolated, shared, intensive moment that would shift once we returned to our normal lives in Nashville in a couple of days. Nathan wasn't a "settling down in one place" man, and I refused to be a fool in love again. I would heed red flags this time.

Our fundamental differences about our respective futures were my cue to shut down any growing feelings toward him.

Propped against the wall, my guitar glowed in the moonlight peeking through the drawn linen curtains. I could no longer deny that I needed to perform again. Returning to Amara and The Crew didn't appeal, though I missed my friends terribly. The image of myself as a superstar didn't gel with my slowly evolving vision. Country music didn't move me as much as the blues that had been permeating my space over the past five days.

"Go to sleep. I hear your thoughts," Nathan mumbled, and shifted to lie beside me.

I slid deeper under the covers, and he placed his leg over mine and hugged me. As much as I wanted to resist the warmth and comfort of his arms, I accepted my fate, at least for now, and snuggled under him.

Nathan pulled behind my private garage and turned off the engine. "I want to walk around your place and make sure it's safe."

The night hid most of his face, though I knew this wasn't a ploy to spend the night with me. He sincerely cared about me. It'd only been a week since we left Nashville, yet I felt our time together had been much longer. What started off as lustful fun became more. We'd grown closer and bonded during our brief time in Memphis. A tie that would forever run deep, no matter whom either of us ended up with.

"Okay." I held my guitar case while he grabbed my bags from the trunk.

He followed me inside. Placing my guitar inside my door, I dropped down on the chaise longue as Nathan walked around my apartment. I liked him here in my space and didn't want to think about tomorrow. I wasn't quite ready to figure out if there was anything to decide about us.

"All clear." He approached me and jammed his hands in his pockets. "I'd better head out. Tired from the road, and it's another twenty minutes before I can walk through my own doors."

I looked up at him. "Then stay and leave in the morning."

His jaw tightened. "I wasn't trying to find an excuse to spend the night."

Gripping the bottom of his shirt and pulling him closer, I replied, "Even more reason for me to ask you to stay."

"We're not in Memphis anymore." He lifted a brow when I toyed with his belly button and the soft hair leading to the large imprint visible through his khakis. "Nothing has changed about who I am and who you are."

"Duh. It's been a week—of course we haven't fundamentally changed what we want." I smiled as he partially knelt on the side of the chaise longue. "That's the best part. I have no expectations of you and of us. I like you, Nathan Price. That's it."

"I like you too." He pulled his shirt over his head and tossed it aside before easing my leggings and panties down my thighs. "I was hoping to fuck you on this lounger."

I giggled. "Did you have that thought the last time you were here?"

A mischievous smile crossed his lips as he unbuckled and unzipped himself. "Naw."

"And here I thought you were an honest man." I admired his body while he finished stripping.

"I am," he reassured me as he eased between my legs, a condom in his hand.

September was slowly ending, and we were still going strong and seeing each other whenever we had a chance, which had become daily. Either he spent the night with me, or I slept at his home, though we had yet to define who we were or what we were doing. We stayed up late laughing, talking, and organizing the information we'd gathered. My pictures and videos illuminated his thoughts on the direction and flow of his writing and his pitch to filmmakers. We debated rather than argued, and though we could be pigheaded, usually one of us would concede to the other when we reached an impasse, like deciding to title the project *The Lost Souls of Memphis Blues*.

Amara had finally finished her first tour, which had been successful, and would be home in a few days, ready to focus on her upcoming December wedding. Nathan and I had been working steadfastly on putting together a collage of pictures to accompany his pitch to present to Jake and Amara. The focus had become Memphis, as I suggested, though Nathan wasn't wholly satisfied. He annoyingly fretted over being unable to convince Claudette Saint to tell her story.

At an Italian café next to Jake's studio, we discussed how best to present our collaborative effort. Nathan wanted to submit packages to studios to review at their leisure. I thought he should arrange meetings to discuss what we found and next steps, including whether he should pitch it to potential producers rather than Amara and Jake, since we'd done the groundwork. He had spent the night with me and driven me to the studio to pick up my tambourine, since I'd been trying my hand at music again in the comfort of my home. Before I picked up my instrument, we'd decided to grab a bite, and then I would use my access code to the studio.

Nathan perused his phone. "The pitch is still missing something."

I rolled my head back and groaned. "Listen, I've read it at least five times. You don't need to do anything else to it. Not one more word or edit. It's perfect."

He frowned and held up his phone, which displayed his manuscript. "Sophie, I need you to be brutally honest. Does this compare to what I did with Stoney's story?"

"You think I'm not honest with you?" I ignored his screen and twirled the last of my delicious pasta around my fork. He had barely touched his lasagna or his tea.

"I don't." He shook his head. "You hate hurting my feelings. We're two creatives, and we can't stand criticism. Except this time. I welcome anything you have to say."

"Then accept that I think this piece is thoughtful, truthful, gripping, heartbreaking, yet inspiring." I reached across the table and pushed up his glasses on his nose. "The two stories don't compare because you create masterpieces each time you put pen to paper or finger to key. Each and every one of your writings is brilliant on paper in its own way. I know because I read them all."

The lines in his forehead cleared. He captured my wrist and gently pressed his lips to my beating pulse. "I can't believe you read them."

"I love your writing," I breathed, mesmerized by the softness in his brown eyes.

Nathan's chest swelled. "And I love your voice and your pictures. Without you, none of this would be possible."

We gazed at each other, caught in the new emotion that danced around us like a feather floating in the breeze—the persistent need to be around each other like we were magnets drawn together through forces out of our control, while the reciprocity of unspoken feelings bounced between us.

"Well, looks like someone had a good day." Jake's sarcastic tone startled us.

"I thought you weren't back yet." Nathan squeezed my hand when I instinctively wanted to release his, stunned at Jake's appearance before our small table. We'd still planned to keep our friendship with generous benefits on the downlow from our friends.

Well, we were *supposed* to keep us a secret.

Jake shrugged. "Mari and I finished earlier than we planned. Wanted to chill a little before life gets crazy again. Thought we would surprise you." His gaze pointedly landed on our entwined hands. "Looks like I'm the surprised one."

This time, we released each other's hands, and I stood up with a shaky smile. "No surprises. We had a moment."

Fuck. Wrong choice of words. Why was I nervous?

He opened his arms to me, though he lowered his eyes at Nathan. "A moment? What happened?"

I hugged him tightly, realizing how much I'd missed Jake, because he had been a constant in my life once I arrived in Nashville. He had become my family, and I had abandoned him without any real explanation. Tears pricked my eyes, and I briefly buried my head in his chest before pulling back. "Working through this project, especially the civil rights angle, has been emotional. I was telling Nate that this story is exceptional. His best work."

"So she says," Nathan scoffed. "Still hoping to get Claudette Saint on board. In the meantime, one monkey won't stop our show. The angle is more civil rights than I intended. Being at the Lorraine, visiting the memorial of Ida B. Wells, and hearing the stories of Black musicians not given their due was a reminder of our past—and, in some cases, our present—and it got to us. May have biased my writing." He suddenly shook his head. "We can talk about all that later. Glad to see you." He rose to dap and hug Jake briefly. "Where's Mari?"

"In the studio. Said she missed it, and just coming home inspired a song. I came over to pick up manicotti and salads." Jake's glare remained on Nathan, and an awkwardness shrouded the space between us.

I shifted on the balls of my feet to my heels. "Umm…is it okay if I go see her?"

Jake tore his eyes away from Nathan to frown at me. "Why are you asking? She's been itching to see you. Nate and I can catch up while I wait for our to-go orders to be ready."

I walked away sensing that the conversation between the two men would be about me, and probably wouldn't be friendly. I might talk a good game, but Jake really did feel like my big brother—a disapproving one at this very second—and I didn't want any part of whatever words he would say to Nathan. I prayed that Nathan maintained his patience with Jake's sharp tongue.

As the glass door closed behind me, I finally dared to look back. They were already talking. Jake spoke with his hands while Nathan unclenched and clenched his jaw, quietly listening.

How could we have been so careless? We were affectionate in public, so near where people could recognize us.

I hurried to the studio and used my code. The familiar twang of country music greeted me, and the anticipation of seeing Amara rushed to the forefront of my mind. We'd become best friends almost immediately after Jake invited her to Nashville. Neither of us had ever had a best friend, and I had missed our conversations, laughter, and the music we created together.

Amara was alone inside the booth with her guitar. When she saw me, she placed it on the stand and hurried out. Our bodies seemed to sigh in relief as two best friends embraced. Tears covered both of our cheeks while we apologized to each other and incoherently sobbed.

Sniffing, I pulled back first. "I missed you so much."

Amara wiped her eyes with one of her knuckles. "We all missed you. Tavion especially. The road just wasn't the same. I wondered how we would make it without you."

"From what I hear, you did just fine. You had Jake, and all I'm hearing are rave reviews." I dismissed the guilt and her words with a wave of a hand. "I'll call Tavion as soon as I leave today and go see him too."

Amara frowned and placed her hands firmly on her jean-encased hips. "Whether I have Jake or not doesn't change how I felt about performing without you…being on the road without you."

"Look, I'm sorry for letting everyone down. I needed a break, that's all." I balled my hands into fists, tempering my growing frustration that I wouldn't be able to explain my actions and could lose my best friend.

Amara noticed and folded her arms. "I'm sorry if you're getting upset, but we wouldn't be friends if I let you get away with what you did to me… to the band. Too much time has passed with no sincere effort on your part to explain for us to pretend that your leaving as the tour was gearing up wasn't a big deal." She rattled off angrily, "You were our social media person, our background vocalist, and our guitarist. You signed a contract. You told us you were going home for the weekend and never returned. We all depended on you, and it's not like you to shirk your responsibilities to the band, to me, or to yourself. What *happened*, Sophie?"

Allowing my defensive walls to crumble, I slumped down on the sofa. "I'm sorry for bailing. I really am. I just couldn't be with the tour anymore."

She eased down beside me. "I don't understand why you couldn't tell me you needed time off because you and Omar broke up. You don't think I would've understood that?"

"Of course you would've understood. I didn't want to bring you down. You were and still are deliriously happy." I opened my arms wide. "How could you not be happy? The man you never knew you dreamed of wants you to be his wife, and your career is white hot. Meanwhile, I can't get a man to commit, and my career isn't going anywhere." I sniffed loudly and shook my head. "I don't mean to sound like this jealous woman, but I knew it wouldn't be easy to be around you and Jake when we first broke up."

Amara pulled one leg underneath her on the plush purple sofa. "So, I don't get to have my best friend because you don't have what you want yet?"

"I didn't say it was fair." I blew out a breath, and a few loose tendrils of my wig flew up. "I hated feeling that way. Nate peeped that I could be jealous of you and Jake before I did. I never wanted to be this selfish woman who can't truly rejoice in her friend's happiness."

She tapped the space between us. "Glad you know that what you did was selfish. You disappeared and barely responded to my texts or calls, as if I had done something wrong. You didn't seem to care that I was genuinely worried about you, miles away, and I had contractual obligations preventing me from leaving the tour to check on you. So yeah, I have to call a spade a spade."

Shifting to face her, I crossed my legs on the sofa. "I'm sorry, Mari. But everything just went to shit real quick. One second, I thought marriage and family were in my grasp, and the next, I had nothing. And the emotional pain hurt like hell. It's like the kind of unrelenting pain you don't believe you'll ever come out of. I'd been waiting for weeks to see Omar, and then he told me he didn't want to be in a relationship anymore, that we wanted different things—though before I left home, he kept calling me 'wifey' and talking about a future. I left for the weekend to fight for him. To fight for my future with him. But when I came home, he looked at me with such pity, as if I were the stupidest woman in the world. We had words, and then…" My stomach twisted as I prepared to—

The door suddenly burst open, and Tavion and Domino rushed in with wide smiles. Partially relieved to delay the hard conversation between Amara and me, I jumped up from the sofa, excited to see them.

Amara heartily laughed at the joy flowing from our unexpected reunion in the studio. "We can finish talking later. Seems I wasn't the only one to miss you."

"Sophie." Domino, the tall, slim drummer who barely spoke, lifted me off my feet in a bear hug.

I hugged his neck, still shaken by my conversation with Amara and what I was about to say to her. "Hey, Dom. Missed you too."

Domino placed me back on my feet, and before I could say anything else, Tavion embraced me tightly before pushing me away, wagging his finger. "Don't ever shut me out again. If you don't want to talk about it, we don't have to. Just don't do that shit anymore. None of us deserved that." The anguish and relief in his usually boisterous voice drew more tears from me.

I nodded vehemently, allowing the tears to fall. "I won't. I promise. I allowed my pride to get in the way of reaching out to you after Omar dumped me."

"You mean your stubbornness," Tavion corrected me. "Omar was trash anyway, girl. I could've told you that."

"Why didn't you?" I asked, half teasingly.

Domino raised both brows, picked up his drumsticks, and entered the booth.

"Because he had your nose wide open, and I didn't want you hating me. I knew how much you wanted it to work. You used to gush about him like he was the one. Who was I to burst your bubble? Good riddance, I say." Tavion waved his hand and flopped down on the sofa, swinging his legs to rest on an amused Amara's lap. "What's up, Sophie? I hope your unexpected appearance here is a sign that you're coming back to the band."

I wasn't ready to have this conversation yet. I didn't quite know my next steps, and I didn't want to make promises I couldn't keep. I looked at Amara, and she quirked one sculpted brow, waiting for an answer.

"Don't pressure her. We don't want to run her away," Domino called from the booth. "Whether you want to be in the band again or not, you'll always be my girl. We can still jam like we used to."

"I'm not going to run away." I smiled at him in appreciation. He did a quick run with his sticks on the drum, expressing his happiness at seeing me again.

I turned back to a waiting Tavion and Amara, who were still anticipating an answer they deserved to hear. Shifting so that I could address the three of them simultaneously, I clasped my hands together. "When I left the tour, I stopped playing. What happened between Omar and me hurt worse than I ever thought possible. I didn't pick Princess back up until Memphis last month."

"What did he do to you?" Tavion asked, and Domino's easy smile vanished.

"It was just a bad breakup. He didn't hit me or anything. Just went through a spell where music didn't matter." Thoughts of Memphis and Nathan evoked warm thoughts. "Y'all, Memphis inspired me to try something new. I'm not sure what my career will look like, but I know I have to play. Trying a new sound. A little blues, a little soul, mixed in with country. Would love your support and patience as I start this new journey."

"You know I love you and will support any of your music." Amara's arms rested on Tavion's legs. "I guess I'm scared to ask if you still want to be with us."

"I'm always with you," I reassured them. "It may not be in the way that you prefer, but I'm not going to abandon you again. You're my best friends. My family." I gestured to the studio. "For five years, this was my world, doing whatever Jake or The Crew needed. Not sure if I lost myself in the process. When everything went down with Omar, my world shifted on its axis. I needed a change and didn't know how to explain it to you. Still trying to figure it out."

"I get it," Tavion said, and sank lower into the sofa.

Domino walked out of the booth and nudged my shoulder with his, smiling. "Already told you how I feel."

Amara tapped Tavion's legs, and he removed them so she could stand. She hugged me tightly. In her embrace, I sensed understanding and forgiveness. After all, she'd been me not too long ago, stepping into a new world, afraid to leave the old behind and not knowing what that would mean.

"Thank you," I whispered.

She nodded. "We'll talk more later when you're ready. I can tell there's still more."

"All right, all right, enough of the blues, because this is Nashville." Tavion clapped to get my attention. "You're here now. Might as well kick it with us like we used to."

I reached for his hand and pulled him up. "That I can do."

As if reading my mind, Domino grabbed one of the guitars hanging on the wall in the studio and passed it to me. Amara pulled the strap of her instrument over her head. "Been working on this new song for my second album, struggling with the last verse for a minute now." She plucked a few chords. "What do you think?"

I listened intently and matched her sound. Before long, we were all in the booth, beginning the tracks to a new song. I had missed them. I had missed this—the collaborative spirit, the fun, and the harmony of our voices and our instruments. Somehow, I would learn to incorporate everything I loved into my life.

TWELVE

Nathan

Jake didn't wait for Sophie to take two steps out of the café before he lit into me. "I thought I told you to stay away from her. You acted like I was tripping when I warned you. Like, I didn't know you or her, and then the next time I see you, you're all in her face, holding hands in public and staring at each other like a happy couple. I trusted your word." He drew in a much-needed breath before continuing. "Sophie might come across as this woman who can handle someone like you, but she can't. You appear to be a nice, stable man willing to give anything a shot. Even a relationship. In the back of her mind, she probably believes that you'll want to settle down sooner or later. We both know you'll leave as soon as the next big gig happens. She doesn't need your shit. I've known her for years, and she has never dipped out on her commitments until this man hurt her."

He stepped closer. "And sooner or later, if you keep seeing her, you'll hurt her too. I can't let you do that."

My temples throbbed during his mini-tirade. Because he cared about Sophie—loved her, judging by his anger—I allowed him to speak without interruption. I glanced around the café at the curious gazes of the patrons. We were two men in the middle of a restaurant on the verge of an argument. I suppressed my indignant anger and calmly replied, "Are you done? Have you gotten everything off your chest? Because I can shut up again and let you continue while you disturb these people's meals."

Jake's nostrils flared.

I tried again, my tone cool and calm. "I'd rather we finish this conversation over drinks and not in the middle of a café. I'm not trying to be fodder for social media. They may not know me by face, but they're starting to know you. So sit down, Jake."

He looked around and grudgingly sat down.

I waved at the waitress, who promptly appeared before us. "Two glasses of your best red wine. Sorry for any confusion. We're two old friends who have a misunderstanding."

Jake scowled at me while he waited for the waitress to leave and for me to speak.

Pushing my long-forgotten lasagna to the side, I steepled my hands on the table. "You can't *let* me date her like you're her father? Like she isn't a grown woman? Sometimes I forget how arrogant you can be," I scoffed. "You honestly think you can stop me from seeing Sophie if *she* wants to continue seeing me? I'm not that wet-behind-the-ears schoolboy you met when we were eighteen. You don't intimidate me. Not then, not now, not ever."

Jake's scowl eased a little. "So, our friendship means nothing?"

"Are all our years of friendship on the line because I'm seeing one of your band members?" I hunched forward. "She told me that there was never anything between you, and you never came across like you were interested in her. Was I wrong? Tell me now. This is you and me talking. Amara won't ever hear a word. Sophie is a gorgeous and sexy woman, and if you ever wanted her, I need to know that right now."

His face relaxed more. "Never anything between us, and never wanted there to be anything. She's the sister I wished I had."

I settled back in my chair. "Then why threaten our friendship? Sophie and I are grown and having fun. That's it. We both agreed that we wouldn't let whatever we're doing right now interfere with our friendship. And if it seems like it is, we're back to how we used to be. I'm not her type anyway. That ex of hers did a number on her, and she was locked away all alone, trying to get over him. I'm here for her, however long she'll let me be there for her. All this anger you're throwing my way is unnecessary."

Jake jabbed the table twice. "Because I can't knowingly allow you to hurt her when I could say something about it. Outside of Amara, you and Sophie are my closest friends, and I know both of you. Be honest with yourself. You think she can walk away from this unscathed?"

"I do." As the days passed, we'd become more entwined, and my need for her grew. I worried I would hurt her, but I kept that thought to myself.

He shook his head. "Bullshit."

"Jake, she and I have talked about this. When I addressed my concerns that I could hurt her, she said she could handle whatever happens between us."

"She probably only said that because she knew you wouldn't touch her if she admitted the truth, that she can't."

A prick of guilt that Jake was right sharpened my tone. "Just like you have always done. You place women in these categories. Ones to fuck and ones to take home to Mama. I don't see women the same. They're no different than us, capable of making decisions about their bodies and their hearts. I care about her and would never do anything to hurt her. She and I have been honest with each other. Sophie is fully aware of the man I am, and I know she wants to be married and have children. I didn't pursue her, nor did I fight my attraction for her. We're both single, were feeling each other, and we acted on it. Simple."

He quirked a thick brow.

"Let me put it another way—you keep this up, then regardless of what happens between me and Sophie, I'll walk away from this friendship. One thing I hate more than lies and dishonesty is hypocrisy. I'm not going to defend my actions to a man who did whatever he wanted to do with women for years, breaking some father's daughter and brother's sister's heart with no regard. At least I'm honest with any woman I've been with." I tapped the linen tablecloth. "Who at this table has done more dirt to women, me or you?"

"Two glasses of the best house wine." The pretty waitress smiled flirtatiously at me as she placed our glasses before us, though her gaze lingered on Jake. "Anything else?"

"Yeah, anything else?" I echoed, grinning at the obvious attention he tended to receive from women.

"No," Jake replied without looking at the woman, who took the hint and quietly left.

I pushed his wine toward him. "Drink up and stay the fuck out of my business."

A reluctant smile finally curved his lips, and he picked up the glass. "Better be glad that Mari and my mother would disown me if I ever stop being your friend. Those two are always Team Nate."

Chuckling, I grabbed my own glass. "Because they know your ass ain't worth shit."

"Can't argue with that." Jake held his wine up. "Glad to be back home."

"Glad you're back too." I swallowed my wine and internally breathed a sigh of relief. Although I wasn't intimidated by Jake, I didn't want to make an enemy out of him. More importantly, I didn't want to lose my best friend. He'd been the only person to truly accept me and my desire to roam the world in search of truth. We could go months without speaking, but whenever we did, it was like time hadn't passed.

"So now what?" Jake picked up a piece of bread from a basket on the table and chomped on it.

"Are we talking about Sophie or Memphis?"

"You just put me in my place about that woman. What do you think I'm talking about?" His amber eyes twinkled.

"Memphis fucked with me a little bit." I stretched one leg to the side of the table.

Jake chewed on the bread, watching me.

"I went there with all these ideas bursting inside. Ready to talk to the musicians, explore the history of blues. Mississippi Delta, not far from Memphis, where the legend of bluesman Robert Johnson, who allegedly sold his soul to the devil for fortune and fame, lived after spending his formative years in Memphis. I wanted another Robert. Another Stoney. I was searching for that elusive musician or song that needed a light. Thought I had it in Claudette Saint."

"What happened?" He sipped more wine.

The tug of an unwitting smile escaped my lips. "She reminded me of my grandmother from Charleston. All feisty, bossy, and no filters. She seemed to like me and Sophie, and cooked us one of the best Sunday dinners I ever had."

Jake chortled loudly. "Better not let my mother hear that."

"Shit, if I ever want to eat Ms. Tanisha's food again, I know better."

Jake's mom had become my second mother over the years. She loved inviting me to dinner, even if Jake couldn't make it. I dipped my fork into my now probably cold food.

"She seemed to be warming up, openly talking about Stoney and how everyone loved him. She wondered what happened to his wife and son, because they all seemed so close. Then, when I asked whether Stoney had written a song for her, she low-key denied it. A short while later, she admitted they wrote a song together, maybe two. When I pushed a little about the songs, she shut down, saying she never recorded them and lost the music over the years. The way her daughter protested, I know she still has the music and probably remembers every single word."

Jake reached for another piece of bread. "Why do you think she didn't want to admit that?"

"She was also heavily involved in the civil rights movement as a teenager. She was at King's last speech. The one when he prophesied that he may not make it to the mountaintop with us." I shuddered involuntarily. "Still gives me chills that he was killed the next day. Seeing his motel room, the unmade bed, and the dishes reminded me of all the hotels, motels, and hostels I've inhabited over the years. Reminded me of all the people who woke up one morning and never saw the day's end at the hands of someone else. Reminded me of the cruelty humans inflict on others, as if our pain is somehow different."

Jake nodded slowly. "That museum is a tough one, but necessary."

I took a deep breath, returning my triggering emotions and thoughts to the present. "Ms. Claudette got spooked. The best way I can describe it. It wasn't just a woman being stubborn and reluctant to relive the past. She was *afraid* to go back there."

The waitress approached us. "Do you need anything else? Maybe more bread, or our olive oil for dipping?"

"I think I might want to dip my bread. And can you hold on to my food a little longer? I don't want it to get cold like his." Jake reached into his pocket and pulled out a twenty-dollar bill.

She grinned and took the tip. "Sure. I'll be back with fresh bread."

"You think she was threatened?" Jake, the ever-busy manager, pulled out his phone and texted someone.

"Maybe, or maybe she just didn't want to relive the past. She still has those songs. She loved music too much to throw away songs she wrote with Stoney."

"Then why did you give up?" He looked up.

"Honestly?"

"Is there any other answer?" Jake replied wryly.

"Sophie," I breathed without thought.

He tilted his head. "Maybe *you're* the one I need to worry about."

"Whatever." I looked away from his discerning gaze. "You could feel Ms. Claudette's pain and frustration over a career that didn't materialize as she envisioned. If I'd gone alone, I would've probed more. I've been in that space before with other people I've interviewed. I can sit in their pain, even empathize with most, but if you're not used to witnessing someone else's hurt, it gets uncomfortable. Sophie started crying, and I don't even think she realized it at first."

"Then why not ask for another meeting without Sophie?"

I shrugged. "Ms. Saint doesn't want one. I called her daughter, who apologized again for our trouble. She told me her mother had been quiet and lost in thought since we were there. So we decided to center the story around Memphis and its strong roots in our culture."

"Is it enough to sell it?"

"Yes, you know I can write the hell out of anything you put in front of me," I boasted.

"Yet you know this story can be more." Jake smiled in appreciation as the waitress returned with the bread and oil.

"Yep." I reached for the crusty, hot bread.

"All right, Mari and I will look at what you already have, and we'll take it from there." He whistled and dipped his bread. "She's going to love that you and Sophie are hooking up."

"Shit." Jake looked at me sharply, and I quickly explained, "We were trying to keep it from you two. Didn't want it to be a big deal. Her decision. Not mine."

"Then maybe you shouldn't have been all googly-eyed in the café next to my studio if you wanted to keep it a secret. Cat's out the bag now."

Pushing back from the table, I complained, "I told her we should go to another restaurant. But no, she had to eat here because she loves the shrimp scampi."

"It's the best." Jake smiled, displaying his dimples. "I can't wait to tell Mari."

"How do you know Sophie hasn't told her?"

"Because Tavion and Domino are at the studio too." He rubbed his hands together. "This is going to be good."

"But we're not *together* together."

"Bruh, you can't even say her name without a smile. We're planning for a wedding, you're our best man, and she's the maid of honor. You think you can hide that shit when we're all together, like we're about to be in a few? Besides, I need her other brothers to keep an eye on you too."

I folded my arms, sat back in my chair, and cursed again.

THIRTEEN

Sophie

Wedding dress shopping. I used to try on wedding dresses and imagine my groom for fun when I first moved to Nashville at eighteen. Then, when my younger sisters planned their respective weddings, I'd traveled back home to help them and my mother pick out the dresses of their dreams. Now I was in this upscale boutique, sipping champagne with Amara's and Jake's moms, who were tickled pink about the pending nuptials while Amara tried on her eighth gown. The two women bonded over their long marriages, careers, and successful children. I contributed to the conversation when I could.

Would my housewife mother fit in with these refined and educated women, who had good lives with men and didn't struggle like my working-class family had? Amara didn't come from wealth, but her parents were college professors and lived an upper-middle-class life. She didn't have the slight airs these two women had, though I knew they welcomed me as Amara's friend. If she'd behaved as if she had a privileged life, we probably couldn't have become best friends. She was as down-to-earth and friendly as they come—even brought the privileged Jake down a peg, giving him a semblance of normalcy, reminding him that most of us didn't have silver spoons. Maybe that was why I preferred Nathan. He'd traveled the world, been recognized as one of the best investigative journalists, and spoke more than one language, yet remained practical and humble.

Nathan drove a 4Runner, though he could afford more. He preferred sneakers to Louboutin and whiskey and Cuban cigars to fancy wines. Cargoes over slacks. Despite his casual preferences, he knew how to dress and fit in to the occasion. His three-bedroom split-level home was modest and had been decorated by his mother, who'd arrived in town to make his house a home. He knew that was her way of subtly telling him that it was time to settle without explicitly telling him so. Nathan also said that his mother would like me, and he would introduce us the next time she visited, as if we were a couple.

The two mothers' chatter became background noise as I pulled out my phone and texted him.

Coming over later?

Nathan responded a second later.

I need to work.

I sent him a selfie I'd taken, modeling my burgundy halter maid-of-honor dress that clung to my body. I used the mirrors to capture the bow that tied around my neck, flowing down my bare back, past my ass. As soon as the satin material caressed my body, all I could imagine was Nathan's hands on my skin and him sexing me in the dress.

My phone beeped.

When you get here, I'm going to show you how wrong you are. And don't complain if I wake you up in the middle of the night, too.

My lady parts tingled. Nathan might be reserved in public, but the bedroom was another matter. I smiled, and my cell buzzed again before I could put my phone away.

Bring some clothes. Might not let you leave for a couple of days, especially if you sing for me.

I pressed the phone against my chest, an anticipatory warmth of being with him spreading through me. I really liked that man.

Amara opened the door to the changing room. She stepped on the raised, mirrored circle to admire the ivory strapless, diamond-studded crepe and lace bodice that hugged her dips and curves and widened past her knees into a glittery, sequined, embroidered train.

"Stunning," gasped her mother.

My best friend glowed with happiness and love. All I could feel for her was pure, unadulterated joy. I jumped up, clapping my hands. "This is the one."

Amara shifted her questioning gaze from me to the mothers, whose eyes were glossy with approval. She looked back at me. "You think Jake will like it? You know he's picky. He's threatened to send his stylist."

"And I had to threaten him to stop and trust his future wife's taste in her own gown. I swear he's more excited about this wedding than I ever thought possible." Mrs. Barnes chuckled before holding up her champagne. "The dress is perfect."

"Jake's going to love you in it. Guarantee he's going to cry when he sees you for the first time on the other end of the aisle. He's become a big ol' ball of emotions since you came into his life." I clasped my hands together over my heart. "I am so happy for both of you. You deserve each other."

Amara exhaled and reached for my hand. "Thank you for being here with me."

"No place I'd rather be." I moved to stand next to her. "We are beautiful together. I love this dress, too."

Mrs. Barnes approached from the other side. "Gorgeous." She caught my eye in our reflection. "Your time is coming soon. I saw the smile on your face as you texted a man. And before you try to say it wasn't, only a man can make you that giddy."

My gaze slid to Amara, and her mouth twitched. Although she, Jake, and The Crew knew Nathan and I were hooking up, we hadn't told anyone else. It was enough that we would get knowing glances anytime he stopped by the studio to listen to Amara, much as he'd done in the past. We were careful not to give each other lingering gazes or touches. We wanted to keep it light and friendly, with no expectations from our friends. Telling Mrs. Barnes, who treated and loved Nathan as a son, would be a recipe for disaster. Her invites to him would include me, and she would start in on us like she'd done with Jake and Amara, who were a real couple. I liked the way Nathan and I were. Neither of us wanted to label our time together as the summer green of August became the orange autumn of October. I had a friend and a lover with whom I enjoyed spending time and who inspired me to keep evolving and growing.

"He's just someone I'm seeing. No one special." Even as I said it, my stomach burned with the lie. Nathan was beginning to mean everything to me, and I didn't know how to stop the intensity of my feelings without stopping the intimate part of our friendship. Correction—we were becoming a *situationship*.

"If he keeps making you smile like that, he'll soon be someone special," Mrs. Johnson chimed in, beaming at her daughter. "I used to feel that way about my husband. He was too stuffy and formal. With me, he was different. Didn't think we would end up married."

"And you know I didn't think a white man would ever get my attention. I love me some Black men, especially ones that look like Jake's father. All big and strong. The kind that gets you in trouble and makes you forget the sense your mama gave you. Mm…hmmm." Mrs. Barnes shimmied her shoulders.

We all laughed while Amara and I bumped fists.

Mrs. Barnes suddenly sobered. "That man hurt me deeply, and I never thought I would ever love again. Didn't want to risk my heart, and didn't want to bring a man around who might abandon Jake like his father did. Then I met this man with piercing, kind eyes who won me over with his respect, his friendship, and his consistency. He slowly crept into my scarred heart and loved me and my son." She looked at me. "Trust me when I say, when a man makes you smile like that, hold on to him at least for a little while. Who knows what the future holds?"

"Told her the same thing." Amara twirled. "So, are we all agreeing that this is the dress?"

The three of us gave our enthusiastic assent.

"Let me tell the seamstress that she needs to take your measurements. The dress could be taken in a little bit." Mrs. Johnson walked out of the large changing room to find the owner of the small boutique.

"After this, can we *please* go get something to eat?" I asked before swallowing the rest of my champagne.

Amara chuckled. "You're always hungry. I can't imagine what you'll be like whenever you get pregnant."

Her backhanded comment hurt like a bee's stinger, and I reflexively touched my stomach. Feeling the yearning ache of desired motherhood, I bit back my sadness to joke, "Oh, I plan to eat for three. My husband better be ready to keep me fed and happy."

"Speaking of babies…" Mrs. Barnes gave Amara a pointed look. "Have you started talking about starting a family with my son?"

"I'll let you ask him the next time you see him," Amara said with a forced smile.

"You know Jake doesn't like to tell me much." Hurt coated Mrs. Barnes's tone. "That's why I look forward to you being my daughter. Now maybe we all can be the family we used to be."

I shot a glance at Amara. Apparently all wasn't completely well between Jake and his mother. He had been livid when he found out that the money his stepfather had given him for Stoney over the years was, in essence, hush money for the songs Evelyn Hart stole. Around the same time, Amara broke up with Jake, leaving us with a brokenhearted man who took his frustration and pain out on us, until I stood up to him and told him he would lose the band, too, if he didn't get it together.

Amara stepped down from the platform. "We do want children. At least two, since we both wanted siblings. We're working on the second album. Considering doing another tour once that album drops. Right now, we want to enjoy our careers and marriage before we start a family."

Mrs. Barnes nodded approvingly. "As long as you plan to have children one day."

"Um…think I'll see what's taking your mother so long." I quickly moved out of the changing area before my dam of tears broke.

Mrs. Johnson was admiring the crowns with the designer at the counter. Furiously blinking back the tears, I slipped outside and texted Nathan.

Rain check on tonight. Call you tomorrow.

I needed to be alone. Didn't want Nathan to see me like this: a weeping mess. I leaned against the store's brick wall and drew in settling breaths. I remained happy for Amara and looked forward to the day I could hold her and Jake's baby. I just wished I could hold my own baby, too.

Staring from my bay window at the starry sky, I reclined on my chaise longue holding my guitar, plucking strings randomly, allowing myself to get lost in the familiar. Waves of emotion swelled over me if I thought too hard about what I'd lost and not what I'd been finding since Memphis. I didn't want to go back to that hollow place, thought I had moved on from it until today. Had Nathan only been a temporary balm for a pain that would never heal? For the past two months, I'd felt so much more joy than pain working on the Memphis project, being with him and my friends, that I hadn't believed talking about babies would upset me.

A knock on my door startled me, and I rose, already knowing who was on the other side. He hadn't responded to my text when I said I needed a rain check. I should've realized that he wouldn't accept what I sent him at face value.

I opened the door without acknowledging him and returned to the chaise longue. I picked up my guitar and watched him as he dropped his work bag inside the door, slipped off his Jordans, and lifted me up enough to sit on his lap while he reclined. My side rested against his bent knees. "Told you I wanted to hear you sing."

"Not in a singing mood," I sullenly said, despite his presence brightening my mood, confirming my earlier worry. I didn't want him to be a Band-Aid to my scar. I wanted to be healed.

"Then play." He traced circles on my forearm with his finger. "I need to be inspired. The writing is slower than I want, and Jake's ready to send my pitch to the studios."

I strummed slowly. "Still having trouble wrapping your brain around Memphis as the heart?"

Nathan tilted his head to see my down-turned face. "Think I need to try Claudette Saint again."

"What good would it have done to push her? You saw the pain on her face." I bit back my annoyance that he remained stuck on Ms. Claudette after all the research, interviews, and photos we'd compiled, organized, and reviewed. He refused to release the pitch to Jake, though in my opinion, he'd finished it two weeks ago.

"Like many others. I wouldn't be a journalist if I didn't go with my gut. I didn't pressure her because of you," Nathan admitted softly before kissing my forearm.

My fingers stilled. "What?"

He sighed, long and drawn out. "You were upset, and I didn't want to push her with you there. You wouldn't have been able to handle it."

"So, is that what you do? Push people until they break to fulfill your need to be right?" I glared at him. "Like right now. Told you I didn't want company, and yet you're here."

Nathan looked away from me. "No, you told me rain check. When I told you I needed to work, you ignored me."

I retorted, "I would've accepted it if you stood your ground."

"You would've texted or called me later to see if I'd changed my mind."

Since I couldn't refute the truth, I replied more sharply than I intended, "Your point?"

"Whatever you and I are doing, it can't be one-sided. Sometimes I need you too."

I frowned. "What does that mean? I'm there for you."

He pushed his glasses up on his head like shades. "You want me around because I help you forget. Sometimes I want to forget, too. You don't care what I'm doing when you need me."

Anger and sadness entwined into a knot that even he believed I hadn't healed. Fearing he might think I'd used him, I placed the guitar beside the window and promised, "If it bothers you when I text or call, I won't."

"I'm not saying that." Nathan sat up straighter. "Just making the point that this thing between us needs to be reciprocal."

I shoved at his chest to get off his lap and put distance between us. "Don't make me sound selfish when you only half tell me your feelings. I don't know what goes through your mind to be there for you like you apparently want me to."

"Yet you can tell when I'm going through something." He swung his feet back on the carpet. "Does it matter what I'm going through when I need your attention…your affection? Just like I know when you need me without saying a word. Today was hard because Amara was picking out her wedding dress, right?"

My heart squeezed at his accuracy once again. Was I that obvious? Was I becoming this helpless, dependent woman who couldn't function without him? Did Nathan see me like that?

Hating that any man could perceive me that way, I defiantly replied, "I don't need you, Nate."

He narrowed his eyes almost to slits and clenched and unclenched his jaw. Silently, he whipped his glasses off his head, moved past me, slid on his shoes, picked up his bag, and allowed the door to slam behind him.

I closed my eyes. "Fuck."

I hadn't meant to take my pain out on him. When Nathan seemed bothered, he would mentally drift away from me. I gave him space and didn't push or prod like I would have if he were my boyfriend. I didn't want to assume he ever needed me, though sometimes I could tell he did.

This past year, I'd been selfish when I shut everybody out. It wasn't intentional; I just couldn't seem to pull myself out of it. If it weren't for Nathan, I might still be stuck nowhere. I was wrong to treat him the way I just did when he'd been there for me without question these last few weeks. Whatever screwed-up thoughts I had about myself were mine only.

Rushing to my door, hoping he hadn't driven off, I swung it open and screamed. His fist was raised, about to knock. Nathan's eyes widened before I slammed against his chest and hugged him tightly.

He chuckled and lifted me off my feet as the door closed behind him. "Can we start this night over?"

I nodded in relief and tucked my head into his neck, loving his cologne. "Yes. Sorry if I haven't been a good friend. It bothered me that I might be depending on you too much to make me feel better, and I *can* tell when you're going through something. I'm just trying to respect your need for space."

He put me down on my feet and pecked my lips. "Until you need my attention."

"Stop making me sound like this spoiled child." I pouted teasingly.

"Never that. You're just honest and clear about what you want when I don't always reciprocate. And it's my fault anyway. I have a hard time telling you no when I should."

I led him to the sofa and patted the space next to me. "Nathan, I never want to interfere with your career and what you've been building. The next time I want to hang and you don't, tell me and I'll respect it. No matter what, your friendship is everything."

He kissed me slowly, his lips lingering on mine. "That's the problem—I like being with you."

I kissed him back, sliding in my tongue, relishing his moan. "Oh, I'm a problem?"

"Mm-hmm." He sat back and picked up my hand. "Were you mad with me because we're not really together? Is that why you didn't want to see me tonight? It can't be easy doing all this wedding planning, and we're not a couple."

I looked down, and he tilted his head to see my face.

"Tell me."

I tugged on his beard. "Would you believe me if I said it wasn't about her trying on the dress? I was actually bored, since I'd done it a couple of times now. And when she found the perfect dress, I was genuinely happy. Not a jealous or envious bone in my body."

Nathan smiled. "Good."

"But when they started talking about Mari and Jake having children, it hurt when I would love to have my own baby." I closed my eyes. "I didn't want to see you tonight because I didn't want you to see me cry. I don't want to always lean on your shoulder when I'm upset."

"Twinkle, I'm here for you. Period. And I promise, your time will come sooner than you think," he pressed his forehead to mine.

I smiled softly. "For the first time in a long time, I believe it will. Today wasn't all bad. Being around those working mothers who still love their husbands, and knowing the change I see in Jake because of love, gives me hope." I kissed him again. "You give me hope that there are men like you in the world, who are good, sweet, attentive, and open to my dreams. Add that he's ready to marry, then he's the perfect find."

"Naw, that's not going to work for me." Nathan suddenly grabbed me up and marched toward my bedroom.

I squealed and hit his back. "What are you doing?"

"No man wants only to be considered 'sweet and good.'"

"I meant it as a compliment."

He dumped me on the bed and pulled off his sweater, revealing his toned chest and arms. "What if I said, 'I have hope that a woman will truly get me because there are sweet women like Sophie in the world. She's such a good woman'?"

I wrinkled my nose and eased off my panties. "Doesn't sound sexy at all."

"Glad you recognize." He dropped his pants, his throbbing manhood at attention as he pushed up my long t-shirt, wrapped himself in a condom, and thrust deep inside of me.

FOURTEEN

Nathan

The brown and red leaves of October fluttered in the wind as I hopped out of my 4Runner and headed inside the building that housed Jake's management office. He'd decided to keep his studio separate from his company headquarters when he branched out independent of his stepfather.

Tangela, his administrative assistant, told me to go into Jake's office, and he nodded when I entered, still on a phone call. He reached across his desk to fist-bump me as I plopped down in the leather chair, admiring his elegantly designed space as I often did. Floor-to-ceiling windows covered one wall, and a plush sofa and a large marble coffee table were centered on the opposite wall. Two expensive paintings from some talented Black artist adorned the third side.

Jake would've done well even if his mother hadn't married a wealthy talent agent. His biological father might not have been in his life consistently, but his high-powered attorney mother was no struggling single mother. With his charm, intellect, and drive, I had no doubt he still would've ended up just where he had—running his own management and production company, with multimillion-dollar entertainers attached to his name.

He hung up with a huge grin. "We have a buyer."

"Was that who was on the phone?" Excitement filled my chest.

Jake frowned for a second and then shook his head. "Naw, that was the planner for our engagement party. I spoke to McClain Studios right before that call. They really want to produce and distribute the documentary. It's a good deal, and I think we should take it. You can finally get yourself another car."

"Fuck you. You know I can afford more than what I drive. Just never been into cars like you." I rested my forearms on my thighs, rocking slightly. "They like the story as it is?"

Jake looked down at his cell, reading a text. "Didn't you tell me you can write the fuck out of anything?"

"I believe I said 'hell,'" I corrected him teasingly.

He finished his text and gripped the arms of his chair. "Well, they love it. They particularly love the photos you attached to tell the story. According to them, you basically gave them the storyboard on how they'll film it. Your idea to include Sophie's work was genius. Even the video she posted of Claudette Saint cooking and humming went viral. Sophie has an incredible eye. That pic of you staring at Ida B. Wells is the chef's kiss. They want to buy the rights to your book and include her pictures, so it's like a coffee table book. McClain also wants you to work with them in L.A."

"I don't know if I want them to buy the rights to my book." My initial excitement shifted to apprehension. Nervously, I rubbed my hands on my thighs.

Jake genuinely seemed perplexed. "Why not? The advance is good money, and I can help you negotiate for more. They only want the rights for five years. It's a crazy deal that you shouldn't pass up."

"I'm not sure how I want to publish it."

Jake stared at me like I'd lost my mind, and I didn't blame him. As far as he was concerned, the book was already perfect, though I knew otherwise.

"You can use whatever you want in the pitch I gave you for the documentary. But the book is mine."

Jake's forehead puckered and then relaxed. "You still holding out for Saint?" His cell phone pinged again, and he glanced at his screen. He then shifted to his computer and typed something on his keyboard. "Sorry, I have an album launch in three days. I'm listening."

"I wanted to try again now that the documentary looks like it's a go and the holidays are coming up. Ms. Claudette seems the type who loves to cook and celebrate. She can probably make a mean sweet potato pie."

Jake tugged on his goatee. "If you do find what you're looking for, are you going to tell McClain?"

"It's up to Ms. Claudette, as far as I'm concerned, how she wants her story to be told. If you feel differently, I won't approach her again, because I need to reassure her that whatever she decides to do will be honored."

He nodded and picked up his cell again. "Then I'd better have my lawyer review the contract to make sure that you can publish your book separate from the documentary and that the material may differ." He grinned. "And let Sophie know she gets a nice cut for her pictures. I'll send her the terms later and see if she agrees. She might want to consider a career in photojournalism. You two are a dynamic team."

"Agreed."

This time, pride instead of excitement expanded my chest. After our argument at her apartment, Sophie and I had resumed seeing each other with the understanding of our respecting boundaries. Though we'd tried not to spend every night together, she or I would inevitably fail. We'd started to rely on each other for more than sex and companionship. I didn't want to write without her photos and videos guiding me, and she needed my opinion on the pictures she would take around the city and her voice, since she had been writing music more closely aligned with blues than country.

He whistled. "Crazy that she took all those pics with her iPhone. Imagine what she can do with a real camera."

"Yeah, imagine." I smiled. The wheels turned in my head.

A live band played on the other side of the darkened restaurant, lit only with strategically placed candles and chandeliers. We enjoyed prime, in-house dry-aged steaks, loaded potatoes, and fancy cocktails. Sophie bopped her head, her newly straightened hair swinging slightly around her face. The halter top of her teal dress emphasized the slope of her neck and the swell of her full breasts. She emitted a natural glow of contentment and seemed like the Sophie I once knew before her heartbreak. We were celebrating the documentary deal that we'd finalized yesterday. We'd both earned a nice check once everyone agreed to the negotiations. I would be allowed to keep my book separate from the documentary as long as I gave them first look, and Sophie received ten thousand more than originally offered for her photos.

"The manager of The Un-Godly Hour just asked me to do a regular gig every Wednesday," she announced once the band took a break, and our hearing had adjusted to the typical din of a Michelin-starred restaurant on a Saturday night. "He heard I was back."

"Great news, Twinkle," I said, though what I intended to ask her could put a wrench in her plan or mine. "I guess that means you want to pursue music."

She shrugged. "I don't think I'm ready for a steady gig yet. I'm leaning more toward soul than country. I'm playing around with my music from all the influences I had in Memphis. With that fat check for my pictures, I can take more time to figure out what's next."

Although Sophie still jammed with The Crew and helped Amara and Jake with songwriting, she hadn't returned full time, nor had she resumed her small shows. She'd been focused on our project since August, and now we were headed into November and were done, at least for now.

"This might help." I pulled up the expertly wrapped gift from under the table. I'd stopped by the restaurant earlier and asked them to hide it for me.

She clapped her hands in delight. "What is it? How did you hide this big-ass gift when we rode together?"

"I have my ways." I put the lime-green box in front of her.

Sophie shimmied her shoulders. "My favorite color."

Her excitement only heightened my anticipation of whether she would love my gift. "I know. Open it."

She took her time unwrapping the bow and peeling back the foil paper, explaining, "I like to keep the paper of my gifts if I can."

I chuckled. "Somehow I pictured you as the one who would snatch the paper off."

Sophie tilted her head and batted her lashes at me. "Just because I do that to you doesn't mean that's how I approach life."

"Point." My pants tightened at her reminder that she enjoyed rough sex. She enjoyed sex, period. And based on how she'd licked her lips, tonight would be a good night for both of us.

When she finally opened it, she clasped her hand over her mouth, pulled out white Reebok Freestyle shoes, and placed them on the table. The Freestyle was the first athletic shoe designed for women, in 1982. "Oh my God, Nathan, where did you find these?"

"I know some people," I bragged. "That's not the only gift."

She peeked back into the box. Her eyes widened, and then lines appeared on her forehead. "Oh, Nate. It's beautiful."

"You can take it out," I said, suddenly nervous that her tepid reaction differed from the excitement over the shoes.

Her smile faltered, and her chest rose and fell as she lifted the Canon EOS R3 Mirrorless Camera. "You didn't have to. I like my phone."

"I know that." I tried and failed to keep the irritation out of my tone. Her confused gaze lifted to mine, and I reassured her, "Your pictures are gorgeous as they are. Imagine the type of photos you would take with this baby. This one is perfect for documentaries."

Speechless, she stared at the camera.

"I can help you figure out how to use it. I read the manual online." I chuckled self-consciously at her obvious reluctance to accept the gift. "Then again, you're a fast learner, probably end up teaching me."

Her eyes shone with unshed tears. "Why?"

"Why?

Your pictures brought the story alive. Honestly, it helped sell the story better than my words. Your face lights up when you take pics like it does when you perform. I wanted to show you my appreciation for all you've done for me these past few months."

"Is that the only reason?" She lowered her gaze, and my heart beat faster.

What did she want from me? I couldn't tell if she was offended or simply didn't like the gift. "Um…I thought it was a good idea. If you don't like it, I can take it back. I'm not trying to tell you what to do or anything like that. I just believe in you."

Her expression was unreadable when she asked, "You think I should learn photography?" She continued to hold the camera in her hand.

I quickly shook my head. "You never took formal lessons to play the guitar or sing. It seems to be the same for you with photography. You have a gift, Sophie, an eye for seeing the beauty in everything you capture. I think you could be a photojournalist. I already spoke with McClain Studios about bringing you on to assist me and them with the documentary. Maybe we can *both* win the Pulitzer Prize one day."

Her lips curved slightly as she placed the camera back in the box, followed by the shoes. "Something to think about."

Refusing to be deterred by her reticence, I picked up her hands in mine. "*We* have a lot to think about."

Sophie's eyes were guarded, yet I saw hope trying to peek out. "Like what?" Then her gaze shifted to the left of me, and her grip on my hands tightened painfully. "Shit."

"What?" I started to turn my head to see what spooked her.

"Keep looking at me."

The urge to see what or who was behind me became almost unbearable, but I resisted because of the pained look in her expression. "Who is it?"

"My ex."

"Omar?" My stomach roiled as I watched beads of sweat pop across her forehead. Her pulse beat rapidly under my thumbs. "Hey, Twinkle, it's okay."

"He saw me and is coming this way with a woman." She suddenly smiled too brightly and looked up. "Long time no see."

"I didn't expect ever to see you here. Thought you didn't like steak?" the thin, tall man with long locs pulled into a bun responded with a thick island accent. Possibly Barbadian.

Sophie shrugged. "Some things change. This is actually my favorite restaurant now."

The attractive woman by his side hugged his bicep. She didn't look pleased. Omar glanced at her and apologetically grinned. "Oh, baby, sorry… this is Sophie. And Sophie, this is my girlfriend, Fay."

The woman boastfully flashed the diamond on her left ring finger. "He's still getting used to calling me his *fiancée*."

Although Omar seemed uncomfortable with Fay's announcement, the expensive ring and the proud twitching of the smile he couldn't seem to hide betrayed his real feelings. He was in love with her.

My stomach dropped at the deep pain that shadowed Sophie's face. I caressed her knuckles to comfort her. "Congratulations. See, Twinkle? He's good." I addressed Omar with a feigned smile. "She was worried about you, hoping you found love again like she did."

Omar narrowed his eyes to slits. "Jake's friend, right?"

"Nathan Price, his *best* friend," I corrected him.

I now recalled meeting him once or twice when he filled in for Domino. I didn't make the connection that I'd met the man who broke Sophie's heart.

"Yes, Jake introduced us about two years ago, and I finally decided to give him a chance and haven't regretted it." Sophie smiled at me, and the genuine brightness relaxed the spiraling tension inside me. *Good. Don't let this man see you sweat.*

"While we were together?" Omar asked, his voice deeper.

Sophie's brows dipped briefly before she gave him a perplexed smile. "I'm not the one engaged when we only broke up seven months ago."

"Did you cheat?" he asked, and the tension thickened and shifted from discomfort to unjustified anger.

"It doesn't matter how we met," I interjected, glancing at the fuming woman at his side. "It's over now. Your woman is getting upset. Apparently Fay didn't know you still had a girlfriend seven months ago. Go ahead to your table and work that shit out."

"Not until she admits that she cheated." Omar folded his arms, glaring at Sophie.

She raised her drink and nonchalantly sipped on her cocktail, though I felt the tremors in the hand I still held.

"She doesn't have to do a fucking thing except be mine. Take my advice and leave now," I said quietly.

Omar focused his attention on me, and his scowl deepened. I refused to avert my gaze. He would look away first or be prepared to fight.

Fay wisely chimed in and pulled hard on his arm. "Our table is ready. Let's go."

His jaw unclenched, and he seemed to remember his woman. Omar's eyes softened. He kissed her cheek apologetically and nodded at Sophie. "I guess congratulations to you, too."

Once they crossed to the other side of the restaurant, thankfully out of our view, I squeezed her hand. "You okay?"

"No," she replied.

I held her two trembling hands together. "You won't allow him to see you broken. Don't give him the satisfaction."

Her pretty brown eyes were so hollow and sad as she whispered, "Why didn't he choose me?"

My heart pinched painfully at her defeated manner, like the amazing time we'd spent together meant nothing. Tugging her hands to me, I growled, "Because he's a fucking idiot and wasn't meant for you. Don't start this self-doubt bullshit, Sophie. You've come too far to allow that man to live rent-free in your head again."

"Nate…please. I don't need a lecture. I need you." Her lips quivered. "Can I stay with you tonight?"

"Already on it." Instead of waiting for the check, I dropped three hundred dollars to cover everything on the table, then picked up her gift box and guided her by the small of her back.

The moment we made it to the car, she burst into tears. I gripped her hand and pressed it against my heart, while I drove with one hand. I'd underestimated the depth of her feelings for Omar. It'd been months since he ended their relationship, and he was already engaged to marry another. Yet Sophie still loved him—deeply, based on the sobs that racked her body. I wanted to punch the son of a bitch for existing. For making Sophie believe in love and forever. For shattering her heart.

I kissed her hand before bringing it back to my chest. I would continue to be her balm. I would continue to be there for as long as she allowed me to be there.

Even while it broke my heart.

A dejected Sophie dropped down on the side of my bed. I knelt before her and removed her heels, rubbing each foot before I rose. She smiled. "You take good care of me."

Lifting her chin to look at me, I wiped her soaked cheeks with my thumbs. "Always."

She nodded before dropping her gaze.

I tugged on her arm. "Let me help you unzip so we can get some rest. We've had enough excitement for one night."

Sophie stood and turned around. I slowly dragged the zipper down, revealing her honey-bronzed skin.

"So…so fucking sexy," I murmured.

Unable to resist a taste of her, I dipped my head and brushed her shoulder blade with my lips. She stiffened, and I gripped her to me, trapping her arms. "Sorry. Sorry. The last thing you're thinking of is sex."

"No. It's the only thing." Sophie looked up at me over her shoulder, her eyes dark with desire. I took the mouth she offered with my own, plunging my tongue inside, starved for her affection. Her undivided attention. I wanted her all, and I wanted it now.

She shimmied her body until her dress draped around her ankles, proudly standing before me in a red lace bra and matching thong. My breath hitched when she unclasped the front, and her pear-shaped breasts appeared like golden orbs in my lamplit bedroom. I caressed the soft fullness and rubbed her nipples while I kissed her, capturing her moans and breathless pants. In between our mating tongues, I whispered, "I feel like the luckiest man on Earth."

With tear-sparkling eyes, Sophie lifted my sweater over my head and wrapped her arms around me, pressing her breasts against my naked chest. She ran her hand down my nape and implored me, "Please, Nate. All I want to feel is you. All of you. I don't want anything between us."

I was rendered speechless by what she asked of me, but denying this sexier, more seductive Sophie wasn't an option. She seemed different—a difference I couldn't quite pinpoint.

I nodded and stepped out of my clothes as she positioned herself on her stomach, with her round, thong-clad ass in the air and the side of her face resting on the bed. Her eyes were closed, and she gasped when I lowered my head to take a sip of her sweet nectar before I slid into her slick, tight walls. We shuddered at the feel of our connected bodies without any barriers.

Neither of us moved, savoring the moment or afraid that completion would happen too soon. Maybe both.

Curving my body over hers, my chest to her back, I held her, hoping that I was her comfort more than ever. For what seemed like an eternity, we were locked together as one before my sexual instinct to move within her overwhelmed.

Flipping her over, without breaking our entwined bodies, I thrust and thrust, urging her to scream, to yell that it was my dick…my body…that it was *me* that could make her feel like no other man had before.

Her encouraging moans and panting spurred me to fuck her relentlessly, my sweat leaving stains on the sheets. We were wild, frequently switching positions, using every inch of the bed to expunge all the hurt, confusion, and pain that we both felt on some level, grateful that we were in my home and my bed, where we could be and were as loud as we wanted. Sophie painfully dragged her nails down my back, leaving temporary scars, begging me for more.

Gripping her waist, I began pounding her again. The bed rattled viciously, threatening to break. With every punishing stroke, I demanded that she scream and tell me that I'd taken her hurt away. When I fisted Sophie's hair with one hand, her body stiffened and then uncontrollably spasmed. She keened loudly as she unleashed her demons before I spilled inside her with the mightiest roar. I collapsed on top of her briefly before shifting and pulling her into my arms. Sophie tucked her head into my shoulder, snuggling deeper under me, despite our sweat, as if I were her blanket, and drifted off to sleep.

I remained awake long after she had fallen asleep. Sophie had captured my heart, and I had no clue how to retrieve it.

Or if I even wanted to.

FIFTEEN

Sopthie

In the wee hours of the morning, I eased out of his bed when he shifted in his sleep, his arms falling away from me. The cold surrounded me, and I desperately wanted to return to his heat. The reality that he and I would never be more than this forced me to remain where I stood. Nathan had been my comfort these past few months, but ultimately, our end games differed.

I looked down at his sleeping form, surprised he didn't sense me. He'd been attuned to me since the first night we slept together.

Tears pricked my already swollen eyelids. I had to stop this thing with Nathan. When he surprised me with the gift, I'd hoped it was something to symbolize how much he loved me. And the thought shocked me. I'd been holding back the growing emotions that had snuck up on me. The thoughtfulness of the shoes and the camera had stunned me, and when I believed the gifts were only a kind gesture, he grabbed my hands like he needed to tell me he wanted a relationship with me. Butterflies of happiness had fluttered in my stomach as I anticipated his question. But then Omar walked in, and I realized that we would never have what he and his woman clearly had.

With Omar, from the very beginning, we'd talked about the future. For two years, we were two musicians on the same path, or so I'd thought. Maybe I did ignore red flags, that he would throw my career in my face, though he never considered me when he took gigs all over the country. Or when I broke up with him that first time because I suspected he was cheating, and he pleaded for me to give him another chance, since I couldn't prove anything. He'd promised to give me his all, and that I would never doubt him again. For a while, I didn't. Now, another woman wore his ring. A woman he'd probably started dating while he was with me.

Nathan was a different sort of man. A man of his word, through and through. If he ever had thoughts about another woman, he would tell me. If he actually did step out, he would tell me the truth and deal with the consequences.

A man of his word.

Even if Nathan wanted to be committed to me, he didn't want marriage or a family.

My tears in the car were for all I'd lost, and I'd once again fallen for a man not meant for me. Though Nathan had taken me long, hard, and unprotected at my urgent request, I kept my heart from further succumbing to his warmth and comfort. His passion. My body had quivered long after the exhilarating, ecstatic high that I doubted I would ever feel again. Nathan had been a fantastic lover and friend to me, reminding me of my worth. I would always cherish him for that. But our time together was officially over. I couldn't continue to accept the status quo. I wanted what we both knew he couldn't give me, and for an impulsive, reckless moment last night, I hadn't cared that we ultimately wanted different things. Now, shame covered me.

Watching him sleep peacefully on his stomach, I longed to kiss his soft lips and feel the scratchiness of his mustache and beard one more time. But that would only wake him, and he would want to know why I was leaving like this. I quietly picked up my clothes, marveling again that, as light as a sleeper I'd known him to be, he didn't notice my absence in bed. Maybe it was a sign that I needed to walk away from him. I shook off my remaining sadness that soon he would adjust to being alone again, while I struggled moving on like I did with Omar.

Seeing Omar with that woman had devastated me in ways I had yet to share. And I wasn't sure if I would ever share. Not even with Nathan, who had become my confidant and haven in the last few months.

I eased out of his home, grateful we'd been in my car. I needed to get away again. I needed space so I wouldn't crave Nathan so much. Inevitably, he would leave again on a quest to save humanity, and I refused to make him stay out of guilt or obligation. I would be his friend again, as we'd always promised each other. Just not now.

"Squirrel, what in the world is going on?" My father stood above me, his voice drenched in concern. "You can't keep popping up here unannounced in the middle of the night. It's too dangerous."

I squinted to keep down the pain from my aching, red eyes. "Hey, Papa. Didn't mean to scare you. I just needed to be around my family for a little while."

He knelt to be closer to me. The ring of gray around his deep brown eyes told his age more than the crinkles at the corners of his eyes and his bald head. "What's wrong? Now, you came here before and left like a bat out of hell."

Patting his round cheek, I smiled and said, "I'm home. Everything is good; if it isn't, all will be well soon."

Papa studied my face. "Mm-hmm. I get it, you'd rather talk to your mama. I'm here, too. I understand some things."

"I know, Papa. I couldn't ask for a better father. It's why I wanted to come home." I hugged his neck and kept my tears at bay. Papa was a good husband and father. A good man. And like Nathan, a man of his word.

"All right, Squirrel. I need to get up—my knees aren't like they used to be." He patted my back to release him and used the sofa to push up to stand. "I have to get ready for work."

Papa had been an electrician for as long as I could remember. He was highly skilled and always in demand in a touristy area like Gatlinburg and nearby Knoxville. Papa made enough to give his wife and daughters what we needed, even if we didn't always have what we wanted. I admired my father for being the protector and provider he'd been to this family. Grateful that, though my biological father had been long gone, Mama had found a good husband for herself and an amazing father for me.

"What time is it?" I shifted on my back. My head and body ached like I'd only slept for an hour.

"Almost six. Everybody'll be up in a minute."

My body was right.

"You want me to hide you? Your sisters will want to stay home from school, and you need to be alone with your mama."

I nodded.

"Come on." He headed toward the back of the house, and I wrapped the throw from the sofa around me to follow him.

We crept back to my parents' bedroom, just big enough for a queen-sized bed and chest of drawers. He closed the door after I entered. I crawled into bed next to my mother and wrapped my arms around her from behind.

"Sophie?" She sleepily turned her head. "What's wrong, baby?"

"I need to feel like the girl who could still climb in bed with her mama." I rested my head on her pillow. "I don't want them to know I'm here until they come home from school."

"Papa knows you're here?"

"Got here around five in the morning. I used my key and fell asleep on the sofa. He woke me up and hid me in here."

"Good, then he knows to take the girls to school this morning. I didn't feel like it anyway." My two youngest sisters were seventeen and eighteen. "Promise me you'll tell me what's happening once they leave."

Yawning, I snuggled against her like I often had as a child. "I will, Mama. Just need to sleep right now. Only had an hour."

"This is the second time you're running home like someone is after you. Ain't no woman after you for messing with her man? I raised you better," she said over her shoulder.

I chuckled. "I know, Mama. I don't deal with taken men."

"Okay then, because I don't want to have to hurt somebody for messing with my baby." She shifted in bed to face me.

"Even if I'm in the wrong, you would defend me?" I asked in surprise. Mama could be very sanctimonious, though she'd had me before marriage.

She quirked a brow. "Wouldn't *you* defend *me* against a stranger?"

I hugged her. "You know it. Love you, Mama."

"Love you, my firstborn." She kissed my cheek.

Sleep found me in the coziness of my parents' bed before I could say anything else.

I called Amara to tell her that I was visiting my family in Gatlinburg for a little while and that Nathan and I had decided to stop seeing each other. I told her I would explain everything once I returned home and wouldn't disappear this time. I would allow her to be the friend she'd been to me. For now, I needed my family.

Having a mother who didn't work outside the home had been a blessing. I loved that she was always accessible to us. If we left something we needed for school at home, she would bring it with a threat not to forget again. She would whip something up at the last minute for a forgotten bake sale or an impromptu birthday party. Raising five girls with different personalities and dreams had kept her busy in and out of the home. It was a good thing we all loved her cooking—a meal for seven was expensive, especially living on one salary. Although three of her daughters had moved out, and the last two would probably leave soon, Mama would remain busy taking care of my father and her various committees in the church and community.

Today, her chosen profession of being a stay-at-home mother served my purpose. I spent the day in bed with her watching mindless TV and listening to her spill on the latest gossip and happenings with family, friends, and neighbors.

We sat up with our backs against the crushed velvet headboard when Mama tugged on the ends of my cornrows. "Your sisters and Papa will be home soon. Are you ever going to tell me what brought you home like you were being chased out of town for the second time in months?"

Grabbing the pillow from behind me, I hugged it tightly and finally admitted, "Omar is engaged. I ran into him last night while I was at dinner."

"I'm so sorry, baby. I know how much you loved him."

"I did. Assumed he wouldn't find somebody so soon. It shocked me and hurt like hell." I rested my chin on the pillow and stared unseeing at the TV. "He probably started it up with her while we were together, and that's the real reason we broke up, and not the reason he gave, that I put my career first."

Mama hit her palm with her fist. "Ooh…I hate a cheater. That's the most selfish type of man. I know it hurts, but be glad you're not the one with his ring on your finger." She patted my thigh. "Erase that lowlife out of your heart. You'll meet someone else who's better for you."

"What if I already did?" I tentatively asked.

Mama's face brightened, and she sat forward. "Is it Jake's friend? That man you went to Memphis with?"

I drew my knees up to my chest. "Now, Mama, don't make a big deal about it. He's been a good friend, and I'm glad he was there last night. He stood up for me." Then the thought of how I'd left like a thief in the night brought tears. I covered my face. "I really like him."

Mama gently pushed down my hands. "Then why the tears? Is it still about Omar?"

"No. Some are for him. Finding out he was engaged stung my ego. Like, why didn't he ask *me* to be his wife?" I held my hand up before Mama could protest. "He's not the one for me without a doubt, but seeing that ring that could have been mine cut to the core. I know my worth. I'm just being honest, okay?"

Though she still frowned, Mama nodded. "Okay."

"I'm crying because the man who made me forget about Omar isn't a real possibility for me. He's a big-time investigative journalist who travels the world and has risked his life several times. He doesn't want to be obligated to anyone or have his woman and children at home worried about him when he chooses dangerous assignments." I peered at her sympathetic face. "Been going through a lot, Mama. Getting over Omar, trying to figure out my career because I'm not happy being in the band anymore. I could do photography, since everyone keeps saying I have a knack, and I do enjoy it. I'm just not sure if it's the career for me. Then I developed feelings for a man I shouldn't have. I knew how he felt about marriage and children before we started kicking it and convinced myself it didn't matter, since we were friends first."

Mama rested back against the headboard. "Is he good to you?"

"The best. Never met a man like him." I smiled. "We have so much fun together, and he inspires me."

Mama brushed her hand over my head. "Then for once, Sophie, stop beating yourself up over these men. Enjoy this experience until you meet the right guy, if it's not him."

"It's easy for you to say because you were married by the time you were twenty-two to a man who still loves you deeply. It's hard out here being single and going through heartbreak after heartbreak. It takes a toll."

She opened her mouth to rebut me and then shut it.

"Go ahead, Mama, and say whatever you need to say." I crossed my arms.

"Of all my children, you go around with this smile on your face like you're so happy. Then I see this." She gestured at my folded arms. "Are you happy out there in Nashville, or are you pretending? Because you're doing things that this family can only imagine. You've traveled the country and visited a few places outside because of your talent. You've never asked us for a dime and have been taking care of yourself even before you left home, plus sending money home for your sisters. You have a beautiful life, but you keep focusing too much on what you *don't* have."

"Why can't I have what you and Daddy or my sisters have with their husbands?" I swung my hands up.

She tilted her head. "Why can't me or your sisters have your talent or your career? We may have made other choices besides getting married and starting families young if we did. Yes, we may be happy with the men in our lives, but we also long for things we don't have. Your sisters would kill to sing and travel like you do, and your baby sisters envy you more than they do the ones who are already married. No matter how much we try, we'll never have your talent. You can still get yourself a husband if that's what you want. Yet you're the only one walking around with your mouth poked out."

Her lips formed a thin line while she stared at me, daring me to contradict anything she'd said. My pride kept me staring back, though her words resonated deeply. I *had* been too focused on what I didn't have and imagined that my mother and sisters were happier than me simply because they had husbands.

When her lips twitched from suppressed laughter—probably from her recognizing that my stubbornness had kicked in—I rolled my eyes. "God, I hate when you make a good point." I slid back down until the comforter covered my head.

Mama poked my stomach. "Still haven't answered my question—are you really happy, or are you pretending?"

For most of my life, I'd believed I was happy, even when life struck back. After everything that had happened this year, I now questioned whether my happiness had been learned behavior or a true reflection of my emotions.

"I don't know," I finally answered.

"Once you know, everything else will fall into place." Mama kissed the top of my head through the comforter. "I need to go cook. Pot roast, potatoes, and green beans. If I'd known you were coming, I would've cooked brisket."

"Make it tomorrow. I'll be here for a few days," I mumbled.

"Now that makes *me* happy." The mattress lifted on one side. "Go on, get cleaned up, and then help me in the kitchen. Your sisters will be home soon. We'll talk more later."

"Yes, ma'am." My head was still under the covers.

Her question settled over me as Ms. Claudette's had.

Had I been pretending that I was happy with my life?

SIXTEEN

Nathan

Slowly waking into consciousness, I reached for Sophie, and when I didn't feel her warm body, my eyes popped open. Frantically, I searched the room for a sign that she hadn't done what my gut told me she'd done. If she wasn't next to me, she was gone. I almost always woke first. I reached for my phone on my bedside table.

Thank you for everything. Time for us to go back to the friends we once were. Need a break. Will reach out soon. Take care.

I tossed my phone on the bed and stalked to the other parts of my house, hoping to find her, though I knew she was already gone. Too harsh and judgmental when she needed my empathy, I had been gruff at the restaurant and in sex because I ached with the need to hurt Omar. Too caught up in his love for his new lady and the audacity to check Sophie about me, he couldn't see how his behavior had drawn a rain cloud over Sophie, how she became a shell of a person right before my eyes, though she tried to present a brave front. I'd been pissed and, honestly, jealous. The anger that could have easily become rage was pure, unadulterated envy that he'd had her heart. Maybe still did. I no longer existed when her eyes caught his. I could've disappeared right then, and she wouldn't have noticed. All of her attention centered on her ex.

Needing to remind her of the current man in her life, I'd wanted to brand her with my dick once we were in my bed. I'd sensed she wanted solace in my arms.

Until she didn't.

She hadn't wanted me to use a condom. And I hadn't insisted. We'd never gone without protection, and the natural feel of her body wrapped around mine erased all rational thought of possible consequences.

The sex had been hot, passionate, rough, and utterly satisfying.

Now she was gone.

My temples throbbed painfully, and I dropped my head between my knees when I returned to the bed, trying to understand why she would leave like she had.

You fool. She left because she was in love with another man, and no other would do. I understood her actions, because if I'd been with another woman after seeing Sophie and her man, I would've snuck out in the middle of the night too.

"Fuck," I yelled. I loved her. No…I'd loved her before. Now I was *in* love, and she was in love with someone else.

I flopped back down in the bed and stared at the ceiling. I would leave her alone. It was for the best anyway. McClain Studios wanted me to be hands-on in L.A. They would travel to Memphis to film, which would take a few weeks, and I'd planned to ask Sophie last night to go with me, until she told me about her new weekly gig. She'd been so bubbly and bright-eyed about the possibility, and I couldn't take that from her, so I'd adjusted my plans to invite her to go with me for a few days to Los Angeles. Maybe try our hands at a relationship.

Everything shifted when she saw Omar.

I screwed my eyes up tight, trying to block the image of her stunned expression and the wailing in the car and to control the fiery rage that boiled within me. Nude, I stalked back to my office and sat at my desk. I fired up my laptop and released the need to destroy with my words.

And for the next four days, I only left my office to use the bathroom, jealousy and disappointment stealing my appetite.

By the fifth day, with no word from Sophie, I became restless and went to her apartment. I sensed the stillness before I knocked. She wasn't home. Might not have been in a few days. Maybe Omar had had a change of heart and sought her out. He'd seemed bothered that she may have stepped out on him, but that was a man simply being territorial. Even if we loved another, an ex was still somehow *ours*.

I called Jake as I left her apartment. "Hey, is Sophie at the studio?"

"No. Haven't seen her since the other day." He paused. "I was about to call you. I read a little of what you sent me last night Bruh…like seriously, how do you manage to get even better? Glad you didn't give up the rights to this book. It's going to be a bestseller. Wouldn't be surprised if this didn't get you the prize."

"Thank you," I answered, unable to truly receive his compliment. My mind raced with worry about her whereabouts. I needed to drive with a destination in mind. Maybe Sophie was with Tavion. Jake would've told me if she were with Amara.

"What's up with you?" he asked, his tone shifting to concern.

I didn't want to hear his mouth about Sophie. "Nothing. Been up for almost seventy-two hours writing. Exhausted."

"Get some rest. Call me later. I still owe you a beer." My partial truth had seemed to satisfy him, and I clicked off my cell, anxious to call Amara.

"Hello?" she answered on the first ring.

"Where is she?" My gut told me I didn't have to explain myself.

She sighed. "Nathan."

Her confirmation settled one part of my anxiousness. Sophie was alive somewhere. "Does Jake know she left again?" I had to know if my friend had become that good at lying to me.

"Not yet. She told me she would tell him herself. Giving her another day to do so before I tell him. I don't keep secrets from him."

"Tell me where she is. I can't keep driving aimlessly." I had been on the road for ten minutes, and my eyes burned.

"I can't," Amara replied. "She's my best friend first. It's enough that I'm keeping it from Jake."

"She asked you not to tell me?" My heart clenched painfully.

"No. She told me that you two were no longer seeing each other and that she found out Omar was engaged. We talked a little bit. She needs time away from Nashville and swears she'll return in a week or two."

"You believe her?" I checked my side mirrors before switching lanes. The last time Sophie told everyone she would be back soon, she'd cut off everyone but her family for months until I showed up at her doorstep. Would she cut me off if she planned to disappear again?

"I don't know, Nate. I still want to give her the benefit of the doubt that this is just a setback. She seems like herself again."

"I'm going to find her, whether you tell me where she is or not. You didn't see her face or hear her tears. And *we* didn't decide not to see each other. She just up and left without telling me a damn thing except she needed time." Gripping the steering wheel, I inhaled and exhaled deeply, trying to ease the burning in my stomach.

Amara pleaded, "Nate, wait until she gets back to talk. You sound angry."

"I am. I'm also hurt and worried about her," I responded, terser than I intended.

"She's fine. I'm sure she'll talk to you. Give her a moment like she asked, okay?"

My mind started spinning, thinking of the places Sophie mentioned she liked to go when she was troubled. "She's with her parents, isn't she?"

Amara didn't answer.

"Please." I stopped at a traffic light. "Amara, I need to see her."

A beat later, she replied, "I'll text you their address. Just take care of our girl."

"Always," I promised, and hung up.

My cell rang a few minutes later as I pulled onto the highway heading to Gatlinburg. Jake again.

"What?" I answered, not trying to hide my frustration.

"Go home," he ordered me.

Amara must have told him. They may have been together when I called them separately.

"We're not about to start this shit again," I sneered. "Swear to God, we're not friends anymore if you warn me about Sophie."

The fast-passing trees on the side of the highway urged me to look down at my speedometer, and I eased off the pedal. The last thing I needed was a ticket.

Jake said, "I let that go the day at the café. I'm worried about *you*. How much sleep have you had?"

I reluctantly answered, "I told you the truth. I haven't slept in days. Been writing nonstop."

"Then get your ass home and go to sleep. You won't do any of us any good if you kill yourself or someone else, trying to be this hero."

His logic and rationality fucked with my own sensibilities. I weakly protested, "It's not that far."

"Go home and get up in the morning. You know where she is now. Chill." He lowered his voice. "You need a cooler head, Nate. I hear the hurt and irritation. You go there with no sleep and she says something to piss you off, it's only going to drive a deeper wedge."

"Fine," I bit out, and clicked off the cell. He was right. I was livid with her. She'd left like I meant nothing to her and didn't bother to tell me she was good. I would never treat her like that. Yet, despite my simmering anger, at my gut level, I knew she needed me and I wanted to be there for her.

At nine the next morning, I knocked on her parents' door. A woman who looked like a darker and older version of Sophie answered with a beaming smile, as if she'd expected me.

"Sorry to disturb you this early. I'm Nathan Price, a friend of your daughter."

She planted her hands on her hips. "Which one? I have five."

I gave a sheepish grin. "Your eldest one, Sophie. We worked together in Memphis. I wanted to check on her if you don't mind. Is she home?"

"No." Her eyes twinkled, and I realized she was messing with me. "She's here."

Before I could utter another word, I locked eyes with an excited Sophie, who seemingly came out of nowhere and slammed into my welcoming arms.

And just like that, all was right in the world.

SEVENTEEN

Sophie

Saturday mornings in the Turner household were reserved for cleaning to music. Sometimes, it would be the radio, a record player, or one of the streaming channels—and if we were lucky, Papa would play his guitar. After cleaning, we would have a huge breakfast, and whoever had kitchen duty would clean again as soon as we finished.

My two youngest sisters, Sasha and Sonia, adored me, and we'd been staying up late laughing and talking, though they had school. They were still asleep now. My two other sisters and I were in the kitchen helping Mama cook breakfast while their husbands and my father were watching ESPN in the den. Both infant granddaughters, only months apart, were together in the nearby playpen, fascinated with their toys.

The house was extra noisy and alive. I needed the kinetic energy of my family to keep me from drowning again. The last time I was here, I'd been overwhelmed with envy for my sisters, Sarai and Shae, and their babies. Now, I celebrated that my sisters had found men who loved them and their children. I might have had a setback seeing Omar, but I had healed as much as anyone could once you had been scarred. This break had been good. I would stay a few more days and then go back to Nashville, test the waters with Nathan, who was probably either pissed with me or relieved that he didn't have to pick me back up this time. I missed him. I wanted him to meet my family. They would love his quiet demeanor and his unassuming nature, and that he was protective of me. Except that would mean something different for us.

"Squirrel, go get more bacon from the freezer," Mama instructed me. Her hands were covered in flour.

"I'm scrambling the eggs." I held up the large plastic bowl.

Sarai, the second eldest, bumped my hips hard enough to make me move, adding water to a large pot at the sink. "You shouldn't be in here in the first place."

"Hey, I've gotten better over the years. I can make good cheese eggs. Mama, let me try."

"Just go get the bacon. We're hungry and don't have time for you to mess up the eggs." Mama shook her head as she finished pressing the dough for biscuits.

It was a running joke that in a house full of women I couldn't cook worth a damn and was always on cleanup duty or setting the table. I stomped off to the small storage room that Papa had added on when I was a teenager to keep the deep freezer and our junk. I'd just lifted the top to grab the bacon when the doorbell rang.

A man's deep voice echoed through the house, and I gasped loudly. The concern and earnestness in Nathan's voice captured my heart. Without any thought, I rushed from the freezer to the living room, and when our gazes collided, he opened his arms to catch me. He held me to him, and I sobbed on his chest as he rubbed my back and kissed me over and over on my forehead and cheeks. He continued to hold me as he led me to the sofa, and I melted into his side.

I whispered, "I'm sorry I left like I did. It was too much. I didn't want to make it harder for you. I had to come home for a little while to regroup. I planned to call you and talk once I got back."

"Shh…" he soothed me. "We can talk later. I think your family is trying to figure out what's going on."

He tapped my back, and I looked over my shoulder. My entire family, including the spouses and babies, gawked from the kitchen in the corner of the open area. They all waved at Nathan.

He grinned. "I'm Nate."

"Hi, Nate," everyone chorused as if on cue.

I dropped my burning face on his chest.

"Too late to be shamefaced, Squirrel. We'll just set another plate and he'll join us for breakfast. Are you hungry?" Mama asked Nathan.

I kept my head tucked into his.

"Starving." The rumble of his deep voice traveled to my core. I really did love this man.

"Does my daughter feed you?"

Popping my head up, I glared at my mother, who smirked in return. Mama thought she was slick. Cooking for each other indicated intimacy. In the last four days, I'd downplayed my feelings for him and focused on my family.

Nathan chuckled. "Cooking isn't her strong suit. I usually do it."

My family murmured their agreement with my lack of culinary skills.

Mama cut her eyes at me and sucked her teeth. She believed in feeding the men in our lives.

I lifted my palms. "Don't look at me like that. I asked you to let me do the eggs."

"Squirrel, let that man go and get the bacon like I asked you." Mama waved dismissively before telling Nathan, "You can sit back with the men until breakfast is ready."

"Twinkle, I think I like Squirrel as a nickname better." He nudged me. "Do what your mother said before she's mad with me."

I groaned and held my head high as I walked past the rest of my smiling family.

My youngest sister cooed, "He has a nickname for her and everything. I like him already."

"Y'all are so annoying," I grumbled, though I couldn't stop my grin. He'd come for me.

"I love your family. Today was fun." Nathan opened the door to his hotel suite after he'd spent the day with us watching college football and getting to know my people. "So loud and loving. Dinnertime for us was always a quiet affair. Both my parents are reserved. My brother and I were the same."

Hugging myself, I followed him as he settled our bags near the bed. "My family is loud. *Too* loud. Sometimes I longed for the quiet. One reason I left home after graduating from high school was all the responsibility toward my sisters. I wanted to be free for a while, be a normal young woman. Mama wanted me to be the first to go to college to be a role model for my younger sisters, but it wasn't for me. Not going to lie, being around you, Jake, and Mari makes me rethink my decision."

"It's never too late. My mother went to college once she separated from my father, and loves her job in D.C."

"Does it bother you that I didn't go to college?" I perched on the end of the bed, tapping my feet, wondering when we would *really* talk. We'd kept everything surface level on the ride over here, though what we both needed to say bubbled just underneath.

"No. I've met brilliant people who never finished elementary school. I'm a firm believer in living your dash to the fullest." He walked to the balcony and opened the door, and the cool night air wafted through the room. The Great Smoky Mountains loomed in the near distance. "Let's sit out here. Nature has a way of keeping us grounded. We need to talk."

I nodded. "It's chilly. Better keep my jacket on."

Nathan grabbed the comforter off the bed and pulled the two chairs together on the balcony. Once we both sat down, he covered us, and I laid my head on his chest. Once our bodies were protected from the night air, I relaxed at the beautiful, familiar sight of the mountains I'd grown up admiring.

"You warm enough?" The vibrations of his voice comforted me. Everything about him felt like home.

"Yeah. He squinted.

Where are your glasses?"

"In Nashville."

I lifted my head. "Nathan, you shouldn't be driving without glasses."

His jaw tightened, and his nostrils flared. "Then don't ever leave me again like you did."

Gazing into his dark, angry eyes, I promised, "I won't ever do that to you again."

"Then why did you ghost me?"

I lowered my head, unable to meet his probing stare. "Some of it was embarrassment that you saw me lose it. I didn't handle myself well. All that crying over another man. Do you know how many nights I replayed our breakup, thinking we would still be together if I'd done anything different? And to find out he'd already moved on, it stabbed like an ice-cold knife to my heart. I just wanted the agonizing hurt and betrayal to end that night. You only wanted to comfort me, and I begged for more. I didn't want you to use anything because, for an impulsive moment, I wanted to be pregnant. I was once again being selfish."

Nathan lifted my chin with his index finger. "Then I was being selfish, too. I would do anything to make it right…to make you remember that you had me. I didn't care either. And if you're pregnant, I'll accept your decision."

Tugging on his goatee, I corrected him, "It would be *our* decision."

He looked down at me. "In theory…maybe."

"Because you don't even want children." I searched his intense eyes for any sign that he'd changed his stance on a more permanent commitment.

"It wouldn't be ideal, but I would handle my responsibility to you and our baby."

Disappointed, I dropped my gaze. "You sound so clinical."

Nathan shook his head. "I don't know what to say right now. You're on edge, and I don't want to argue with you."

I blew out a restless breath. He was right. My nerves were slowly fraying, and he needed to know everything before I changed my mind. "I took Plan B the next day. We should be good."

"Are you trying to test me?" Nathan's sharp tone tore through me.

"No, no… Not a test, nor am I playing games to see how you feel about children. I was intentional the other night, and I left out of shame for my actions. I didn't care if it was the right decision for you or the best environment to raise a child."

I tightened the comforter around us and shifted in his arms. His heart beat faster than it typically did as he waited for me to continue.

"Seeing Omar again reminded me that you and I don't want the same things, and I couldn't keep pretending otherwise. I watched you sleep, thinking about the amazing person you'd been to me and how I selfishly didn't care about your wants and needs. I've always prided myself on being this good, reliable person. A woman of my word, as you've been a man of yours. Whenever and whatever you need, Sophie is there. It's why my parents rely on me more than the others, though I live in another city. That's why Jake calls me all the time. After everything went down with Omar, I've become someone who runs and quits. I can't be that person anymore."

"Then don't."

"I won't." I unblinkingly stared into his eyes. "I realized that I won't truly heal until I tell the whole truth about why it was so hard to get over Omar."

"He cheated," Nathan replied. "I figured that a long time ago, based on the bits of information you would give me, and he confirmed it the other day."

"Yeah. It was confirmed for me then, too. I suspected it, but didn't know if it was true. Let me talk before I lose my courage."

"All right."

"Um…" I rubbed my beginning-to-sweat palms against my jeans. "Might as well snatch off the Band-Aid. I found out I was pregnant right after he broke up with me."

Nathan's breath hitched, though he remained quiet.

"Omar never knew. He'd already decided he didn't want to be with me. Guess I should give him credit for breaking up with me in person. He told me we just weren't working anymore because of my devotion to Mari and Jake. I found out I was pregnant a few days later. I came home for the weekend to tell him the great news. I was so excited. All I had to do was prove that he was more important than my career. It got ugly between us when he only seemed annoyed and angry at my unexpected appearance at his place." The memory of the cruel taunts we'd hurled back and forth sent a chill through me.

Nathan stiffened. "Did he hit you?" Tension bulged the veins in his neck, and I rubbed his forearms, hoping to calm him. If Omar had touched one hair on me, Nathan was going after him, and there would be nothing I could do about it.

"No. Just words we both said to hurt one another. Hateful words that I hope I never say again to any person. I left him that night confused about how everything got so fucked up." I gently caressed my belly. "My little bean growing inside gave me hope. I figured I would give him space and approach him again in a couple of weeks. Tell him about the baby. If he wanted to work it out, we would. If he didn't, I would raise my baby alone. I had a village between The Crew and my family. I had decided that I would be fine whether Omar was involved or not. My mother did it with me and met Papa when I was two. My story would be similar. Until that awful morning."

The overwhelming gulf of loss coursed through me, and I wrapped my arms around Nathan, debating whether I needed to dredge up that memory of pain that I'd done my best to bury.

His arm curved around my shoulder. "You don't have to say anything else."

"I think I do. Maybe that's why I haven't been able to move on completely." I brushed my lips against the racing pulse in his neck. "You're making it easier to continue."

Nathan kissed my forehead and tightened the comforter around me once more. The crickets chirped, and an owl hooted in the crisp night air. He commented, "We won't be hearing crickets too much longer. Surprised they're out tonight with this nip."

"Nate, are you filling up the awkward silence like I do when a conversation gets tough?"

His chest shook slightly underneath my head. "I guess I am."

Silence drifted over us again while we were entwined under the moon and mountains. This time, I allowed peace to settle over me before I continued.

"I asked Jake for a few more days to check in with my doctor to see if it was safe to travel and get over my initial sadness about Omar. The doctor said that the baby and I were healthy and that I could tour until maybe my eighth month, as long as I took good care of myself. The sun was waiting to peek over the clouds. The first colors of the rainbow were shining despite Omar dumping me with little explanation. I'd planned to return to the tour until my pregnancy made it impossible.

"I became hyper-focused on prenatal care. Looking into the best doctor and hospital to deliver. Started searching for a house because I didn't want to raise my child in an apartment. I didn't want to feel the heartbreak of betrayal, so I went full steam ahead. I didn't sleep much, so worried that I would slip into despair that my vision now would only include a baby and not the husband. That my gut told me that he'd met someone else. That I was the biggest fool. How crazy inadequate I felt. Still feel. I couldn't hold on to my man. Felt like less than a woman."

Sobs broke through my will. Nathan rocked me gently until I was able to speak again.

"Princess became my lifesaver. I wrote songs and played her every chance I had. I didn't share a wall with a neighbor then, so I was up late. Anything, *anything* to focus on the joy I should be feeling. I wanted to call my mother and ask how she'd learned to accept single motherhood. Yet I was afraid that in her desire to help me, she would inadvertently say something that would make me blame myself more than I already did for the end of another relationship.

"Then one dawn, while lounging in bed, I became inspired and picked up my guitar. I started to play, and suddenly, pain attacked my womb. The pain subsided after what seemed like hours, though it was only minutes. I breathed a sigh of relief and planned to make an emergency appointment later that day to make sure I was still good. A couple of hours later, I was huddled in bed, trying to call 911. I'd already lost the baby by the time the ambulance arrived."

"You were all alone through all of that?" Nathan asked.

I nodded. "Came back to an empty place with no hope. Music didn't even matter, because I couldn't be sure that it wasn't music that took everything from me. And until you knocked on my door, another soul had not crossed that threshold in four months." I finally looked at Nathan, who didn't hide his tears. "I had consoled myself that Omar wasn't the right man because he wasn't ready for marriage. I thought it wouldn't matter if I saw him again."

"It did matter," Nathan said quietly.

"Yes, because he just didn't want to marry *me*." I wiped my eyes. "Before you try to tell me to get over it or encourage me to be strong, put yourself in my shoes. The father of my baby, the man I'd wanted to be with for the rest of my life, is engaged to another woman. It fucks with me that maybe if he'd chosen me, my baby would still be alive."

Nathan blew out a rattled breath before he eased out from underneath the blanket. Cool air slipped in as I wrapped the thick material around me. Soon, I heard the shower running. He came out of the bathroom, shirtless, and took my hand. He undressed me and finished undressing himself, and then washed me from head to toe, encouraging me to cry as much and as long as I needed.

"Water is a life source. We're cleansing the hurts of the past and welcoming renewal and abundance." He whispered, "Loss and pain are an unfortunate part of life, just as the sun and the rain. The universe doesn't operate in vain. Whatever happened is supposed to happen."

The soft, gentle touch of his hands, his soothing words, and the warm water pushed out more of the gut-wrenching pain I'd thought I'd already expunged. Unable to hold up my own body, I fell back into him, and his arms went around me.

"I got you until you can stand on your own two feet again."

And in his strong embrace, I finally found a semblance of peace.

EIGHTEEN

Sophie

"We could've stayed in and had room service or something," Nathan complained as soon as we found a love seat in Ramses, a popular local bar and lounge. A blend of country, pop, and soul music played, and soft lighting created the ambiance of a chill vibe. The noise level of the couples and singles chatting forced him to speak louder. "There's way too much going on in here."

"People are just having a good time, like I want you to." I refrained from rolling my eyes. He'd been grumpy since we parked. We'd been in bed all day. Some talking. Mostly quiet. No TV or music. Just sleeping and curled up against each other. By the evening, I'd suggested we go out to break the solemnity. He reluctantly agreed.

"Not really my thing to hang out at hookah lounges."

"Ramses is more than Hookah." Unbothered by his negative attitude, I scanned the QR code on the low table before us. "I needed to get out, to remind me of the life I still have. I hate that I allowed Omar to bring me back to the dark place."

"A real place," he corrected me. "Life isn't always good. It's damn bleak for a lot of people. Stop trying to be this merry sunshine when you don't have to be."

His words mimicked Mama's, and I still hadn't resolved whether I was happy or pretending.

"I want a lemon drop. See if there's something you want." I passed him my cell to look at the drinks menu. "I'm not *trying*. It's how I approach life. Just because you believe the world is cruel doesn't mean I'm naïve if I don't."

"The world *is* cruel. It's not my belief. It's a fact." He held his palm up. "The world is also good. And you're trying to be what you don't even feel yet." A group walked past laughing loudly, and Nathan scowled deeper. "I'm not in the mood. Can we pick up some alcohol on the way back to the hotel?"

"I want to stay. I love this energy." At his skeptical expression, I angled toward him. "How do you know what or how I feel? If I say I'm good, I'm good. Wasn't the point of the shower last night to take away all of my pain?"

"It's a part of the process, Sophie. Hours later, you're healed and ready for the world? You kept what happened to you a secret from everyone you loved, and you have more love than almost anyone I know. You suffered alone when you didn't have to because you'd rather pretend that what happened with Omar and your baby didn't exist."

More talking people walked past us and stopped his words. A barmaid approached us to take our order, and he impatiently waved her off.

"What's wrong with you?" I asked. "Why are you angry? Because I'm not behaving like you think I should? Because I wanted to do more than feel sorry for myself?"

Nathan's broad chest rose and fell. "You disappeared for months with no real explanation, and Sunday morning, you practically ghosted *me*. I could feel your pain. I could touch your hurt. Yet you're here bopping to the noise with a damn smile." He glanced around the room. "You walk around the world like the sun never sets when inside you're wishing for a different life, keeping inside everything that fucked you up. Even the lie you tell yourself that you want marriage and family above all else."

"It's not a lie. You just said you felt my pain. My sorrow."

He placed my cell on the table. "I didn't say you didn't *want* your baby. I said that it's not all that you want. Your face lights up when you perform, and it's even brighter when you photograph. You are an unbelievably gifted woman who insists the moment she meets that man, she throws away her talent. And for what?"

"For what?" Annoyance burned through me. "How did we get here?"

Nathan hit the palm of his hand. "You can't see that one thing leads to another?"

Indignation increased the volume of my voice. "You've seen my parents? That's years of love. Priceless. Beautiful. I wouldn't expect you to understand why having a husband and children are important to me. You want to come and go as you please, have no responsibility to anyone. Might even say you're a selfish man because you keep your heart to yourself."

He frowned. "Are you one of those people? Back in Memphis, I thought you actually got me."

I huffed. "No. I do get you. I left you back in Nashville *because* I get you. And unlike you, I don't judge people's choices, because there's no right way to live the dash."

"I'm not judging you. I'm telling you what I see." He draped his arm across the back of the loveseat. "You left here for Nashville. Why? Because you wanted something bigger than this town. Two of your younger sisters are married to men from Knoxville and Gatlinburg. If marriage is all you ever wanted, then why the hell did you leave home?"

My mind scrambled to find a plausible answer. To say I didn't want to struggle like my parents wouldn't be enough of a reason if my end goal was marriage and family.

"Stop trying to defend yourself when you know I'm right. Just because your dream is bigger than your family's doesn't mean that you're better than them—it's just bigger. The world awaits you, Sophie."

I shook my head. "Don't do that."

"What am I doing?"

"Pushing me like I'm one of your subjects. Trying to get me to think like you, so I'll accept whatever you give me." Annoyed with her pending interruption, I waved away the waitress approaching us again.

Nathan removed his arm from behind me. "I don't want you to accept anything you don't want to accept."

"Bullshit, Nate. You didn't drive four hours to check on me for nothing. How do you feel about me?" I tilted my head expectantly.

"You know how I feel."

"No, I don't. Not since Memphis and then Nashville, and now you're here." I tapped his thigh. "How do you feel about me?"

His nostrils flared. "I care about you."

"It kills you to admit that you want more from me because you're too scared to see if we might actually work. We aren't just fuck buddies. You get jealous when another man looks at me, and you find ways whether we're around others or alone to touch me. It's what Amara sees. It's what Jake knows, which is why he wanted you to leave me alone. You were hurt that night we bumped into Omar because, for the first time since we've been doing whatever the hell we've been doing, I wasn't focused on you. You had sex with me that night without a condom, not just to try to make me forget him. You also wanted to stake a claim on my heart."

As his right temple twitched, he slanted closer to me. "I hurt for you, and I came here because you ran again, and I had to make sure you were okay. Men are territorial. Of course I don't like it when another man looks at you. That's all it means. I'm here right now because I care deeply about you."

I scanned the lounge full of smiling faces and circled back to the man in front of me, who'd worn a frown since I suggested leaving the hotel. He'd wanted to stay locked in that room because he hadn't said everything he needed to tell me. Now he wanted to call me out without accepting any of his contradictory behavior.

"I swear, I want to scream. You're so damn frustrating." I balled my hands into fists. "Amara and Jake care about me too—correction, they *love* me—and didn't feel the need to drive here. Why are you *really* here?"

"Like I told you, I was worried. Don't transfer your love to me while still stuck on another man. Believe what I say—neither of us is ready for more."

Daggers hit my heart, though I said, "I don't believe you. Omar told me he loved me, but his actions didn't reflect that. Since you knocked on my door in Nashville, your actions have shown me how you feel. For God's sake, you cleaned my apartment without asking me that very first day. You told me to trust my gut. My gut says you love me so much you can't function when we don't talk." I jabbed the space between us so hard that a woman walking by jerked her head in our direction.

"Lower your voice," Nathan demanded quietly. "This is why we should've stayed in the hotel. We obviously had more things to discuss."

My stubbornness and pride battled viciously with his quiet truth. Closing my eyes briefly, I calmed my frustration and disappointment enough to speak more softly. "If you want me to admit I want more than marriage and a family, or that I'm pretending to be happy, then you need to admit *you* want more than your career. Admit that you want me to be yours forever. Maybe even have a baby or two with me." Picking up his hand, I squeezed it. "Better yet, admit that you're afraid. That's why you're trying to push me away with some bullshit that I'm still in love with Omar when I confront your ass. I left you in Nashville because you could only promise me now. Anything more than that is too much for you."

Our gazes locked. Resignation and fear settled in his.

"I'll catch a ride to my parents'." I released his hand, picked up my purse, and rose from the table, numb. Nathan loved me. Like I loved him. My heart couldn't take another wound. Not now.

He grabbed my wrist.

"Let go," I said sternly, and he did. "I can't make you love me just as I couldn't make Omar or anyone else love me. I accept that, and I accept that whatever we had is done."

"Sophie, please… You're asking for…" He fumbled for words.

"I'm not asking for shit. You want to be with me or you don't."

His eyes were desperate. "I can't lose you."

Blinking back tears, I calmly replied, "You won't. I'm always your friend. We worked on an amazing project together, and I'll never forget our time in Memphis." I patted his shoulder. "See, I told you I could handle us not becoming more. I'll text you when I return to Nashville. I won't disappear anymore. You healed me, right?"

I lifted my purse higher on my shoulder, placed my shades on my face, and glided out of Ramses.

Later that night, I sat alone with my guitar on the porch of my family home, playing around with a chord sequence, using my sorrow of losing my baby and Nathan. I'd only held tight to Omar because he'd been the father of my baby. We had nothing in common beyond music, and even with that mutual interest, we'd never shared ideas or played together like I did with Amara. All these months, I'd grieved losing my baby and confused those emotions with the loss of Omar, entwining my grief and music like a ball of yarn that had slowly unraveled because of Nathan.

I had an ease with him that I'd never had with anyone else. We could talk and laugh about anything for hours. He'd already promised to wait in line for both of us whenever the next greatest shoe dropped, and he fit in with my rambunctious family. I loved Nathan, and realized how deeply the moment I heard his voice in Mama's living room. I also knew that he loved me too, but that he'd rather return to our old friendship than a possible new relationship.

He'd once told me to take something from every man I dated, and I would. I wanted a man who would be my friend and lover. I wouldn't cry over Nathan. I would learn from him.

"Squirrel, I hear the blues. Everything okay?" Papa held Queenie in his hand and sat in the rocking chair near me. "Mind if I join you?"

"Only if it remains just me and you." I tugged the lapels of my coat closed to block off the night air.

He chuckled. "I told them I needed some quality time with you."

"Until we start playing and everyone wants to request a song." I strummed quietly.

"You can't blame them. We don't see you enough. And then you ran off with your man friend." He began tuning his guitar. "When you're ready for the family to join us, we'll call them. Right now, it's just us. Is that a new song?"

"No. It's one of Mari's songs. I'm in a thinking mood. Not creative. Wondering why I haven't found love like you and Mama."

Papa snorted. "Simple. You weren't meant to yet. Who was that big-headed boy you used to be crazy about in high school?"

Laughing, I replied, "Jamie Woods just had a lot of hair because he wanted locs."

"To cover that big head." He raised his brows. "You were writing his last name on all your notebooks."

"Ugh," I groaned, laughing again at the memory. "You couldn't tell me I *wouldn't* be Mrs. Jamie Woods. He ended up marrying a girl from Jackson, and they have three children. From what I hear, he might have a couple more somewhere in these streets."

"And if you married him, that would be your story, and you would've never moved to Nashville." He plucked his guitar languidly. "You've experienced things we'll never experience. Me and your mama talk about you all the time, about how proud we are that you did something with your life besides having babies. Now, you know we love our grandbabies, and there's nothing wrong if you want to stay at home with your children and make your home special for your husband. But one day, those babies grow up and have their own lives." He beamed proudly. "We have five girls because your mother loved the toddler stage so much. I had to put my foot down when she started in on me about baby number six."

"I thought it was about having that elusive boy?" I hadn't realized Mama loved us as babies so much that she was willing to have more.

"I would've loved a son, but nothing compares to my daughters." He looked back at the house. "I wouldn't trade anything in the world for you and your sisters, and especially that short woman who loves to terrorize me." Papa slanted his gaze at me. "I told your mama that you left home because it was too hard to be here, because no matter what I did to show you that I loved you, you felt like an outsider. It didn't help that your skin is lighter than everyone else and that we live in a small town where all secrets come out of the shadows. Had to be tough at times."

"It was," I admitted, thinking of the murmurs and grumblings of people at church or school. There had been speculation over who was my real father—someone I'd never cared about finding or knowing anything about, even when Mama wanted to tell me. The only father I needed was Papa.

"Do you know why I only taught *you* to play the guitar?" He patted my hand that rested between us. "Your sisters share my blood. I wanted you to share my passion so you would always know that my love for you is no different than if my blood traveled through your veins."

Papa's eyes softened. "You were the chubbiest and sweetest child, and I loved you from the start. I didn't understand how any man could walk away from his innocent baby." He glanced back at the door and whispered, "Don't tell your mama, but I wanted to be your father before I wanted to be her husband. Shh." Papa's eyes widened. "I will deny, deny, deny if you ever tell her what I said. I have to live with her while you're miles away in Nashville. You know she don't play about me."

I chuckled through my tears. "She really doesn't. I can't wait to have a man who don't play about me."

He focused on Queenie and played a few more notes. "Nathan."

I sank back on the bench. "No."

His head shot up. "Did something happen with Nathan? I really like him, and I can tell that he cares for you."

"He's my friend. Of course he cares."

"Nathan loves you because of how he takes *care* of you. He does it without thought, like an old, familiar habit. Picking up your bag before you could think about it. Grabbing your jacket and helping you put it on. He made us menfolk look bad when he fixed your plate in a house where men wait for their women to do it."

"He prefers his career," I said.

"He prefers you."

"Daddy, you don't—"

"Little girl, don't tell me what I do and don't understand. I've been on this earth longer than you. Give me some credit. I get you might downplay that man's feelings because you don't want to be hurt."

The sternness in his voice silenced my protest. My father seldom raised his voice or spoke harshly to me.

"No man drives hours to check on a woman and then spends even more hours with her family when all he wanted to do was be alone with you. I don't know if this man is in your future, but he is in your present. Whatever he needs to work out within himself to get right, he will. Mark my words."

"Okay, Papa," I replied. "I hear you."

He narrowed his gaze. "In the meantime, you'd better not wait around for him. It'll be his loss if he steps to you too late. Continue performing or taking those beautiful pictures, or whatever else your heart desires. Let marriage be the icing and not the delicious cake." He winked. "Tell Nathan I'm pulling for him whenever you speak to him again."

I kissed his stubbled cheek. "Thank you for choosing me to be your daughter."

"Thank you for choosing me to be your papa."

I picked up my guitar. "Can you guess this song?"

As I played, my family slowly filed out of the house and found a spot on the porch.

Mama responded, "'My Girl' by the Temptations."

"The first song I taught you." Papa touched his heart before he joined me on the guitar, and we all sang together. Joy spread through me as I looked at my smiling siblings and parents.

Right now, at this very moment, I was happy.

And maybe that was all any of us could expect—those rays of sun that chased away the clouds.

NINETEEN

Nathan

Two weeks had passed since the day Sophie walked out of the restaurant in Gatlinburg. True to her word, she'd texted me a few days after I left to say she'd returned to Nashville. I hadn't heard from her since. I'd messaged a couple of funny videos that reminded me of her and told her that Jake and I had a meeting with an independent film company for a new idea, possibly a story set in New Orleans. She'd hearted the message.

Each morning, without Sophie, it became harder and harder to pull myself out of the void that threatened to swallow me. My days seemed long and dull. In the expansive tapestry of life, three months wouldn't be considered a long time for any relationship by any stretch of the imagination. Yet I knew that no matter the length of the relationship, not time I would ever spend with another woman would be as meaningful.

I couldn't leave the car to walk into Jake and Amara's engagement party. He'd leased a sprawling estate in the hills of Nashville. Before Stoney Johnson's story, he would've had the party at Hartland, Evelyn's compound. Evelyn Hart had been like a grandmother to Jake, and though he didn't speak of his current relationship with her, I recognized that he had lost someone he loved dearly.

A knock on my window startled me. I looked out and rolled the window down.

"Are you ready to park?" the valet asked.

"Yeah. Just need to finish a call."

"Okay, sir. When you're ready, we'll be over there." He pointed to three other men waiting to park cars.

I looked down at my cell and scrolled through the pictures, finding the one of me and Sophie the morning she snapped our pic in Memphis. We were happy because we were having fun and had no expectations. Now I sat in my car, nervous to see her, unsure of how we would interact. Would she be my Twinkle, or would she be the woman who opened the door to her apartment back in August, reluctant and cool toward me? I prayed for the former, though the latter was what I deserved. She was right—I was afraid. Afraid that love would anchor me to one place when my soul wanted to soar. I didn't want to feel sadness, regret, or remorse every time I had the opportunity to travel. As Sophie had so aptly noted, I wanted to feel free. I didn't want any obligation to anyone except for deadlines imposed on my assignments.

I also didn't want to give up aspects of my career to be her second choice. My mind wouldn't erase the image of her woundedness caused by another man. Though she'd accused me of using Omar as an excuse not to love her, I couldn't fully shake the fact that she was still attached because they had shared love and a baby.

Her laughter tickled my ears, and I scanned the cars and guests before me. Sophie grabbed Tavion's arm while he relayed something funny. My stomach ached with longing to be the man beside her. Sooner or later, it would be a man other than her gay best friend. Perhaps she'd get her wish, and the next man she was with would become her husband.

I waited until she and Tavion entered the mansion before giving my keys to the valet, then sought out Jake as I entered the party. Soul music from the live band blasted through the crowd. The mansion was covered with balloons and streamers in the red, gold, and blue colors of their wedding. Now that I was here, I longed for home. I didn't feel up to making conversation with strangers or his family, so I would show my face and dip.

"Nate?" someone called. I glanced in the direction of the sound and smiled when I recognized my college friend, Elijah Parker, a gifted pianist, bopping his head to the music, leaning on a pillar near the door.

Grateful to see a familiar face in this throng of people, I took long strides toward him. We clasped hands and pulled in for a hug before releasing and snapping our fingers. "Who invited you?"

He flung his head back with laughter. "You asking me like you can't believe I'm here. Jake invited me. He must still not like me."

"He's always been jealous that we met and were friends first," I admitted. "Seriously, what are you doing here? You don't care for him either."

"Amara loves my music, and when she found out that I attended Tulane with Jake, she asked to meet me. She wants me to arrange the music for their wedding."

I lifted a brow. "He must want something from you too. He loves Amara, but he has something up his sleeve if you're here at his party. You still based in New Orleans?"

"Yep. You know that's my city."

Putting two and two together, I clapped my hands. "I know why he has you here. Over the last year, we've been uncovering lost musicians and amplifying their legacies."

Elijah grinned widely and pushed his locs out of his face. "Of course. Stoney Johnson and now a story on Memphis blues, right? He told me how you're writing a kickass book about the influence of music and civil rights on the city."

"Jake has talked to you a little bit." I scanned the party again and saw Jake and Amara standing beside each other in the main ballroom. A small crowd surrounded them, which had become the norm, as they were slowly becoming the latest power couple. I didn't see Sophie or Tavion, though I saw Jake's and Amara's parents sitting together at one of the many tables. I would speak to them before I left.

"He did." Elijah gestured with his empty whiskey glass toward Jake. "We only spoke for a minute. He said that he wants to talk more after the wedding. What angle are you looking at now?"

"Still working it out. Could use your help to flesh it out. Smart thinking on his part to reach out to you."

"We'll see." Elijah moved from side to side with the rhythm of the band. "Packed-out party."

"Yeah." Internally, I sighed. I needed to do better by him, too. Check on him more. Elijah didn't have the family support that Jake and I had. His music and friends were everything at one point. "How long are you in the city?"

"Until tomorrow. Got a gig in Chicago." He refocused on me. "We need to keep in touch better."

"Was just thinking that. Got to do better." We locked hands again and snapped upon release.

Jake noticed us, excused himself from the small group, and strode over.

"Be good, Jah," I warned.

"As long as he is." Elijah picked up another glass as the barmaid passed by. I quickly grabbed one too, just in case. In college, the three of us rarely hung out together. It was either Jake and me or Elijah and me. Given that they were both into music, I'd always thought they should have been the closest of friends. Instead, a rivalry for my attention had developed. I'd grown closer to Jake because we were roommates, and Elijah could be painfully self-involved.

Jake dapped me and passed me a cigar. "Why is my best man always late to my events?"

I quickly gulped my whiskey. It was already starting. He rarely told anyone or mentioned that I was his best man. "Didn't know I had to be here at a particular time, since this isn't your wedding."

"He was always on time when he was my best man." Elijah smirked. "No cigar for me?"

"Only had one for him," Jake dryly remarked.

"You want this one?" I offered, knowing full well Jake carried cigars in his inside jacket.

Elijah took it out of my hand. "Sure, he'll just give you another one once I leave." He pointed the cigar at Jake. "You petty bastard."

"And where is your lovely wife?" Jake quirked a brow, knowing that Elijah's marriage had been short-lived.

Elijah grudgingly nodded. "You won't ever change, will you?"

"I'm thirty-five. Thinking this is pretty much me." Jake indicated the opulent, decorated mansion and the abundance of food and alcohol. "Enjoying yourself?"

"Not bad." Elijah shrugged. "I've been to better."

"Woah," I intervened. One thing Jake hated was anyone insulting his parties. "Can both of you act your age?"

"I told you if he started, I would finish," Elijah retorted.

"Finish what? That drink in your hand?" Jake scoffed.

Before he could further insult Elijah, who tended to be singularly focused on music and let everything else around him fall apart, including his marriage, I signaled a timeout. "Jake, you invited him here, remember? Stop it. Did you want to ask him about the documentary we're thinking of doing in New Orleans?"

Jake twisted his mouth. "Yeah. He knows the landscape better than anyone I can think of. Amara and I will be on tour again. Maybe he can be a part of our next story."

"Why are you talking to Nate like I'm not here?" Elijah put his hand up as if to block Jake's face. "You know, he and I are like oil and water. How the fuck are we supposed to work together? Helping Amara with the music for her wedding is a one-time deal…doing a film with this dude is another story."

"That's because both of you are arrogant bastards who are more alike than different." I grasped both of their shoulders. "Let's table this discussion and speak on it after the wedding. For now, let's enjoy this expensive party."

"Fine with me. The less he and I speak, the better for me." Elijah sipped on his whiskey. "They do have some beautiful women here, like that sexy-ass woman over there next to Amara."

Jake and I followed Elijah's nod, and Jake almost choked on his drink. *Sophie.* A slick grin crossed his features as he took a puff of his cigar. "Yeah, she's something else. Go for it."

"Talk to her and I'll hand your ass to you like I did when we were sophomores," I said. Elijah had a way with women that even Jake didn't have. His bright, charming smile, creative edginess, and mad talent kept women chasing after him. The last thing Sophie needed was another musician.

"You only got the best of me because I was drunk." Elijah smirked as he continued to stare at Sophie. "She is gorgeous."

"I'm serious, leave her alone. Too many thirsty women here who'd love the company of a jazz musician." My hands balled into fists.

Jake and Elijah exchanged amused glances. I forgot that the one thing they *did* bond over was getting under my skin.

Elijah speared a piece of fried lobster using a small silver fork when a tray passed us. "She yours?"

"Nope. He won't claim her," Jake replied. "She's one of my musicians. Single and ready to mingle. You two will probably make beautiful music together and shit."

"Fuck both of you." I glared at them before Jake cracked a smile, and then the three of us broke out in laughter.

Elijah grinned. "We might just work well together." He dapped both of us. "I need to grab a drink at the bar and check out the band. Next time, Jake, call me and I'll recommend a better one. Or you can just pay me to play."

Jake grunted and continued puffing on his cigar as Elijah grooved to the music on his way to the bar.

"And stay away from Sophie," I called after him. Now I would have to stay longer to make sure he didn't try to step to her just to fuck with me.

He waved, and soon Elijah blended into the crowd.

"Why didn't you tell me you invited Jah?"

Jake pulled another Cuban out of his jacket and passed it to me. I put the cigar in my mouth, and he lit the end.

"Molasses with a hint of spice?" I asked.

"Yep." Jake nodded in the direction that Elijah had disappeared. "I wasn't sure he would come. I knew he would do anything you asked. Had to see for myself."

"That's fair. Maybe now I can have my friends getting along so I don't have to feel like I do when I'm dealing with my parents." My gaze drifted back to Sophie, gorgeous in a long-sleeved fitted red velvet dress. She didn't wear a wig and had her hair blown out, and I wondered if she'd done that purposely to get at me, since she knew I preferred it when she wore her hair that way.

"Stop with the long face. It's your fault you didn't come here with her," Jake said. "I told you to leave her alone, but you didn't listen. Now I have to be way over here with you instead of with Amara because she's talking to Sophie. I'm not ready to start splitting friends."

I dropped my forehead briefly on his shoulder and lamented, "She said we could be friends. Why isn't she acting like it? She hasn't reached out to me at all, and when I ask to hang out, she politely declines. If the roles were reversed, I would still be her friend."

"Give her time. Sophie doesn't stay mad long. She'll come around. Meanwhile, have fun. Maybe meet a new woman with no strings. Plenty here. It's my engagement party. Smile."

Holding my fist for him to dap, I said, "My bad. This is your night. I'm happy for you and Mari. Go ahead—I'm going to roam for a while."

"We good. Enjoy." Jake wandered off, smiling and talking to his guests.

Two hours into the party, I still couldn't drag my eyes away from Sophie longer than a moment, no matter whom I conversed with. She had to feel my stare, though she never glanced my way. She looked like the old Sophie, the reason Twinkle became my nickname for her—dancing, smiling brightly, and having a good time. She seemed happy.

I just wanted her to be that way around me.

Even when Jake and Amara gave speeches and introduced us as the best man and maid of honor to an approving crowd, she smiled politely at me like we were strangers.

Before she could step down from the raised stage area where the band and DJ were located, I gently grabbed her elbow. "Can I have a moment?"

Sophie turned slightly, the lines around her mouth tight. "Sure. What's up?"

"We haven't spoken all night."

"At any point, you could've walked over. I thought you were friends with everyone I've been hanging out with tonight. It would've been cool." She looked at me rather impatiently. "You're the one making this more than what it is, acting like I have beef with you, and I don't. I kept my word to you. I let you know I was back. Whenever you text, I respond. I heart your posts or your funny memes. What more should I be doing? Before Memphis, we only hung out as a group. I thought we were being the friends we once were."

When I only stared back, helpless to contradict the truth, Sophie tapped my chest lightly. "You look good in your suit. There are plenty of women here who don't mind temporary. Take it easy, Nathan."

She sauntered away from me and joined Domino on the dance floor. They smiled at each other as they grooved together. I jammed my hands in my pockets to keep myself from grabbing her up, sneaking into one of these rooms, and reminding her of how amazing we were together. But what good would that do when nothing had changed except I missed her?

I strode to Amara and Jake, sitting together at their special table in the center of the ballroom, murmuring. I stood behind them and leaned down to hug them both. "I'm about to head out."

Amara kissed my cheek. "I haven't spoken to you all night, and you're about to leave?"

"Yeah. I've been circulating."

She looked up at me. "We need to talk. I've read the latest version of *The Lost Souls of Memphis Blues*, and I have an idea."

Jake tapped my forearm. "We can talk business tomorrow. I have a surprise. You can't leave yet."

She frowned. "What surprise? Jake, what did you do?"

He rose and held his arm out for Amara to take. "Come on."

"I guess we're both about to be surprised," I said. "He didn't tell me either."

She rolled her eyes hard, though I still detected the love for Jake. They were committed to each other despite any differences. For once, I envied that Jake had Amara for as long as they both lived.

I glumly followed them outside to the back lawn lit with tiny white lights and heated with lamps to fight off the November night air. Taking the hosts' lead, the party moved outside, and people started dancing and mingling. I searched for the surprise, assuming it was a large gift.

I nudged Amara's shoulder. "Was the surprise coming outside?"

She smiled. "Maybe he wasn't ready for you to leave."

Jake was on his phone on the other side of me. When I gestured toward the door, he held up one finger.

Then a large boom erupted over the night, and people squealed.

Startled, I covered my ears, lowering myself closer to the ground as I immediately searched for Sophie.

"Hey, you good?" Jake's voice dripped with concern from above.

I gawked at the sky, trying to make sense of what was happening. Colorful lights sprinkled the air. Fireworks.

"What just happened?" Jake pulled me up carefully by the elbow. Amara and a few curious people looked at me with worried expressions. Most were captivated by the lit-up sky.

"Nothing… Um…I need to find Sophie. This was fun. I'll call you later." I walked briskly away to avoid answering any more questions, because I needed to touch Sophie to ensure she was still here. I scanned the lawn and marched toward where she gleefully pointed up at the fireworks with Tavion and Domino, standing slightly apart from the crowd.

"We need to talk." I didn't wait for a response and gripped her hand, pulling her away from her friends.

"Hey," she protested, tugging against my grip. "Ta, Domino, you're going to let him snatch me away?"

A smiling Domino shrugged, and Tavion waved. "Bye. She's been dragging for you the whole night. Might as well tell him to his face."

"Such a traitor." She stuck her middle finger at him as I walked toward the front.

"Love you too." He laughed behind me. "You better get your woman."

His taunt and her irritation barely registered. Fireworks were my worst trigger. I had to escape, and my irrational need to protect Sophie wouldn't allow me to leave without her.

"Nathan, I'm serious. You can't jerk me around. You made it clear where you stand, and I accept it."

I glanced over my shoulder at her displeased face. "Then if you accept it, why are you cold toward me? Don't pretend that this is normal for us."

"Give me a little bit more time." She tried to pull away, and I only held tighter. "I'm not ready to go, Nate, and I don't feel like talking when nothing has changed."

I jerked her into my chest and gazed down into her beautiful face. "I need you."

Sophie assessed my eyes and finally relented, allowing me to lead her.

Another boom, followed by multiple shots. *Afghanistan.* The suicide bomber who'd self-destructed near me. I cringed, though I kept walking.

Sophie leaned into me. "Hey, you okay?"

I shook my head, trying to fight the overwhelming panic.

"Where are we going?"

"Anywhere but here. I hate fireworks."

An explosion and more scattered pops. *The Sudan.* A bomb had landed several feet from me.

"Ouch. You're hurting my hand."

"Sorry. Sorry." I loosened my hold and meandered through the multitude of cars, looking for mine. Then I remembered a valet had parked my car. "I need a valet."

"Hey, we can take mine. I parked my own car," she calmly suggested.

"No." I needed familiar.

"It's right here. I don't think you can take much more." When I resisted, she reassured me, "It's okay, please." She opened the passenger door. "Get in. We can go to your place."

"Your place is fine." I slumped down in her car, still reeling from the flashbacks. I practiced breathing and squeezing my thighs with my hands to stay in the present and not drift to the past, like my old therapist told me.

When she'd parked in her garage, Sophie turned to face me. "Are you going to tell me what happened back there?"

Wiping the moisture from my brow, I asked, "Can we go inside?"

"Only if you're finally telling me what's with the nightmares and the sweating. Like right now, your shirt is sticking to you in November."

"Yes. I just don't want to sit in this little-ass Porsche for too much longer. I drive an SUV for a reason."

She unlocked the doors, and as I'd always done, I hurried to her side to open her door. Sophie's eyes softened.

We entered through the side door of her apartment, and a hurricane must have blown through here. Papers and photos were scattered throughout the room and covered the table. I chuckled. "Well, at least I know you're just messy and not depressed."

She planted her hands on her hips. "Keep talking about my place, and you'll be catching an Uber right out of here."

"Fine. Fine." I snuck a kiss on her neck. "I missed you. Like, so fucking much."

She grudgingly replied, "Me too," then flopped down on the sofa and pulled me down beside her. "Look, I'm here as your friend, like you have been for me. Talk."

I rested my head back on the sofa. "Never had to say it aloud except with my old therapist. Kind of how hard it was for you to talk about... Well, you know." I whistled in frustration when words kept getting caught in my throat.

She cradled my hand. "Take your time."

Ruefully, I shook my head. "You're such a good woman. A good person. Jake was right. I shouldn't have ever stepped to you. I was selfish and I'm sorry."

"I don't have regrets, Nathan. You told me to learn something from every man, and that Omar may not be my last heartbreak. You were right."

I lifted my shoulders and dropped them with a loud sigh. "Still, I should've been a real friend and not gotten you all caught up."

She squeezed my hand tightly. "Nate, stop avoiding what you really need to say. I'm good. I'll meet a man perfect for me in time. Can we please stop rehashing us? You don't want to be with me. I've got it and am moving on."

"I want to be with you. I just..." I rubbed my head.

"Nathan Price, if you don't tell me what wakes you up in a cold sweat and makes you afraid when you hear fireworks, I swear to God, I'll slap the shit out of you." Her warmth and concern for me tempered her angry words.

"I don't think you should curse and use God's name in the same sentence," I teased, then blocked my head with my arms, anticipating her licks that never came. "All right...all right. I'll talk."

Suddenly, telling her about the violence I'd witnessed in the last twelve years poured out of me.

TWENTY

Sophie

The crying of the baby next door awakened me. I slowly opened my eyes to the dawn light, expecting the accompanying ache that usually followed that sound. Two months after I miscarried, my lucky neighbors had brought their infant home. I often woke up, confusing the wailing with the dreams of my own baby. Grief had paralyzed me for weeks. I was mad at God and the world for stealing my joy and then teasing me through my very own walls. I became attuned to the sounds of my neighbors, hoping and scared to hear their baby.

Once Nathan knocked on my door in August, I'd no longer heard the cries. My focus had become the Memphis project and him.

I turned my head and watched him sleep through the cries, and his buzzing phone on the bedside table. His back faced me as he continued to sleep, probably emotionally spent after confiding in me. He'd rested his head on my shoulder while he shared some of the horrors he'd experienced. Nathan didn't go into details but relayed enough of what he'd seen for me to marvel at how he even functioned normally without being paranoid about people and places. We'd retired to my bed a little after midnight. He'd stripped to his boxer briefs and his undershirt, and I'd worn baggy pajamas when we preferred being nude. It was also the first time we'd slept in the same bed and didn't have sex. Ironically, in our attempt to avoid being intimate, we'd seemed more like a real couple.

I eased out of bed, closed the door, padded to my chaise longue, and picked up Princess. I needed my instrument to help me process that I no longer felt pain from simply hearing the baby next door. Hitting a few notes that soon formed a melody, I smiled. Mornings were beginning to be my favorite time of day again.

"Nice. Is it yours?" Nathan, wearing the shirt and slacks from last night, walked out of my bedroom. He hadn't donned his glasses nor brushed his hair yet, giving him a rugged look that I found extremely attractive.

"Yeah." I continued to play. "Your phone has been ringing."

He looked back toward the bedroom. "It's Jake. Probably pissed because I left early. Weren't we supposed to do a speech or something?"

"I hope not, because Mari will be mad at me too."

Nathan walked to my refrigerator and grabbed a bottle of water before he plopped on the barstool, listening to me play. He closed his eyes and smiled contentedly.

I stopped playing and quietly asked, "Why haven't you told Jake about what you went through?'

"He knows some of it. I've never told him how it affected me." Nathan opened his eyes to look at me. "I didn't tell him for the same reason you didn't tell Amara about your miscarriage. We didn't want them to worry about us."

"And they're supposed to be our best friends." Reclining back on the chaise longue, I stared up at the ceiling. "The funny thing is, I believe Mari would share anything with me."

"Jake definitely has shared more with me than I have with him." He wryly chuckled.

"We're both pieces of work, you know that?" I rested my arms over Princess. "I told her everything once I returned home. It was good for me." I softly admitted, "You were right about trying to keep this façade up about being happy when there were times I really wasn't."

Amara had cried with me when I confided in her, and instead of being mad that I'd kept the miscarriage a secret, she'd empathized and told me she might have made a similar decision. We were tighter than we'd ever been, spending more and more time together as her wedding neared.

He moved closer to me. "Listen, I didn't handle Gatlinburg right."

I waved my hand. "You don't owe me anything, Nate. You brought music back to me. You opened my eyes to photography and helped me through the worst time of my life."

"I only came in at the end. You'd done a lot of the work. I just came around at the right time."

I placed my guitar beside me and reached for him. He bent down to hug me, lifting me enough to replace me on my lounge and pulling me on top of him. I protested, "Hey -"

"Hey." He brushed back the tendrils that fell over my face. "I am in love with you."

As much as my heart sang at his declaration, I could hear the silent *but*.

My cell rang, and I could see the screen from where my phone lay on the sofa. "It's Mari. Let me answer. We did leave abruptly, and they might be genuinely worried about us."

Nathan nodded and dropped his hand. I eased from beneath him, saved by a ringing phone, unprepared for whatever followed his declaration of love.

"Morning," I said brightly when I answered.

"Good morning. You sound breathless." Amara giggled.

"No, I don't." I rolled my eyes and walked back to the chair where he'd scooted over so I could lie beside him. "Stop fishing. Yes, I'm with Nate. And no, we're not a couple."

"A matter of time," she said firmly. "He was like a lovesick puppy last night."

Blushing, I quickly informed her. "He's sitting right here and can hear you."

"I can, and I was a mess," he said. "Morning, Mari. Tell Jake I'm good. He's been trying to call me too."

Amara replied, "Well, I'm glad the two of you are together."

"We're not together," I repeated. "This is why I didn't want you and Jake in my business. He needed a friend, and I was there for him. We've made up."

"I was never mad," Nathan chimed in. "She was the evil one."

I popped his shoulder, and he yelled loudly before grinning devilishly at me. I did love him. But love also meant accepting a person for who they were. He'd never lied to me, and had been there for me. After knowing what he'd been through, I understood even more why it was hard for him to settle down with a woman who would undoubtedly worry about him. Nathan loved adventure, searching for the truth, and helping others. He'd grown up in a military household on bases worldwide where danger lurked. Storms and pain were his norm. Mine was sunshine and joy.

"You know, that really hurt." Nathan rubbed his shoulder.

"That's what you get," I retorted, and returned my attention to the phone while Nathan grabbed me in a headlock. "Quit it."

"Do I need to call you back? Sounds like he still needs you." Amara laughed.

I groaned and stopped resisting him to lay my head on his chest. "Naw, I'm listening…we're both listening. You're on speaker."

"I've been reading the notes from Memphis about Ms. Claudette. I think I need to pay her a visit and talk to her myself. She's the story."

"It's what I keep telling Sophie," Nathan added enthusiastically.

"She's a part of the story. We can't put all our eggs in a basket with a big hole at the bottom," I insisted. "You know I like Ms. Claudette. In a lot of ways, she reminds me of me."

Amara continued, "The video you posted of her cooking Sunday dinner and humming went viral. She believes no one wants to see her perform. I know otherwise. I just have to convince her. Correction, *we* must convince her to sing one more time."

"Jake too?" Nathan asked. "You know he can charm the rattle off a snake."

"Says the man who had Ms. Claudette wishing she were ten years younger." I smiled at a now-red-faced Nathan. "Mari, that woman would have had his babies if she could. He just didn't want to push her to talk in front of me. You weren't there. She was visibly upset and shut down on us. I have pictures I never showed you."

"It was because she got spooked. A little more coaxing and she would have told us everything," Nathan said. "I think a visit from her old friend's granddaughter might do the trick."

"Good. Glad we're on the same page," Amara replied. "Just call her for me or her daughter and tell them about the viral video and that I want to meet the woman who wrote with my grandfather. I'll keep Jake at the hotel while we meet with her. Sometimes he can come on too strong when he sees talent, and he wants her to be the focal point too. We don't want to scare her away."

Nathan and I smiled in agreement about Jake's tendency to be bullish and persistent when he was pursuing talent. Then Nathan tapped my back and whispered, "Where are those pictures?"

Pointing to the coffee table, I shifted so he could get up. "All right. I'll call her back and set up something. Send me your schedule and we'll make it happen." I hung up the phone and joined him on the sofa.

Nathan picked up the scattered photos and began placing them in neat rows. "This is crazy…that none of these pictures made the cut when all are so good." He whistled in admiration and pointed to a picture of Annie looking at her mother. "This one right here. See the wistfulness in her expression that you caught perfectly? She wants to be a badass like Ms. Claudette. There's a story that she knows her mother is hiding."

"Or maybe she just wished she could've known the performer her mother was? I know that's what Mari misses the most about her grandfather. Never seeing him play." I straightened another picture on my table, then asked Nathan a question that nagged in the recesses of my mind: "Did you ask me to be a part of this project because you wanted me to see myself in these musicians?"

He looked up from the table. "No. I didn't know you'd given up music when I first approached you, remember? Once you told me, I did hope Memphis would remind you of your greatness. And I can see that it did. The blues fit you." He nudged my knee with his. "Talk to Jake."

I gathered three pictures that had fallen on the rug. "About what? I don't know if I want a musical career."

He held up a photo of us from that first night at B.B. King's restaurant. "Maybe you don't want a career like Amara's, but you do want to be recognized for your talent. Ms. Claudette is you forty years down the line with unrecorded songs. Trust me, you'll regret not at least seeing what Jake can do for you. Maybe he didn't see you because you didn't want him to. Show him now."

"All right, I'll talk to him once we get back from Memphis," I agreed, mostly to avoid an argument. I still wasn't quite ready to approach Jake. Looping my arm around Nathan's neck, I pulled his attention to me and gazed into his brown eyes. "Thank you for everything."

For almost three months, I'd woken up to this face—the sexy almond eyes, the broad nose, and this treacherous mouth that had indulged on my body. Melancholy assailed me, and I pressed my lips to his lightly. He slid his arm around my waist, and the imprint from his growing desire became visible. I murmured, "I've missed and will miss this part of us the most. How being intimate with you felt so natural and easy. Right."

Nathan groaned. "I can tell where this conversation will end. Just stop." He cradled my face in his hands. "You think this is easier on me than it is on you. And it's so fucking not, especially when I know being with you is mostly on me. You make me happy in ways I never imagined. I love you, Twinkle. I was halfway in love before we ever went to Memphis, and I couldn't resist being with you. It was selfish of me when I'm not ready to be in one place yet, like you need me to be." The corners of his lips drooped. "I've been invited to L.A. for a while to work with the documentary's director and network with some people who want to help me start my music magazine. I would love for you to come with me and be my photographer. We make a great team, and we can see if commitment works for us. It's what I wanted to ask you that night we saw Omar."

Pressing my hand to slow my rapidly beating heart, I digested what he was asking of me. My stomach twisted painfully in knots as he awaited my answer.

He gestured to the pictures. "You told me that you're more than music. Then come with me to L.A. What do you have to lose?"

"Everything." I spread my arms out. "I'm still figuring out my life, Nate. You just told me to talk to Jake. This is where he's based. This is my home, and Nashville is close to my family. Why can't you stay here and fly back and forth?"

"Because I don't want long distance to be our norm. I want you in my bed every night," he said, his voice ragged with frustration and love for me.

Silence dragged between us.

His eyes pleaded for me to agree. To settle. Stubbornness and fear catching the joy of being with him that threatened to slip through my lips.

"Why torture ourselves more, Nate, when you don't want forever?"

When he didn't contradict me, I shoved down the sadness that threatened to overtake me. I didn't want to waste any more tears on men who weren't meant for me.

I rose from the sofa. "I think it's time for you to go. Y'all don't need me in Memphis anyway."

Nathan tugged on my wrist. "We do need you. *I* need you. At least come with me to Memphis. Let's not end like this."

"There was nothing to end," I replied. "The worst thing that could have ever happened to me already did. So go ahead and do you. I'm good."

His eyes were sad, and he cursed under his breath before standing up and gripping my hands. "What do you want me to do to make it better?"

"I told you that I'm good."

"No, you're not. I'm not either." He kissed my hand. "Let's be different and go to Memphis to celebrate that we found each other when we most needed each other. If you believe there was nothing to end, then why can't we have a little more time?"

"Because it feels like I'm getting the short end of the stick once again."

Nathan's brow scrunched together, and his eyes darkened. "If that's how you feel, then you're right, I do need to leave now. I have never used you and never will."

An exasperated sigh escaped my lips. "I didn't say you used me."

"Then what the fuck does 'short end of the stick' mean in your world?"

"Everything is going just like you planned," I reminded him. "You never wanted a relationship. Your career is on the up and up. Soon, you won't think about me. Meanwhile, I'm still here trying to figure out my life without you."

Nathan looked back at my table full of photos. "These are gorgeous. Your voice is flawless. There's really nothing to figure out."

"Ugh. There we go again with you believing you have the right to tell me anything about my life."

He squeezed my hands. "I do because I'm your friend. Just like you read me correctly the last time I saw you in Gatlinburg, I'm doing it to you. I asked you to be my photojournalist and girlfriend. You only told me no because you're scared to try something new. Scared to take a risk on me. Just like you're scared to tell Jake you want a shot, too. You can do it all. Or you can try something completely new. Just don't stay stuck like you've been." He tilted his head. "And I'm always there for you, however you want me to be while you work it all out."

"What's the point of a relationship with you if you don't want forever?"

"And how do you know you want forever with me when you haven't given us a real shot at now?" He released my hands. "I better go, because I know you hate to be wrong. I'll wait for my ride outside, call you later about Memphis, and work out the details."

I resisted folding my arms like I so desperately wanted to do. "I never agreed to go."

Nathan grinned. "You have to go to stop me from making a fool out of myself around Ms. Claudette. If she cooks for me again, I might just move in with her, happy to be her boy toy."

A smile tugged at my lips before I could stop myself. I wagged my finger. "Even if I go, it doesn't mean I'm sleeping with you again."

"Oh, good thing sleeping isn't all we did." He stole a kiss and backed away before I could hit him. "We're going to Memphis with our best friends—let's just have fun. We did the hard work, and now it's time to enjoy the city. Come on, Twinkle." Nathan danced by himself and spun around. "One more time before you let me down gently for the hundredth time."

"Fine. I swear you're worse than Jake." I did miss just being with him when it had been simple and easy. One last weekend with him wouldn't hurt any worse.

"Yes." He pumped his fist before he touched the doorknob. "For the record, I'll always love you even if we don't end up together." His smile vanished. "I'm hoping you'll give us a real shot."

I walked to him, slid my arms under his, and melted into his comforting embrace. I wasn't ready to tell him that my vision of happiness was slowly morphing into something different—something I couldn't yet touch or see, yet I knew it would happen, and that gave me hope.

TWENTY-ONE

Nathan

Cold air struck my face as I adjusted the earmuffs. I looked ahead at the paper targets at varying distances while Jake finished a call. We were at an outside shooting range, spending a rare moment with just the two of us. He had rented out the entire area for two hours so we could talk and shoot.

"I promise not to take any other calls." Jake slid his cell into his cargo pants. "So what's up with you and Sophie?" He picked up his earmuffs. "Y'all good?"

We bumped fists before loading our array of guns that the ammunition specialist had set out.

"I love her." I smiled as I finally announced my feelings to someone other than Sophie. Telling Jake validated that my love for her was real.

His forehead wrinkled before he relaxed into a grin. "Finally."

"Not finally. We're still not together." I grabbed a loaded magazine.

He pulled his baseball cap down further on his head. "Why not? You're just going to L.A. She can come with you."

"I asked her. She's been hurt, Jake, and isn't ready to leave here. At least not with me. Hell, I might be her rebound and the guy who helped her heal for the next man. End of our story." It'd been more than twenty-four hours, and Sophie still hadn't reached out to me except to agree to travel with Amara and Jake this weekend. Memphis could be our swan song.

He sucked his teeth. "It sounds like *you* don't want to be hurt."

"I don't. I'll be in Los Angeles for a few months, except for your wedding. Space might help her figure out if she's really in love, too."

"Bruh, that woman loves you." Jake adjusted his earmuffs and blew out air that formed puffs of steam in the cold.

"I've told her twice now and she hasn't said it to me." Her reluctance to tell me she loved me had fucked with me. Did it mean that she wasn't sure? Or that she still loved Omar?

"Maybe because she's protecting her heart. We all know you love to roam the world." He picked up a box of cartridges. "Do you want a future with her?"

A vision of waking up to a pregnant and glowing Sophie evoked a peaceful contentment. The selfish part of me wished she hadn't taken that Plan B.

"I do. Not sure if I'm ready for marriage. But I want to be in a relationship with her, and if it progresses to that, it does." I grasped the gun's grip with both hands and pulled the trigger, firing off six shots at the cardboard person. All six hit the head.

Jake whistled. "I forget how good a shot you are.'

"Hazard of being the son of a soldier and hanging in these mean streets."

"Shit. Remind me to hire you for Mari's security." He then proceeded to shoot. Two hit outside the head, and the other four hit the chest. "Why are you so against marriage? As you pointed out, you've been a fairer man to women than I was. Being monogamous has never seemed like an issue for you."

"For so many years, I've been the temporary guy. It's the record I play in my head and what I tell any woman who wants to date me. Maybe it's because my parents didn't have the best marriage, or maybe I just don't want to be responsible for anyone but myself for my career. Yet these months with her have been the best time I've ever had. Sophie made me *feel* again. I'd been numb for so long. All I want to do is be there for her…to care for her. I don't know. She has made me reconsider everything. Period."

Jake aimed his gun at the target and then lowered it. "Then tell her you're open to marriage too."

"I don't know if I'm quite there. Besides, I'm not what she needs right now. *You're* who she needs right now."

"Why?" He shot once and struck right next to where the ear would be.

"Friend to friend"—I took a deep breath—"be honest. Do you think that Sophie has what it takes to have a career as a solo singer?"

"Does she *want* that type of career?"

"The woman used to perform all around Nashville. What do you think?"

Jake frowned. "She always told me she preferred the background. Likes being a part of The Crew." He tilted his head. "Or she did until this year."

I refrained from sighing. "You still haven't answered me. Does she have what it takes?"

"She does." He nodded slowly. "Is that why she doesn't want to be a part of The Crew anymore?"

Relief I hadn't expected to feel eased my constricted lungs. "No. Or maybe partly. She needs to know you believe in her."

He placed his gun down and turned to face me. "I believe in anyone who works for me."

I pushed the earmuffs down around my neck to hear him clearly. "Yes, you do. But when Amara entered the picture, no one else mattered, making Sophie doubt her talent."

"Why? She knows she's always the first I call whenever I need a vocalist or guitarist."

"That's exactly the point. You're persistent when you believe in someone's talent. You were never persistent with her. You only envisioned her one way. Working on this Memphis project woke something up inside Sophie. She wants more than she used to. Marriage and family may not be her priority anymore. At least, not now."

Jake rubbed his goatee. "Did she tell you to talk to me?"

Placing the earmuffs back on, I picked up my gun again. "No. I'm afraid she won't do it herself. Just wanted you to know."

"Got it." He lifted his gun and shot multiple times, landing most of the shots. "You done with the dangerous stories? Which better be the case, because you can't keep going around scared of any loud boom."

"I can handle it if I know." I removed my earmuffs again and shot a round at a target further away. "See, I can handle it. It's the *unexpected* loud noises, and that fireworks sound like bombs exploding, which trigger me. I avoid them at all costs."

Jake indignantly jerked his head. "How was I supposed to know that if you never told me? I didn't have to have fireworks, or I could have told you so you were prepared."

"I know. I know."

Jake grunted. We both picked up our guns and shot more rounds. He yelled in victory when two of his shots finally hit the head.

Picking up a 9mm Glock, I fired too.

Jake squinted to see what I'd hit in the distance. "Fuck you."

I chuckled. "You can't stand when I win."

"Nope. I can't." He looked at me and pushed off his earmuffs. "The other night, it wasn't just that you ducked. You were scared. We've been friends too long for you to not tell me how the shit you've been through affected you."

Telling Sophie first made it exponentially easier to speak to Jake.

I rested my knuckles on the table and explained, "I was tired of all the violence and death around me. Tired of the nightmares, always looking over my shoulder, and jumping anytime I heard a loud noise, believing that I was the next to die. I don't like to think about the things I witnessed, so I don't want to discuss them. People can be so diabolical in ways you can't imagine."

"Why didn't you tell me you were going through all that? I knew you'd seen some rough shit. You always seemed like you were okay."

"I'm good most days, and then something will trigger me. Memphis affected me more than I imagined it would. Seeing and remembering the pain of our ancestors, parents, and grandparents affected me more than I realized. Working on Stoney's story didn't prepare me for the emotions I've felt since we started this project. Stoney just unleashed so many untold stories. His legacy might have been stolen because of love, or maybe it was racism, or both. But the undercurrent and overtness of racism permeates all the other stories."

Jake tapped the table in understanding.

"I studied wars on the streets of Chicago, L.A., and in Somalia and the Congo. We talk about the civil war to end slavery, but we never talk about the civil war between Blacks and whites during our fight for equality. Just because we never labeled the civil rights era a war, trust me, it was one, and I'm still not sure who won." I picked up a Desert Eagle and aimed. "Been in therapy, learned some strategies, and I'm better now. No worries."

"Therapy?" Jake placed his gun down. "You've been going through all this and still wouldn't have told me if we weren't having this conversation. You scared me the other night. I didn't know what the hell was happening. You're ducking like you heard guns, visibly shaken, and then you run off with Sophie during my party without any explanation. I thought we were boys."

Releasing a long sigh, I quipped, "Whose idea was it to have this conversation at a shooting range?" When he folded his arms, I explained, "You've always seemed invincible to me. Never thought you would be hurt at my omission that I have PTSD." His scowl grew deeper. "I was embarrassed, okay? My father has seen much more shit than I ever have, and he's good. I hate that I can't control when I have these nightmares or the intrusive thoughts of people hurt and dying. I don't like talking about it, and I never wanted anyone to know. Sophie only found out because I had a nightmare while we were in bed together, and she saw how I reacted at your party. She helped me through it."

"Naw…not good enough." Jake backed up. "I don't think I've kept anything from you, and you would've kept Sophie a secret, too. Now I find out she wants to be a solo singer. What do I do to make people I love believe they can't be honest with me?"

My shoulders sagged at the hurt he didn't bother to hide. "It's not about you, Jake."

"Agree to disagree," he retorted.

I stared at my best friend since college. "Sometimes it's not easy being your friend. It's hard to admit to you that I have problems. Everything just seems to work out for you. Money has never been an issue. Women throw themselves at you. Evelyn Hart's scandal didn't even impact your business. You remind me of a benevolent king deciding who's worthy of you. One mistake and I'm out of your kingdom. I didn't want to seem weak to you. I used to feel so lucky in college that you chose me to be your friend, and I never wanted to lose that."

Jake poked my chest. "Did it ever occur to you that I felt like the lucky one? You were already friends with Elijah. You didn't need me. You've always been levelheaded, even when you decided that risking your life for the greater cause was your path. I envied you because your father raised you, and you knew what it meant to be upright and good. No matter what I did, I had a void that I couldn't fill. Before Amara, you know, I was a wreck. Drunk all the time and not giving a fuck. And that was before I discovered my stepfather, the only man I claimed as a father, used me to give hush money to another Black man."

My chest ached at the raw pain in his voice and the unshed tears.

"He and I are still trying to work through that shit. I haven't spoken to Miss Evelyn in months, and she was like my grandmother. I'm about to get married. I need you in my corner more than ever. I need to know I can rely on you to be truthful even when it's downright painful." He spread his arms. "I'm telling you now, before nature and God, if I ever find out you kept something else from me that directly involves you or me, then you get the fuck on."

I blew out a puff of steam before announcing, "Right before I came out here this morning, I was asked to interview a former teenage gang leader in Haiti who wants asylum in the U.S."

"What?" Jake dropped his arms. "I thought you were tired of all the violence?"

"I am." I stepped closer to him. "I haven't gotten all the details yet. Maybe he's being kept in a safe house, since he could connect with the U.S., so I won't be in danger. I'll make sure it doesn't impact our documentary or your wedding. This could be the piece that hits it out of the park." I slapped my palm with the back of my hand.

He studied my face for what felt like a long time. "I can tell you're already considering it. Doesn't matter that you now have a community of people here who love you, especially Sophie. But I can't be mad. You are who you are. Now I understand why you didn't fight for her more."

Jake donned his earmuffs and started shooting again.

His cool dismissal of me stung. I stood there, unsure what to say or do. No one had seemed to care what I did or how I chose to live my life before

I moved to Nashville. Jake had said his piece and would still be my friend through his disappointment. Would Sophie?

I dropped my head briefly before picking up a gun. I fired until the sadness that I hadn't fought harder to be with Sophie dissipated like the puffs of cold air I breathed.

TWENTY-TWO

Sophie

This time when we drove up, Claudette Saint awaited on her porch. She had her hair freshly done, and was dressed in probably her Sunday best. Amara, rocking a turtleneck, jeggings, and expensive boots, strode up the pathway like the star she'd become and greeted her with a warm hug.

Ms. Claudette teared up. "You look like him when he was around your age. Just as beautiful as he was handsome."

"Thank you. They say I sound like him, too." Amara hugged her again. "Thank you for allowing us to come back."

Claudette turned to me and Nathan. "I'd hoped you'd give me another chance. I didn't like how I behaved the last time I saw you. I apologize."

Nathan hugged her and kissed her cheek. "We were only respecting your wishes. And we still want to respect whatever you decide after today."

She grinned at me. "He gives strong hugs. I warned you last time about him."

I smiled and leaned my head on his shoulder. "He does give very nice hugs. I have heeded your warning and take it *very* seriously."

Nathan squeezed my side. "How lucky can a man be to have two beautiful women willing to fight over me?"

Laughing, we all moved inside, and this time, Ms. Claudette chose the living area. She sat between Nathan and Amara on the sofa. I lifted the

Canon and alternated between taking pictures and recording video. I'd been practicing since I was in Gatlinburg and could use the camera with ease. Annie supported her mother from the recliner, clasping her hands near her mouth as if she were praying the entire time.

Ms. Claudette turned to Nathan. "Thank you for allowing me to read your manuscript to understand better how you want to use my story. I couldn't put it down. I laughed, cried, and recognized places and many musicians I'd forgotten about. You represented Memphis well."

"Thank you. That means a lot coming from you." Nathan bowed his head briefly.

He hadn't told me he'd decided to give her the manuscript. Nathan was very sensitive about his writing, yet he'd trusted Ms. Claudette with his words and guessed right that she needed to read what he'd already written to ease her mind and cultivate a safe environment.

Amara turned toward her. "I didn't know my grandfather until after his death. I found out that we were kindred spirits and that he was the one who taught me how to play the guitar when I was a little girl. We're discovering that he was a prolific songwriter, and finding all that he composed is like putting more and more puzzle pieces together. It's okay if you tell us you found the songs since the last time they visited. No one will judge you for wanting to hold on to them, since you wrote them together. We only want a copy of the lyrics and music, and we will pay you for them." She glanced at me, and I nodded. "I understand you might have two songs you wrote with my grandfather?"

"It's three, and I know where they are. My life was threatened by racist white men at the time, and I've been afraid all these years to say I had the third one," Ms. Claudette admitted shyly. Her daughter gasped.

Nathan and I locked eyes. He quickly twisted his lips to hide his triumphant smile, and I raised a sardonic brow. *Fine. You were right, Mr. Price.*

Annie reached for Ms. Claudette's hand. "I'm so sorry, Mama."

Nathan scooted to the edge of the sofa. "I would like to know what happened with those men, if you don't mind. I won't use your name or likeness for your protection. I have had to protect people before from dangerous people. I can do it again. For you."

Ms. Claudette nodded and started rocking. Nathan beckoned to Annie and switched places so she could comfort her mother. When Ms. Claudette remained tight-lipped, he suggested, "Let me ask you questions to guide you. Would that be okay?"

Annie placed her arm around her mother's shoulders. "We won't let anyone hurt you anymore."

"No, we won't," Nathan reassured them. "But if you keep the truth that has been attacking your soul little by little for the last fifty years, you will never truly be free, and those sons of bitches continue to win."

"*Nate*," I said, pulling the camera away from my face.

Ms. Claudette chuckled through her tears. "They *were* son of bitches, and I'm tired of being afraid."

"Yeah, they were," Nathan said. "We're about to expose them and show them you couldn't be broken. Can we do this, Ms. Claudette?"

She took a deep breath and lifted her chin. "Ask away."

Nathan picked up his notepad. "Were those songs about the civil rights movement?"

"Two were love stories that Stoney and I wrote together. The third song that my daughter didn't know about was a song about the ongoing lynching and Jim Crow here in Memphis. I first met Stoney when we were at the Mason Temple listening to Dr. King speak the night before he was assassinated. We stood next to each other with tears falling down our faces. So many of us cried at being in the presence of someone so dynamic." She looked straight ahead, past my lens. "I chose to move here as a teenager because I loved the blues and believed in our civil liberties. I was a fighter, willing to die to end segregation. My parents worried about me because I was always outspoken about racial injustice."

Her brown eyes glistened with her pride and strength. *Poise* had become her middle name, with her ramrod posture and hands primly clasped on her lap.

"A fan of Ida B. Wells, I wanted to be close to the ongoing movement. Anytime there was a protest, I was there. Moved here at the end of 1967. Went wild with anger like everyone else and was a part of the short-lived riot in Memphis in protest of Dr. King's death. The National Guard was already on alert because of the last time Dr. King had been in town, a few days prior, due to a fight that broke out during a march for the sanitation workers, and a Black teenager had died. My parents begged me to come back home, and I refused." Ms. Claudette smiled at her daughter. "You would've been so proud of me. I was this young, fearless warrior."

"I've always been proud of you," her daughter said.

"Not how I would've wanted you to be proud of me," Ms. Claudette retorted.

Nathan asked, "Did you and Stoney write the song around the time of the assassination?"

"No. We were standing next to each other, excited about seeing Dr. King speak, and we started talking. We were both singers, though he had more clout, since he was from Memphis. He promised to help me. I ran into him maybe three years later. Funny that, as small as Memphis was, we didn't see each other. I had started working with Stax Records in the studio, and they sent me to Wattstax in 1972." Her smile grew wider. "Being around thousands of beautiful Black people and all the celebrities, proud and unafraid of our heritage and our skin, I became inspired to write a freedom song. Richard Pryor, hearing Reverend Jesse Jackson speak, the Staples sisters, and of course, we were all there for Isaac Hayes. It was also his birthday, and we were all clowning with him. For us Black folks back then, we didn't get to be all together like that, just celebrating ourselves. I ran into Stoney there and asked him to help me write a song once we returned to Memphis."

"My granddad was at Wattstax?" Amara asked, her tone a mixture of awe and curiosity. Wattstax was a benefit concert in Los Angeles organized by Stax Records to mark the seventh anniversary of the Watts Riot. At the time, it was a cultural phenomenon for the Black community. Over one hundred thousand attended.

Ms. Claudette beamed. "And your grandmother was there too. They were the baddest couple in Memphis. I wish you could've seen them back then. Ooh, they were a good-looking couple."

Amara's eyes watered, and she replied wistfully, "Me too."

Ms. Claudette patted Amara's hand before she stood up and moved to a tall gold vase in the corner. She reached into the hole and pulled out folded papers, then held them out to Amara. I moved closer to her and adjusted the lens to capture the moment as she carefully unfolded the papers. Nathan was on the edge of his seat, trying to peek at what had to be the songs.

Amara was careful not to touch the ink on the papers. "It's his writing."

"My handwriting was horrible." Though I could see the tremors, Ms. Claudette kept her hands behind her back. "We were so proud of all three. But 'Wild Flower' was our 'Strange Fruit.'"

Annie patted the space next to her to encourage her mother to sit.

Ms. Claudette shook her head. "I need to stand."

"Whatever you need to do to tell your story," Nathan said.

Ms. Claudette closed her eyes, a soft smile gracing her face. "We played that song together once at a bar he frequented. We sounded magical together. Of course, with his voice and his guitar skills, he made anyone sound good."

We all chuckled in agreement. Stoney Johnson had truly been an unsung musician until Amara found his journal, letters, and guitar in his closet.

"I debuted my song alone at one of the bars one night and received such a warm reception, I decided to sing it again a few nights later, at a Black civic group. We were protesting unfair economic situations that hadn't changed much since Dr. King's fight for the sanitation workers. I received a standing ovation, and a talent agent from Chicago was in the audience and wanted me to meet him at one of the local studios the next day because he was headed back to Chicago that night." She looked at Nathan and boasted, "He raved about me, wondering why I hadn't been scooped up yet, and even promised me an all-expenses-paid trip to his studio after I told him of the experience I'd already had working in the music industry in Memphis. Finally, I could taste a record deal. I was newly married and didn't yet know I was pregnant with this one."

She squeezed her daughter's hand. Annie had been enthralled with her mother's story as much as we were. She rocked slightly while she stared at her mother as if seeing her for the first time, as a young woman who had a big life before she became a mother.

"Did you get a chance to go to Chicago?" Nathan gently prodded. His demeanor was disarmingly open. His eyes were empathetic, focused, and bright. He'd long stopped taking notes and angled his body closer to the ladies on the sofa. He knew she'd never made it. This was his way of keeping her talking.

Ms. Claudette clasped her arms, and tears slowly fell down her face. I lowered the camera, wanting to hug her. Nathan slid a warning gaze my way, and I returned the Canon to my right eye.

"Why didn't you go to Chicago?" he asked.

"The next night, I performed at Judy's, a club that no longer exists but used to sit right off Beale. I walked to my car alone, like I did most nights. When I got in my car to head home, two white men were in the back seat and told me to keep driving, that they had a gun and would shoot me if I made any sudden movements or tried to call for help. Somehow, they knew about 'Wild Flower.' They also heard that I had been involved in protests and was a local activist." Ms. Claudette's hands balled into fists at her sides. "They forced me to drive an empty part of the highway."

"Mama, no," Annie cried out, and bolted from the sofa to hug her. "No more. She can't take any more." She looked at Amara and Nathan. "You have the songs now."

I lowered the camera again. Nathan shook his head at me, and I warred with myself for a second whether to scrap it and go to Ms. Claudette or keep recording. He pleaded with his eyes that I keep filming.

"Ms. Claudette, if you prefer to finish this story without me in the room, let me know. Sophie and Amara will take care of you. Or we can stop. Your daughter is right—we have the songs, and we can appraise them and ensure you get every penny. We can look into getting them recorded, whatever you want, okay?"

The songs were on Amara's lap while she hugged herself, her face stricken.

"What do you want to do, Claudette Mae Henderson Saint—or do you prefer to be called Mae Hennie?" Nathan continued softly.

His use of her stage name was intentional, and her head snapped in his direction. Her brown eyes widened. Barely above a whisper, she said, "You did your research. No one calls me that anymore."

"Think it's time we did again," I chimed in, and Nathan's lips curved into the widest smile.

"Yes, it is." Ms. Claudette's tone was certain and strong. She tapped her daughter's back with shaky hands and stepped away from her to stare out her front window. "Those evil *boys* are dead anyway. Used to see them around the city. Their sons and grandsons still lurk. None of them can hurt me as long as God watches over me like he did that night."

We were all so quiet and motionless that you could hear a pin drop, too afraid that any noise or movement would break her confessional spell.

"I could only imagine the worst things possible happening to me as I drove. After the first painful punch to the face, thankfully, my body went numb as they continued to punch, slap, and kick me until I fell to the ground and curled into a fetal position. I defiantly hummed 'Wild Flower' the whole time, ready to meet my maker. I believed they planned to rape and kill me, but one noticed me protecting my womb. Something clicked for him, and he grabbed the other man and said he didn't believe in hurting pregnant women. They warned me never to sing again or attend another protest group, or they wouldn't be so nice the next time. They stole my car and left me on the side of the road."

Ms. Claudette pressed her hands on the window. "I slowly rose and inched my way back to my house, bloody and battered, refusing to cry, though the numbness had worn off. Halfway there, my husband, who had been frantically searching for me, drove up. Someone from the bar had told him I should have been home. I collapsed in his arms."

She looked over her shoulder at Nathan, perched at the edge of the chair as if he were prepared to catch her. "The craziest thing was that I still wanted to sing. Those racist pigs could try to kill me again, but I wasn't going to stop. My husband threatened to leave me and everything." Old bitterness coated her tone. "He never supported my singing anyway."

"You didn't want to stop until you found out you were pregnant," Nathan concluded. "You said earlier you didn't know you were pregnant."

Ms. Claudette nodded and turned to face her daughter. "I protected you before I knew you were on the way. I would die for my music, but I couldn't risk you. I figured it was a sign that it was time for me to give up music and the fight. I changed my dream because you saved me. I folded up those songs and hid them in that vase all these years. I would hum and sing the love songs around you, but I couldn't bear to sing 'Wild Flower.'"

Amara carefully placed the papers on the coffee table, stood, and walked out the door without saying a word.

"Is she coming back?" Annie asked, and hurried to follow.

Nathan nodded with a smile. "Yes, ma'am." He rose from the chair and touched Ms. Claudette's forearm gently. "Thank you so much. The ancestors are smiling."

"They really are." Ms. Claudette beamed. "Thank you for insisting I finish. A weight I didn't realize I still carried has been lifted." She playfully tap-danced, gratitude and relief illuminating her face.

"Can I hug you?" he asked. "It took everything in me not to do it while you told us about that night."

She laughed heartily. "Of course you can."

When he hugged her, Nathan opened an arm to bring Annie and me in. We were still all in a soothing embrace when we heard the twang of a guitar.

Amara stood by the door with her guitar, staring at the music on the coffee table. "Mind if I play in honor of my granddad while you sing, Mae Hennie?"

Ms. Claudette lifted one side of her dress and bowed. "My honor to sing for you."

"Yes," I shouted as I raised the camera.

The three of us swayed, full of elation, while Mae Hennie gave us chills as she performed "Wild Flower" with the granddaughter of her old friend.

Mama used to call me her wildflower
A girl child destined to have power
Despite being unplanned and unintentioned,
Refusing to be conditioned
By the status quo,
Of poverty, sadness, and pockets of woe
Daddy tried to make me a rose
Full of purity, love, and prose
Afraid of the pain and destruction of those
Scared of my inherent power
Because nothing can stop a wildflower

Not even death
From growing and knowing that she was meant to exist
And meant to be seen in all her colorfulness
That's why I love Mama so
She called me her wildflower
A girl child destined for power

I entwined my hand with Nathan's. He winked and returned his attention to the makeshift stage.

This was why he was willing to risk his life for moments like these.

And I couldn't love this man more.

TWENTY-THREE

Sophie

After the breakthrough with Claudette Saint, we celebrated the rest of the weekend in Memphis. The four of us, including Jake, took Annie and Ms. Claudette out to dinner at Flight, where we met with Sweetie Jay, who promised to discuss with her board adding a small exhibit in honor of Mae Hennie, much to Annie and Ms. Claudette's delight. Then the four of us bar-hopped on Beale. Jake knew people, so we got free drinks or appetizers wherever we went, though we could more than afford it. Nathan and I were openly affectionate around Amara and Jake, determined to enjoy our time together. They accepted that we weren't headed for coupledom and didn't force the issue. We were with our best friends, and we were this awesome foursome, dancing, laughing, joking, and teasing each other. Jake kept us in stitches talking about him and Nathan back in college, and their scheming to hook up with women.

Jake managed to get us into a late private party at Raiford's, a nightclub with a few local artists, featuring Memphis's native rap queen, GloRilla. We grooved and rapped along with her and the other acts, reveling in the freedom our ancestors had fought and died for before us.

In the wee hours of the morning, Nathan and I couldn't keep our hands off each other as we tumbled into our suite. He bent me over the desk, pushed up my dress, and thrust deep inside of me, seconds after closing the door. Our heated passion capped off a triumphant day.

Sunday morning, we slept in with room service and ate well at Majestic Grill before enjoying the marching Peabody ducks. That night, the four of us grabbed blankets and set up a tent that Nathan kept in his vehicle on the banks of the Mississippi River, admiring the nightly light show on Hernando De Soto and Harahan Bridges. We drank hot cocoa from a thermos, indulged in sweet potato pie and peach cobbler courtesy of Ms. Claudette and Amara, and chilled.

"Aw, Jake, you should have seen Mari and Mae Hennie tearing it up. They were so good. Stoney Johnson is somewhere in heaven smiling. I know that will go viral as soon as I post it," I exclaimed. "Once I finish editing, I'll show you."

"Why didn't you play with them?" he asked.

"I was there as the photographer." I dusted my hands of crumbs from the yummy sweet potato pie.

Jake shrugged. "Nathan could've taken over. Blending your three voices would've been the chef's kiss."

"Naw…I was where I was supposed to be," I firmly said. "It was their moment."

"So, either Nate is confused or I'm confused," Jake commented, looking between Nathan and me.

"About what?" I asked, and Nathan's arms tensed around me.

Amara frowned and looked back at Jake.

"I told Jake that you want more than to be in the background," Nathan admitted near my ear. "I didn't expect him to bring it up like this."

Jake held up his thermos. "No time like the present."

"It wasn't your place, Nate," I gritted out through my teeth, torn between feeling betrayed and simply annoyed that he couldn't let me decide if and when I wanted to ever approach Jake.

Jake used his thermos to tap the side of my leg. "Hold up now—before you get upset with him, you should've come to me long ago. He was looking out for you *and* me. I never want you to feel that I don't value you or don't consider you one of the most talented artists I know."

Nathan rubbed the chills that suddenly covered my arms, and I willed myself to calm down. "Ask him, Sophie."

Amara clasped her hands together expectantly. "I've been waiting for you to realize you want more."

"The difference is *you* allowed me to decide. This one here…" I tapped Nathan's chest. "Let's just say I see why you two are best friends. So pushy."

"I like to think of it as persistence," Jake said while he and Nathan fist-bumped. "So, what do you want to know?"

Three people looked at me with barely contained smiles.

"I want to know if you think I have what it takes to be a star," I said.

"You have what it takes to do or be anything you want, Sophie. I didn't push you because you've always made it clear you preferred the background," Jake replied. "I just wish you'd felt comfortable telling me yourself. Closed mouths don't get fed."

The positive encouragement and support of my friends emboldened me to explain. "This year has been about loss and my growth. *I* thought all I wanted was the background, so you weren't wrong, Jake. I guess when I saw how much you pushed Mari when she wasn't sure what she wanted, it made me question how you see me."

Jake nodded in agreement.

"Being here in Memphis among all these talented people has been nothing short of amazing. The grittiness and the grind of this city are so me. More than Nashville will ever be. I'm not scared of rejection as much as this one believes." I squeezed Nathan's bicep. "I'm still trying to see where I fit in, which is why I still hadn't approached you. The only thing I'm certain of is that music and photography have to play a part."

"Well, when we return to Nashville, come to my office and let's chat." Jake pulled a cigar from his jacket and gave it to me. "Congrats and welcome to the team."

"Yeah!" I stuck the cigar in my mouth and threw my arm around Nathan's neck.

He smiled. "Mm…you look damn sexy."

"And this is when we start collecting our stuff to go." Amara giggled.

Jake moved to get up. "Yeah…this ground is hard and I'm getting old. We have an early flight, too."

"Hey, before we all leave, I need to say something," Nathan said, looking at me with sad eyes. "Jake already knows."

"What is it?" I asked, trying to prepare for whatever he said, which probably wouldn't be in my favor.

"I've been asked to go to Haiti on a mission to help bring a gang leader hiding out to safety in America. Just found out. I'll go there from L.A. in a couple of weeks. I should be able to get in and out pretty safely."

"But it's chaotic there with all that political unrest, Nate," Amara said. "You could get hurt or stuck there. What about the wedding?"

I stared at him, unsure of what to say. Underneath the sadness, his eyes were alive like they were with Ms. Claudette. He *needed* to do this.

"I'll be back in plenty of time. I have connections and contacts there. And not every part of Haiti is dangerous, no more than parts of any city are a threat. I could really help him, and he personally asked for me."

Amara rose to her feet and pulled Jake up to stand beside her. "I don't know why you insist on endangering your life. I thought everything you've been doing since last year was your new start?"

"It is. I love what I'm doing with these unsung legends. I also want to do this." Nathan reached for Amara's hand. "I know you're worried because we've become friends, but I've been on more dangerous assignments and I'm still here."

"No, we're your family," Amara corrected him, and Jake squeezed her shoulder.

Nathan released her hand and stood up. "Nothing is going to happen to me."

"How can you say that?" I asked from where I still sat. "You can't promise that. None of us can."

"You're right, none of us are promised tomorrow," he conceded. "I can die doing nothing or live doing something." He grabbed my hand and pulled me up. "I love you. Nothing will change that, and it's what will keep me safe. Can't explain it. Just know it." He pulled me into a hug, holding me tight. "Don't be mad, Twinkle."

In the pregnant pause, confessing my love jammed against my tongue, and instead I replied honestly, with a trembling voice, "Just come home safe. I need my escort for the wedding."

Nathan replied with certainty, "I will."

TWENTY-FOUR

Nathan

Carlise Price stepped out of her black Cadillac to hug me. I squeezed her to me and looked down into her face, that for a long time, I'd had to get on tiptoe to kiss her cheek. My mother could have been a model with her height, statuesque build, flawless sepia skin, and high cheekbones that guaranteed a perfect picture every time. She kept her head covered with wigs because she had alopecia that worsened during times of stress. When she and my father were going through their divorce, she had bald patches all over. I would add the ointments to her hair while she held back tears. My father had been bitter toward my mother because he still loved her and wanted his family intact.

"My son." She beamed with a mother's pride. "Handsome as always. Keeping healthy?"

"I try." I smiled and placed my leather bag and luggage in the trunk. She moved to the passenger side, and I adjusted the seat and slid behind the wheel. Soon we were off, and the Washington Monument gleamed bright in the rearview as we headed toward Arlington on the other side of the Potomac River.

"How long are you staying?"

"A few days. Maybe longer." I'd called her an hour before I decided to jump on a flight to visit her instead of Los Angeles. My emotions were getting the best of me, and I needed grounding.

"Can you be more specific?"

"I'm used to staying in hotels if you're too busy." I glanced at her. My mother had had a full life once she left us, between her sorority and the community organizations that she inevitably chaired, and traveling with her longtime boyfriend, Bradford.

"I thought I divorced your father," she quipped. "I have the right to know how long you'll be here, since you called me a few hours ago and said you were headed here without explanation. You know I love it when you visit, especially because your brother doesn't make much effort."

"You did leave when he was fourteen. I think he might feel a way."

"Your father didn't help."

"He didn't," I replied.

My father wouldn't allow us to mention our mother. I left for college soon after the divorce, so I didn't live with him when he was at his worst. My brother, Carlos, had borne the brunt of the family drama. He still lived in San Antonio near my father, working as a computer programmer. We weren't particularly close, though we loved each other. He and my father had always had a tight bond, while I was a mama's boy. Maybe that was why she'd decided to leave when I was preparing for college instead of waiting for my brother to grow up.

We were silent the rest of the drive. Our past troubled family life shrouded our present, and I hoped that after this visit, she and I could fully move past that and embrace our future. The Turners were a strong, tight-knit family, unafraid to love out loud, headed by that rare couple who genuinely liked and adored each other. The expectation of positivity and light was a given. The cruelty of the world didn't exist in their home because they made it so with their teasing jokes, abundance of laughter, and music. It was no wonder that Sophie had isolated for months following the double heartbreak of the end of a relationship and a miscarriage.

"I made your favorite spaghetti bake with ground turkey and extra mozzarella," Mama shyly announced when I pulled into her driveway of her two-story home in an upper-class neighborhood. "It's just us. Bradford is in San Francisco for a convention."

"Surprised you didn't go with him."

We walked through the door, and the lavender scent she'd used to keep our family home smelling good floated nostalgia around me. She strode ahead of me, unaware of my bout of sentimentality. "I was supposed to fly there tomorrow."

An unexpected pang hit me that she might leave me again, and I pulled her into a hug. "I love you, Mama."

"Love you too." She patted my back. "I'm not going anywhere—already told Bradford that you must need me to fly here like this. You're my priority."

I pulled away and averted my gaze, not wanting her to see the unshed tears.

My astute mother lifted my chin. "Nate, what's wrong?"

"I don't know," I said honestly.

She studied me a little longer before she wrapped her arm around my waist, already sensing what I needed. "Come on, let's talk while you eat." Mama's safe space was the kitchen, just like Ms. Claudette. Even with her busy career, she still loved to cook and rarely ate out if she were home.

She sipped on wine, watching me gobble down the loaded plate of food in the recliner in front of the TV turned to Lifetime, her favorite channel. "When's the last time you ate?"

"Probably yesterday. Been busy. I was down in Memphis over the weekend, then back to Nashville, and was supposed to go to L.A. As soon as I started to board, I realized I didn't want to be there, so I came here."

"Is it about your writing?"

I finished chomping and swallowed. "No. That's going well. I was headed to L.A. to work with the documentary producers I was talking to you about, and then focus on the music magazine I want to start. I also got the interview with that singer I wanted in Memphis, and she'll be recording the songs she held on to all these years with Jake soon. I'll expand *The Lost Souls of Memphis Blues* with the new material and might get an agent to shop it to a big publisher."

I put my fork down. "Got another call early last week from a small press in the Dominican Republic. They want me to go to Haiti and meet with one of the gang leaders who's been hiding out. He wants to tell his story in hopes of gaining asylum in the U.S. or Canada. He specifically asked for me. He read my story about that Somalian soldier we were able to move to Ghana safely, and he believes I can write it in a way that will be heard around the world."

She squeezed my wrist and smiled. "Congratulations. This is the type of work you live for. You're going to get that Pulitzer."

Surprised Mama had accepted my potential assignment without any sign of worry, much like Jake, Amara, and Sophie, I leaned forward and asked, "No concern or warning that I'm putting myself in harm's way again?"

"What good would that do, Nate? I was married to a soldier for eighteen years, and the same need to save the world was passed down to my son. You might not have joined the military, but you're every bit the soldier your father was, courageous and determined to fight wrongs. I do what I always do, pray for my sons when I sleep at night. So far, my prayers have worked." She picked up my plate from the folding tray. "You want more?"

Satisfied with her answer, I relaxed. "No. That was delicious. I miss your cooking."

"And I miss cooking for you. While you're here, I'll make all your favorites."

"Yes." I pumped my fist several times.

She laughed. "You used to do that so much as a boy. Despite what your father may have told you, I loved being a mother and taking care of my family."

Mama moved to the kitchen, separated from the living area by a large island. She washed and dried my plate and fork and placed them in a cabinet.

"I know that, Mama. But I don't feel like talking about Dad, okay?" Inevitably, whenever I spoke to either parent, they would make some nasty comment about the other. I'd sworn to myself that if I were ever to marry and divorce, I wouldn't pit my children against the other parent. Being a child of divorced parents wasn't for the weak.

She returned to the beige sofa and gently asked, "Why are you here, Nathan?"

"I'm in love." The soothing vanilla and cocoa butter scents drifted over me just thinking of Sophie.

"You met the one?" Mama exclaimed.

My mother used to worry about my dating status and whether I'd chosen a life of singledom because of her divorce. To allay her fears, I'd told her that I believed in love and that whenever I found the one meant for me, she would know. Since then, she hadn't expressed concern or asked if I'd met anyone.

"Maybe," I conceded, though I couldn't imagine loving another woman more than Sophie Turner.

Mama's look of surprise shifted to an amused grin. "And you don't know what to do with your feelings?"

"No clue. I didn't think I could feel this out of sorts, this weepy, angry, this crazy. I don't have control of my emotions, and it's messing with me. I get Dad more now, understand why he was so mean and unreasonable. Love can make you irrational."

My father once believed he was the luckiest man in the world because he'd landed my mother. He would hug and kiss her every time he left and when he returned. As stoic as my father could be, Mama could always make him smile with a wink, a touch, or a playful shimmy of her hips. For a long time they were happy—until they weren't. Or had their happiness always been a façade that they wanted their children and everyone else to believe? Sophie had triggered me the day after she confessed about the miscarriage, smiling like she hadn't just relived some painful shit.

Mama's smile slipped. "Was he that bad after I left?" She quickly raised her hand. "I know…I know, you don't like talking about him to me, but I need to know at least that much."

"Dad was irritable and mean. He didn't hit us or anything. We could tell he was heartbroken. I was both guilty and relieved when I left for college. Guilty, because Carlos was still there without me as a buffer, but happy to breathe again."

"I'm so sorry. I tried to stay." She touched her chest. "I was slowly dying inside. I tried to explain to your father that I needed more than my family and that I was tired of all the changes and moves, starting all over, and he refused to hear me—until I refused to hear *him* anymore. I didn't realize how much he still loved me. It took me a long time to understand that the bitterness and anger he spewed at me was his realization that I didn't love him as much as he loved me."

"Are you saying you would've stayed if you loved him more?" I poured more wine into my glass. I'd suspected that my father loved her more than she loved him. Since they'd split seventeen years ago, he hadn't been in a relationship, while Bradford was Mama's third.

"I don't know, Nate. I really don't. I loved him enough to create a family with him, to take care of him and our home for years. Maybe a deeper love would've made it easier to ignore what I wanted, or at least maybe my inner voice wouldn't have felt suffocated. The same way you felt when you left home for college was the same way I felt when I moved out of our home. Guilty yet free."

She dropped her gaze to the floor. "I keep trying to connect with your brother. He's always respectful, but won't let me in like you do. I don't know if he's happy or in love, or if he still blames me for the divorce. I'm praying that one day he will forgive me." Mama's lips formed a thin line as she poured more wine into her glass. "Enough talk about that. Tell me about this woman who made you run home to your mama. Do you have a picture of her?"

I scrolled to a picture of *her*—my new favorite. Sophie, smiling in front of the Withers Collection Museum with her arms spread because she'd found her happy place in the iconic photos of Black life taken by internationally acclaimed photographer Dr. Ernest Withers. My Twinkle.

"Sophie is a singer and musician. One of Jake's people. She also worked alongside me in Memphis and took all the photos we used in the proposal."

"Those pictures were breathtaking." Mama admired Sophie. "Talented and pretty. You need sun in your life, Nate."

"I really do." Relief that she got why Sophie mattered so much to me helped me release the breath I'd been holding since I impulsively called my mother and told her I was coming home. "Not sure if I'm the man for her, though. The timing might be off even if we can get past our fundamental differences."

"Why?" She frowned, still studying Sophie's picture.

"She's traditional. She wants a man at home with her, raising a family together."

"I thought she was a musician? Aren't most of them always on the road? It seems like Jake is gone as much as you."

I shrugged. "She claims that she never wanted that life and had been waiting to meet a man to settle down and be a housewife."

Mama tilted her head. "This young woman, who has talents that most don't have, wants to spend the rest of her life taking care of her children and husband?"

"You sound like I did when she first told me." I snickered, loving that my mother and I were usually on the same wavelength. "I met her peeps, and I do get it on some level because they are a happy family. Her parents have been married forever, and her mother never worked outside of the home and seems to love it."

Mama wistfully said, "Some truly do. I did for a while. I loved making a home for my babies and husband. I wish that had been enough."

I sat up straighter and touched the back of Mama's hand. "I'm not saying anything's wrong with any woman staying home for her family. I just don't see it with Sophie. Maybe when the children are babies—other than that, I don't see it. She has such sparkle and excitement when taking photos or playing her guitar. She wants more but is scared to have a new dream."

"A new dream, including being with a traveling man? Didn't you discuss what you wanted from a relationship before you got together?" Mama twisted her lips.

"She and I have been friends for two years. We grew close working on the Memphis project together because she and I vibe. We just flow like we were loves in another lifetime. Initially, we were just casual because she went through a lot with an ex, and neither of us was looking for commitment. Next thing I know, one night turned into three months of exclusivity."

"People still tell themselves that lie." Mama shook her head. "You can have one-night stands and even occasional sex with the same person, but sex with the same person repeatedly changes the narrative. Feelings will develop on at least one person's side, especially if the sex is good."

Internally and visibly cringing, I held both hands up. "All right, all right, Mama. Please stop…stop. I'm still your son who doesn't want to discuss that with you openly."

She smirked. "I love sex, just like you."

I moved to get up, but she laughingly pulled me back down. I asked, "Are you going to stop?"

"Yes, you big baby." She took another sip of wine and looked over the rim of the glass with a teasing smile. "We've established you want different things, though you believe you are more alike than different. Is that the only problem?"

Stretching my legs under the table, I slumped lower in the recliner. "I don't know if I'm her rebound either."

"My son is no woman's second choice." She tapped the table with the bottom of her almost-empty wine glass.

"My thoughts exactly. I don't want to give up what I've been working toward all these years for a woman who doesn't love me as deeply as I love her." Smiling, we raised our glasses in agreement. "So, what do I do? Because I can't stop thinking about her."

She tucked one leg under her. "Have you told her how you feel?"

"She knows I'm there for her and love her."

"You have more of your father in you than you probably like to admit. I knew he loved me, but he kept his insecurities and fears from me. It's hard to have longevity if you can't freely be you. It's the first thing I loved about Bradford—he didn't care if he looked like a fool; he had no shame in expressing what he felt or feels."

"I've shared things with her I've never shared with anyone. I've been vulnerable," I insisted. No one had known about my nightmares until Sophie, not even my mother.

Mama grabbed my chin. "Have you told her what you told me…that you believe you are a rebound?"

"Yeah. She believes it's an excuse, and I don't want to settle down. If she can change her dream, I should change mine." Saying what Sophie wanted from me suddenly seemed reasonable, given how I encouraged her to be open and willing to take risks.

"She has a point." Mama released my chin and eased back in her chair. "Okay, let me ask you a question. Can you be in one place? You've been in Nashville now for over two years. You seem to enjoy being there and are forging a new path with music because you're tired of risking your life. Have you changed your mind?"

Scooting to the edge of the recliner, I explained, "I still plan to focus on music, and Nashville is a large part of that. Haiti is just an opportunity. He's in a safe house, so it's not as dangerous as it may seem. Helping others in need motivates and fulfills me, and if I have to travel, I want to be free to do that without feeling like I'm letting her down."

"To love you is to accept that part of you."

"Well, maybe she doesn't, since she hasn't told me she loves me," I glumly admitted, and dropped my head.

"You also said she went through some stuff with an ex. Heartbreak can make you second-guess every choice and decision. The moment I trusted my gut, I became a happier person. Do I have regrets? Of course—I hate that I'm not close with my baby boy, though I've never given up on him." She glanced around her stylish home. "I love my career, my friends, and my man. How many times do I have to tell you that the dash is what counts, because we only get one in this life? What does your gut say?"

I closed my eyes and pictured Sophie's face when I showed up at her parents' door. "She loves me as much as I love her."

"Then stop trying to find reasons you can't be together and focus on the reasons that make you want to fight to keep her. Just don't forget that you are always evolving, and you must listen to each other to make it work." She reached for a throw out of her wicker basket that she kept next to the sofa. "Come on, let's binge-watch *Scandal* until we fall asleep." Mama used to joke that I was the male version of Olivia Pope, ready to fix any crisis.

Grinning, I settled back in the recliner. "Then you need to make your son some of that good-ass popcorn."

She rose from the sofa. "Set up the show."

I picked up two remotes in the console built into the chair. "Mama, how many times do I have to tell you to sync your remotes so I'm not always trying to figure out which one does what?"

"As long as *I* know, it doesn't matter."

"I'll do it while I'm here. Makes no sense," I muttered. "Can I stay a week? I'll push back my meetings in L.A."

Mama waved her hand. "Boy, you can stay as long as you like. Bradford still has his own place."

The TV now displayed Apple TV. I asked, "Have you ever seen *Swagger*? It's that basketball series with Ice Cube's son. It's good."

"No, but we can watch while you're here. If you like it, I'll love it." She pulled out a pot and grabbed the vegetable oil from the other counter. "Connect my new iPad to the Wi-Fi while you're at it. Bradford hates technology."

"You need to make an honest man out of him, Mama. I like him for you."

"And Bradford and I like us just the way we are." She opened a bag of corn kernels. "A part of me will always love your father. He was good to me and our family. And I don't want to be another man's wife." Mama softly smiled. "It's my way of honoring him and what we once had. You can tell him that if you want."

Maybe my mother *had* loved my father as much as he loved her. And maybe, just maybe, Sophie was in love with me, too.

TWENTY-FIVE

Sophie

Two weeks later

Pushing off my headphones in frustration, I glared through the glass at my nemesis. "Why did you cut it?"

"Run it again, Sophie," Jake barked from the control board. "You need to sing from the depths of your soul every single time. The blues give despair a space to breathe and release. It's gritty and grimy and real. Sing a fun pop medley if you want cute and light."

"I know that." I gripped the mic stand before I strangled him. "I've done that riff at least ten times already."

"And? If you need to do it a hundred more times, you do it." Jake adjusted knobs and signaled for me with his index finger to sing again.

I blew my bangs up and muttered, "Damn that Nate."

Jake pressed the intercom button. "What was that?"

"Nothing." I plastered a fake smile on my face, too exhausted to go toe to toe with Jake when he was in asshole mode.

Amara and Tavion, who lounged on the sofa behind Jake, turned their heads to hide their laughter. They were there to support me as I recorded my new song, "Found Soul."

"If the people behind me can't be productive, they can leave," Jake growled.

Amara and Tavion threw up the middle fingers behind his back, and this time, I laughed loudly. God, I loved these people and this world of music. Stoney may have brought his granddaughter to country, but he'd led me to the blues. Once we had the conversation by the Mississippi River, Jake had treated me like I'd wanted him to treat me.

As a potential star.

He'd wanted to represent me once he realized that Amara and I wouldn't be in direct competition, though there could be times when that wouldn't be the case. The three of us had promised to keep communication open and make different management decisions because, above all, we wanted to preserve the family that we'd built.

The fortune and fame that Amara had steadily amassed didn't appeal. Still, I wanted to leave a lasting footprint in music. For now, a song that I could have and hold to pass down to future generations was enough.

"Why you have to be such a hardass to get the best out of me, Jake?" I asked.

He pointed at me. "You asked me to work with you. I don't know why you seem surprised. This is what it looks like. When you blow like I know you can, then I'll leave you alone. You know the routine. Until then, again."

"Ugh," I groaned, and slammed the headset back on my head. We would be here all night.

Amara winked at me before wrapping her arms around Jake's shoulders and kissing his neck slowly. Tavion whistled, and I clapped my hands at the blush that Jake's brown skin couldn't hide as he growled, "I think everyone needs a break."

"Yep." I ducked out of the booth. "We'll be back tomorrow."

"Be back in an hour." He turned in his chair to face his soon-to-be wife and, at her seductive smile, impatiently waved us off. "Tomorrow."

"'Bout to get us a drink anyway." Tavion entwined his arm with mine before the two lovebirds forgot we were in the room.

The minute we were outside, we burst out laughing.

I looked back at the door. "That man is so whipped it's ri-di-cu-lous."

Tavion tilted his head. "Emphasis on 'dic.'"

We high-fived and shouted, "Facts."

"Pinch, poke, you owe me a Coke," I chanted.

Tavion patted my arm and grew quiet. We passed a few tourists on our way to Broadway. Jake's studio was a stone's throw from all the activity. Many nights, Tavion and I would leave rehearsal and hang out. He'd been my confidant and best friend before Amara and Nathan entered my life. A lot had changed in the past year, and I'd never openly acknowledged how much Tavion still meant to me.

I bumped into his side. "Can I say something?"

He glanced at me. His usual teasing eyes were subdued.

"I owe you the biggest apology of everyone. You're my Day One, and I forgot that. Caught up in the excitement of Amara and lusting after Omar and then falling for Nathan, I neglected you."

Tavion tightened his grip on our woven arms. "It's not like I didn't do the same to you when I fell in love with Ethan. I disappeared on you, and you started hanging out more with Mari. We don't even have to talk about Omar. We've all been fools in love." He scrunched up his nose. "I understood why you clung to Nate. He's that dude who looks after people. If I'm sad about anything, it's that you didn't trust me enough to share your pain."

"It's not that I didn't trust you. I'd never experienced anything like it and didn't know what to do except run."

I stopped mid-stride. *Nathan.* A warmth spread across my chest, and I started walking again.

"What?" a confused Tavion asked.

"It bothered Nathan that I had a hard time accepting that life is gray more often than not. I'm used to the sun, and when a storm hit, I didn't know how to handle it, didn't even know how to voice it to the very people who have shown me love and acceptance." I looked around the bustling street, alive and popping. All I longed for now was peace and quiet. "You want to have a sleepover? I have a lot to tell you, including how I fell in love with a temporary man."

He sucked his teeth. "Omar is for the streets."

"No, Nathan."

Tavion's braided head went back with laughter. He continued to laugh while I stared at him.

"What's so funny? Nathan doesn't want to be tied down."

He wiped his eyes and pulled me back in the direction we'd just come. "Woo, I needed that laugh. Yes, we do need to lie up in your house, order pizza, talk, and get sloppy drunk."

"Still doesn't explain why you laughed like that."

"Nathan is just as whipped as Jake." We shared an amused smirk, and Tavion amended, "Naw, ain't no one as whipped as Jake. But you and Nate have something. To me, you two are like Dwayne and Whitley, except for the 'spoiled bougie' and HBCU parts."

"Really? You know those two are my all-time fave couple besides Spencer and Liv, and Derwyn and Melanie," I squealed.

"He's that friend in the background who's been quietly watching until he got his chance. The man who snuck up on you and that you can't live without. The one who helped you bloom." We made it to our cars parked in front of the studio. "He encouraged you to step out of your comfort zone. You were always good, Sophie. Now, you're even better."

Kicking his tire, I lamented, "Then why isn't he here with me instead of being in L.A. or risking his life in Haiti?"

"The same reason you left Gatlinburg." He hit the key fob for his Corvette. "You wanted more."

"That's my point, Tav. He wants more than me."

"And? So do most people, including you. If he asked you right now to give up the song you're working on with Jake or to stop taking photos to be with him, would you?"

I shook my head. "He would never ask me to do that."

"Then why would you expect that of him? Don't let your stubbornness and pride get in the way of a good man." He opened his door. "Nothing is keeping you from traveling with him when you can. I like you two together." Tavion snapped his fingers. "I want at least five Memphis photos blown up and plastered on my walls. Doesn't even matter which one."

"Ugh," I yelled. "I hate when I'm wrong."

My stubbornness and unwillingness to take a chance with Nathan on his terms had blocked the simple fact that we could figure out how to love one another and have the life we wanted together.

As soon as I settled into my car, I texted him.

When you return from Haiti, let's talk. Before I hit send, I added, *I miss you.*

When I pulled into my garage under my apartment, my phone beeped.

Can't wait to see you, Twinkle. I'm keeping myself safe. Miss you more.

I pressed the phone against my heart and squealed. My phone beeped again.

Can we talk?

My stomach churned when I saw Omar's name.

Two days later, I pulled up beside Omar's black Mustang. I scanned the park and saw him sitting at a table alone, facing the lot. He smiled and waved when he saw me, and I slowly eased out of the car, questioning my decision to meet with him. I didn't want him anymore and had no plans to tell him about the baby. Tavion had wanted to come with me, afraid I would backslide into Omar. I knew otherwise. My heart no longer belonged to him—if it ever had.

The blistering cold of December chilled me, and I wanted to hop back in the warmth of my car. I'd chosen this park because I wanted the cold to force a potentially long conversation into being a quick chat. I tugged down my fur-lined hat, slipped my hands in my coat pockets, and trudged toward him.

Omar stood to hug me, and I shook my head. His smile slipped. Refusing to sit, I asked, "What do we need to talk about?"

"You don't want to sit down even for a second?"

"No."

He sighed. "You're not this person, Sophie. All cold and shit. Please."

"Well, it's pretty cold outside, and I have no reason to be pleasant with a man who hurt me. I'm only here because it seems like you need the closure that I already have." I checked my watch. "I need to get back."

"To him?" he snarled, a scowl crossing his face.

"You don't get to judge anything about him. He's a better man than you'll ever be. Say what you need to say or don't."

"Okay. Okay." He dragged his hand down over his face. "I've been thinking a lot since I last saw you."

"That was almost two months ago."

"I know… I wanted to reach out the very next day, but I figured it was too soon."

I stepped back. "Men are something else. Would you think about me if you saw me at the restaurant with Mari or alone? No. You saw me with another man, and now you can't conceive that I would dare love someone besides you when you have a whole fiancée happily flashing your ring."

"Sophie, I saw how you looked that night. You still love me. Tell me what I need to do to fix things."

I held my hand up when he moved toward me again. "For what? I don't deal with men who cheat."

He weakly explained, "I got caught up because you were gone so much."

I slammed my hands on my hips. "Dude, I'm talking about now, but thank you for finally confirming what my gut told me and what your actions presented the last time I saw you. I bet you're still engaged. You have no intention of breaking up with her until you have some sense of commitment from me, right?" I shook my head slowly. "I was such a fool to ignore those glaring red flags because I wanted to believe in you and love so badly. Thank God you have horrible timing, because I might have taken your ass back if you showed up before Nathan did. Then I would be the poor woman with a ring on her finger, blissfully ignorant that her man is trying to get back with his ex. Go home to her. I'm good." I started backing away.

"Wait… Please." He grabbed my wrist. "I still love you."

Breaking his hold on me, I spun around. "So the fuck what? You have no clue what love really is, and I'm so happy that I don't love you anymore."

Omar stared back at me incredulously. "You were hurt that night."

"Oh, I was. Until I was reminded of my worth later that night… A very *good* reminder, I might add," I taunted him as I strolled back to the car and waved over my shoulder. "Goodbye, and please don't ever call me again."

As I backed up my car, the last of the lingering cloud of grief lifted. I could finally answer my mother's question.

I am *happy.*

Even when my life didn't quite work out like I'd envisioned.

I couldn't explain why any parent lost a child, whether it was on this side or still in the womb—I only knew why it had happened to *me*. If I'd had Omar's baby, I would've forever been tethered to a man who didn't see me or truly love me. I would've clung to my dream of a husband and family and stuck it out through thick and thin with someone undeserving of that blind devotion.

My dream had been that of a nine-year-old who felt like an outsider the moment I discovered, through careless adult conversation, that I was the blood of another man. My dream had been that of a teenager who believed in fairytales. My dream had been that of a young woman who thought her worth was tied to having a husband and a baby.

I still wanted a man, and a family that we created together. But I also wanted to pursue my passions. Right now, they were music and photography. Tomorrow, it might be something else. Whether I ever found my person or had a baby, I was enough as I was.

Sophie Nicole Turner.

TWENTY-SIX

Sophie

Adjusting the lens, I refocused on the city below from my perch on the roof of the Twelve Thirty Club. I loved my camera. I could spend hours walking around the city and snapping, and planned to create Christmas gifts from the photos I'd captured. Amara and Jake's wedding was in four days. Nathan would be back in Nashville in time to join for the family dinner two days before. I'd only spoken to him four times since he'd been in the Dominican Republic. Travel to Haiti had been restricted due to the violent protests and political unrest since the president was assassinated in 2021, but he traveled back and forth on the island the two countries shared by a bus and blended in with the natives because he knew enough Spanish and Creole to maneuver within the countries. Luckily, his contacts were English speaking, and he was able to gather more information about the twenty-year-old gang leader, who feared for his life before he met with Nathan.

We'd kept our conversations light, warm, and friendly, though I could feel the undercurrent of desire in how he would say my name like he had during our more intimate moments. Or how he would pause before he ended the call, like he wanted to tell me that he loved me or that he wanted to hear me say it to him. I didn't want the first time I openly declared my love to him to be over the phone, especially when the connection was often unstable. I hadn't told him about the conversation with Omar, though I planned to once we were together. He was too far away, and I didn't want doubt to creep in because he believed I wasn't over Omar.

I'd thought Nathan's perception that I was still in love with my ex was his subconscious way of keeping me at a distance—until Omar mentioned that he thought I still loved him because of my reaction to seeing him unexpectedly. Thinking back to how I behaved in the restaurant and in the car, which was about what I'd lost and perceived someone else now had, I could see why Nathan was hesitant to commit to me despite his evident love for me, and I had yet to tell him how much I needed and loved him too.

Whenever he showed up at my door, I planned to lay my cards on the table and take the biggest risk I'd ever taken on a temporary man, hoping he would be my forever one.

A notification of a text from Nathan appeared on my watch.

Check your email.

I returned to my table and opened my email on my cell, bouncing in my seat when I noticed the long message.

My Sophie.

You are forever etched in my heart.

This is the last time I plan to ever be separated from you. You are my light. My energy. My inspiration. My sun. My solace.

My Twinkle.

Sleep had never been my friend until you curled up against me. The nightmares I used to have are now infrequent bad dreams. You soothed the pains of my soul with your warmth and comfort. When I hear your melodic voice, I long to hold you and make love to you, to laugh at your silliness, your insistence on making fun of my age or my music. I'm not much of a talker, though with you, I'm a chatterbox. I'm not a dancer, with you, I'm Alvin Ailey. I'm not a singer, with you, I'm Otis. I hate that I was afraid of the depth of my love for you. Hate that I ever caused you any pain. Hate that miles separate us based on a decision I made. A decision I don't regret, yet I won't make again.

He is a boy forced to be a street soldier in a land he loves, poverty forcing him one way that prosperity wouldn't. His heartbreaking story mirrors that of so many others who look like you and me. Who look like the musicians we interviewed. Who look like Claudette Saint. We are all interconnected through our ancestors across the diaspora at the whims of our government or people's political beliefs. I have a couple of connections, and my soul won't rest if I don't at least try to save a man who could've easily been me. After all, it is an accident of birth that we end up wherever any of us end up.

I wanted to call you and say these words to you, but I worry that my phone line may be compromised. My email is supposed to be protected, and I pray that it is, because I had to tell you who I am and why I do what I do, or why I did what I did.

Thank you for the collage you sent of your daily selfies, as I asked you to. I had to see if the love you still refuse to tell me of is evident on your face. If you haven't noticed, look at the photos again. Whether you ever verbalize how you feel, you have shown me that my love is reciprocated. And that is enough for me to give up this part of my life. I can no longer willingly place myself in harm's way, knowing I can cast a shadow on your sun.

For so long, I needed a purpose for my existence.

Once upon a time, my search for truth and justice was my reason, the Pulitzer Prize the ultimate goal.

Then I met you.

Slowly placing the phone down on the table, I searched for the collage that I'd sent him. I'd included the dates under each picture, as instructed. Tears fell. My eyes were unfocused and soulless the day he knocked on my door. The very next day, my eyes were clearer, and a soft smile of hope stared back at me. As I scoured the pictures that I'd begun taking on a whim and continued out of habit, I could observe my journey of healing, growth, and love.

Papa had been right.

Nathan worked out whatever he needed to within himself to be right for me, and I hadn't met the man for me yet because I hadn't met Nathan.

Two days later, with no further contact from Nathan, I walked into the new, sprawling home that Jake and Amara now owned with my head held high. Nathan was set to come home this morning. It was after seven, and no one had heard from him. I'd been his last contact when he sent the email two days ago. We were all on high alert, awaiting news. Yet I refused to worry or be afraid. He'd asked me to trust that he would return alive and well, and I did.

After placing my coat on the large rack at the door, I walked through the foyer to the sitting area. Tonight's guests were Amara and Jake's closest family members and the bridal party's guests. My parents and two youngest sisters hadn't made it here yet. I didn't know if Nathan's mother had. The rehearsal dinner tomorrow would include a few other guests. Despite the two large, festive Christmas trees, a pall shrouded the room and kept the guests quietly chatting instead of laughing and talking loudly. Jake was impeccably dressed, as always, in a dark, tailored suit and was on the phone, probably trying to track down Nathan. Worry bounced off him even from this distance. Nathan was the brother he'd never had, and their love for each other was evident. He would do all in his power to ensure Nathan's safe return.

Amara's face brightened when she saw me. With her freshly straightened hair, wearing an off-the-shoulder navy-blue sheath that hit her dips and curves perfectly when she moved, Amara looked the part of a woman about to marry a wealthy man. A natural beauty, she'd experienced a serious glow-up in the last year because of her burgeoning career and inherited millionaire status. Although Amara could rock the latest designers, she still remained more comfortable with jeans and a peasant blouse.

She greeted me with a hug and concern. "How are you holding up? Jake's been trying to reach the embassy in DR and hasn't heard anything."

"I'm good." I swung one of her hands gently. "This is a big night for you. Nate is fine. He's just delayed. You look amazing, and we have to stop worrying and enjoy."

"You must be Sophie," a woman said from behind me. I turned, and a tall, curvy, Naomi Campbell-esque woman with Nathan's broad nose and bright smile held her hand out.

"Ms. Price?" I asked to be certain as I ignored her hand for a hug, which she returned warmly. "It's so good to meet you."

Her nod was quick, and I knew tears were near. "Yes, it is."

"I know we just met, but he wouldn't want us to be sad. Even if he doesn't get here in time for tonight, he'll be here for the wedding," I reassured her, though my resolve loosened each passing second in everyone's worried presence. "Did you come with Mr. Bradford?"

She smiled. "He's back at the hotel, but he'll be my guest at the wedding. Nate told you about him?"

"He did. Speaks highly of him." I squeezed her forearm, glad to see a genuine smile. "He could've been your guest tonight."

"I wasn't sure if Nathan had invited his father, and I didn't want to make things awkward." She hunched her shoulders.

"His father and brother are coming to the wedding but not going to be here tonight," I replied, feeling the tension rise as we discussed Nathan's other side of the family. I wished I had something to drink. Thank God my parents were still happily tethered. "So please relax, and I'll be back to talk more once I make the rounds."

Both sets of parents, the Barnes and the Johnsons, were already here, sitting together. They were already becoming friends and would sooner or later share grandchildren. A handsome older man stood in the corner nursing a cocktail. I squinted for a second. He looked like Jake, and I gasped. It had to be his father.

Then I remembered the conversation from the dressing room and how Mrs. Barnes loved Jake's dad deeply. I glanced between him and Mrs. Barnes. Her expression lacked the usual warmth, and she seemed stiff, though she appeared focused on the conversation between the couples. Jake's father was alone and didn't hide his interest in his former wife.

"Can I holla at you for a minute?" I eased behind Amara, standing beside Jake, who spoke to someone impatiently on the phone.

She nodded, and we moved into the elegantly decorated grand hall away from everyone.

Amara wrung her hands. "Is it about Nathan?"

I looked over my shoulder to ensure we were out of earshot. "No, it's about Jake's father."

She sighed warily. "I *told* Jake it wasn't a good idea to invite him to the wedding. I get that they're bonding, but there's way too much bad blood between his parents, and Jake hasn't completely let go of what happened between him and his stepfather. I'm not about the drama during my wedding."

"Well, he can't stop looking at Mrs. Barnes," I teased, trying to lighten the mood with gossip.

Twisting her lips, she nodded.

"Okay, now you know how I feel about older men. I barely wanted to give Nate a chance, and he's only a little older than me, but, um… That man in there?" I whistled. "I understand Mrs. Barnes better. And my bestie, you have a bright future if Jake ends up looking like him." A grin eased out of Amara, and I clapped happily. "Yes, a smile. Nathan would hate it if he knew he'd caused all this sadness when all he's trying to do is help others."

"Yeah, you're so right. Nate would be upset if he thought he'd ruined our night." She pulled me back into the main area and announced, "All right, we're all worried about Nathan, but we can't do anything right now except enjoy. He would want us to. Dinner is ready, and if you all can follow me into the dining room, we can eat and be merry."

As everyone slowly left the sitting area, I needed a moment to fight off my own blues and walked outside on the patio, rubbing my bare arms. It probably hadn't been smart to wear a strapless dress in the wintertime. I should go back inside before I catch a cold—I didn't want to greet Nathan with sneezing and a runny nose. Then again, that man would still kiss me and risk catching what I had.

I smiled at my certainty that nothing would stop him from kissing me, just as nothing would stop me.

Why didn't I tell him I loved him when I had a chance? What if he never knows how I feel?

Bending my head back and clasping my hands together, I listened to nature. The quiet and stillness of a cold winter night evoked peace again, and I lowered my head and released my hands. "Nope. He's still alive and trying to get to me. My gut would tell me if something happened to him."

"The last time I heard you talk to yourself, Twinkle, I was the one on the balcony."

I whipped my head around at the unexpected voice. Nathan stood at the door, dapperly dressed in a tailored suit. His hair had grown wild, he needed a shave, and he'd never looked more handsome. My heart sang louder than my squeal of joy.

We collided, and he cupped my face with his calloused palms. "I'm so sorry I'm late."

"It doesn't matter. You're here." I wanted to jump around, do a cartwheel—something to express my happiness that this man stood in front of me.

His eyes hungrily caressed my face. "You don't know what I did to make it here tonight. I lost my phone somewhere between the DR and Miami, and all I could think was that you were worried about me. I barely had time to throw on this suit before I raced over her, breaking all kinds of laws."

I lovingly wrapped my arms around his neck and stood on tiptoe to kiss him softly, interrupting his nervous rambling. I pulled off his glasses, tucked them into his jacket, and stared into his brown eyes. "I knew you would keep your word to me." I gently caressed his nape as I marveled at this beautiful man who'd saved me the day he knocked on my apartment door.

He removed his jacket, smiling proudly. "And I got Jean Pierre to Puerto Rico. I didn't want to say his name over the phone in case my communications had been compromised. The government there will grant him asylum for now."

Nathan placed his jacket around my shoulders, caring for me without thought.

"Proud of you." The warmth and scent of him blanketing me heated my chilled skin. "Like I said, I knew you would keep your word."

Lines crossed his forehead. "You really believe in me."

"I do." He pulled me even closer to him, and I gripped the lapels of his shirt. "And I've been waiting for what seems like forever to tell you in person that I am positively, undoubtedly, impossibly, and irrevocably in love with you. I want to take this journey with you and see where we end."

Nathan's sensual mouth curved into the widest, brightest smile. "So many adverbs. I can add more." He lowered his head to whisper against my lips, "I am madly, emphatically, and happily in love with you too. I also want to see where we go, and I hope it ends with you being my wife and mother of my children."

"Who would have thought that by giving this old man a chance, we would fall in love?" I teased, my vision blurred by my tears.

"I told you to be open." As he slipped his tongue inside my mouth, someone nearby cleared their throat loudly.

"This is supposed to be Mari's and my night. You come up here stealing the show, and you know I hate to lose." Jake scowled, though I could see the twinkle in his eyes from here.

"You better get used to it, because Nashville is my home now." Nathan squeezed me to him. "Well, wherever she lays her head is my home."

I smiled and snuggled under his strong arm. "The same. I actually like L.A.—might not mind living there for a while and flying back here to annoy Jake in the studio."

A glowing Amara could finally enjoy her night. She clapped her hands together. "Now that we know Nate is safe and sound with us, let's move this party back inside and finish eating. It's freezing. Don't know why that man of mine insisted on having a winter wedding."

We broke apart to an approving audience of our family and friends, including my people, who must have arrived while Nathan and I were on the patio. They surrounded us as soon as we stepped back inside. My parents beamed at seeing us together. Questions about all that had happened to help the young Haitian man, and about our future as a couple, were thrown at him while I remained by his side. When we all moved toward the dining room, our gazes locked, and in his eyes, I recognized that we were finally on the same page.

Whatever we decided about our lives together would be on our terms, and for now, that was enough.

Nathan held his arm out for me to hold. "Ready?"

"Yes, I am." I grasped his bicep, and together, we began the next phase of our lives.

EPILOGUE

Sophie

Seven months later

Nathan slowly guided me from the car, covering my eyes. "Better not be peeking."

"How can I peek when your hands are blinding me?" I complained. The sounds of cars passing and the smothering July heat shifted as we moved through some doorway. "I swear, you better not try to surprise propose to me, because I'm not ready yet." I said louder, "So if people are waiting to jump out, then they need to know that I'm in deep, but it's not our time yet."

"Well, it's a good thing I'm not proposing and that we don't have our friends and family waiting, or this would've been embarrassing for me." Nathan chuckled. "Now I'm worried that we may *never* get married."

Laying my head back on his firm chest, I replied, "I like us as we are."

Much as I would probably never openly admit it to him, he'd been right that I could've had that life if I'd truly wanted to be married with children. I'd made choices since I was eighteen, leading to Nathan, who had pushed and encouraged me. He was a man who needed me to feel again, to love deeply, and to embrace his village of family and friends fully. The seven months since we'd committed to each other had been the busiest and creative time of my life. After the glamorous and fun wedding of Amara and Jake, Nathan and I had spent the holidays with our respective families—Christmas with mine and New Year's Eve with Nathan's mother and Bradford. A trip to San Antonio to visit his reserved yet friendly father and brother, whom I met at the wedding, would happen later this year.

At the beginning of the year, we were based in Los Angeles, and I traveled back when needed to work in Nashville with Ms. Claudette, to officially record the three "lost" songs and create two for the documentary soundtrack. To my delight, "Found Soul" had achieved a modicum of success on the blues chart and would be included on the soundtrack to the documentary. Eventually, I planned to produce a country and blues album with Jake's guidance. Still unsure if I ever wanted to tour again, I did occasional shows at bars in Nashville and Memphis of my single and covers of rhythm and blues songs.

We were still deciding whether New Orleans would be our next city to explore for lost musicians. In the meantime, we had busy days of working with McClain Studios on the film slated for release in September and developing Nathan's magazine, *IOLA*, set to drop in November.

On our rare off days, we took mini-vacations, exploring the United States and nearby countries. My camera was a constant companion, just as Princess had been. I was officially Nathan's photojournalist and woman, and we were both in high demand for our respective work. We traveled to New York to capture a still-grateful Jean Pierre on camera. He'd transitioned to the U.S. with a distant aunt who had welcomed him into her home. Nathan's desire for the Pulitzer had shifted after his work with Jean Pierre and the discovery of stories about musicians. Although still a goal, winning the prize was no longer required evidence of his success, as my desire to marry and have a child as a measure of mine had faded into the background.

In June, we'd returned to Nashville, where the music magazine's headquarters would be located for the foreseeable future, since it was there that Nathan's vision was born.

Now, while celebrating my thirtieth birthday, he'd instructed me to close my eyes while we were supposed to be taking a leisurely drive, which had concluded at some place that felt airy and smelled like pine.

"Can I please open my eyes?"

"Yes." He kissed my neck before he removed his hands.

I opened my eyes to a large, empty store. The praline-brown hardwood floor glistened in contrast to the white walls on two sides. One wall was brick, and the other was the glass door and front. I stepped away from him, admiring the look and feel of the store. "Beautiful space. This would make a good gallery." I looked over my shoulder at him. "Is that why we're here?"

Nathan grinned. "I took the liberty to tell the realtor we wanted it."

"Wait…this is ours?" I folded my arms and hid the smile that wanted to burst from within.

One thing I'd learned while we'd been together was that Nathan believed in executing quickly on ideas or suggestions. During pillow talk while we were in L.A., I had shared my ideas about creating a fan book for Amara Johnson. He'd arranged a meeting with a publisher within a few days, and I signed a contract with Amara's permission. When I complained about leaving my purse at my place when I spent the night with him, he'd offered the key to his home and asked me to move in with him. Last week, I'd told him how much I loved the Withers Collection and how cool it would be to present *my* photographs. Now he was presenting me with my own gallery.

His smile faltered. "I told her you would want to add your name to the lease, and we can still back out. It's only ten minutes from Jake's studio." He slowly unwrapped my arms and took my hands. "I thought this place would be perfect to showcase your photos, and there's an office in the back for us to work on *IOLA*."

Trying hard to hold on to my feigned anger, I raised a brow. "We could also add a small stage against that brick wall for me and others to perform."

The pucker between his eyes faded. "Sooo…you like it?"

I slowly smiled. "I love it."

Nathan breathed in relief. "Why do you play so much?"

I tugged him to me and wrapped my arms around his waist. "Because I would've liked to have come with you to pick out this place."

"I wanted to surprise you for your birthday."

"Yes, babe, and I appreciate it. Best gift I've ever received, besides you." I tightened my arms around him. "I love that you like helping others; I just don't want you to feel like you always have to help me or push me to do something."

"I wasn't trying to do that."

I glared at him.

He grinned sheepishly. "Okay…okay. My bad. I hear you."

"Do you?" I asked for emphasis.

"I do. Something I need to work on, because I know you're fully capable of doing whatever you set your mind to do." He solemnly nodded before slowly leading me around the room. "I would give you the world if you asked. So when you talked about the Withers Collection, this was the next logical step. Besides, we needed a formal place to work. Our home is filled with your photos scattered everywhere. Pictures that need to be framed and adored." We stopped at the brick wall at the back of the large room. "I didn't think of this being a place for you to perform music."

"I actually thought of something you didn't?" I grinned. "Gold star for Twinkle."

"It's crazy how much I love you." Nathan shook his head in awe.

Looping my arms around his neck, I teased, "Even crazier for me, since you're as old as dirt."

He chuckled. "Nope, the ageism doesn't work anymore now that we're both in the same decade."

"Oh, yeah, forgot about that part. I'll start it again when you turn forty." We swayed slightly together. "You think we'll always be this happy?"

"Probably not, but it doesn't mean that I don't want to be, or won't plan to do whatever I can to make sure," he said, resting his forehead against mine.

I closed my eyes and started humming "Let's Do It Again."

He held me closer. "Mm… I love when you hum that song."

"I know," I purred. "I thought this song was about sex, but it's so much more. The lyrics celebrate the fun of loving someone, even if only for a moment, and letting the worries go. Maybe that's what we'll do when times get hard—we allow our love to erase the clouds temporarily."

Nathan kissed my neck. "That might just work."

"It'd better, because I'm not going anywhere," I promised before melding my body into his, grateful I'd taken a risk on him.

We danced and twirled to my singing in the middle of our future gallery, lost in each other and the present. Hoping that our love would last a lifetime.

And if by circumstance it didn't, we would accept the lessons learned.

ACKNOWLEDGEMENTS

I will be forever grateful for the opportunity to write this ode to the musical and civil rights legacy of Memphis, a city ironically named after the capital of Egypt, the birthplace of civilization. To our ancestors and leaders who fought the battle and died so that others could see our humanity. To the unsung and heralded blues musicians and singers whose lyrics give us the sun on rainy days. To the brilliant writers, journalists, and photographers who capture our rich past, present, and future through their art.

I want to extend a special thank you to Keisha and the Honey Blossom Team for amplifying my voice as an author and for the unique attention they give to each project. A special appreciation for B. Love, who took the time to share her love of her hometown with me. And to my family and friends who continue to support this auspicious dream of mine to write relatable stories that educate, heal, resonate, and transform.

www.ingramcontent.com/pod-product-compliance
Lightning Source LLC
Chambersburg PA
CBHW031036310726
48969CB00007B/2003